The Demon of
Table Mesa

by John Waddell

DORRANCE
PUBLISHING CO
EST. 1920
PITTSBURGH, PENNSYLVANIA 15238

Dorrance Publishing Co
585 Alpha Drive
Suite 103
Pittsburgh, PA 15238
Visit our website at www.dorrancebookstore.com

ISBN: 978-1-6480-4080-1
eISBN: 978-1-6480-4939-2

CHAPTER 1

The Fast Life of Scott Abrahamson

*I*t was 7:50 A.M. when the doorbell rang. I knew it was Scott, because he always showed up right at ten till eight. It only took five minutes to get to school from the front door of the house. To get there we'd walked across the street, through the field around the bottomless pond up the hill to the high school parking lot.

When I opened the door, I could see Scott was already pissed off about the cold. He yelled at the top of his lungs, "Would you hurry up, Jacob, it's fucking freezing out here!"

I told him not to yell the "f" word, because my dad would hear him.

Scott bellowed, "I don't care if your dad hears me." As he stood there shivering, there was steam rolling around his head from his breath. He was right, it was very cold this morning.

We walked across the street and down the trail through the field. When we approached the bottomless pond, I started to make the turn to go around it. Scott continued walking in a straight line. I could see he had no intention of going around the lake. I tried to explain to him that the ice wasn't thick enough to walk across. He looked at me with determination and said he wasn't walking around the pond. It's faster to walk across the ice than around it.

I started to follow him across but hesitated at the edge. I looked through the ice and could see it wasn't thick enough to hold our weight. I yelled at him to come back. He continued his trek across the ice. I heard a popping sound coming from the ice, then another, then another loud one that went across the lake. Scott broke through the ice. He fell through then bobbed back up out of the hole. I looked into his eyes when he came back up, there was only the demon Zoavits staring back at me.

As he stared into my eyes, sounding like the devil himself, Scott said, "I'm going to kill you next, Jacob." Scott's head slowly sank into the Icy water.

I began to panic. I had this idea that I'd lay down on my stomach and slide out to the hole in the ice. Just as I laid down, I heard a big crash from a ladder that fell next to me. Mr. Cantone my neighbor was yelling at me to hold the end of the ladder, while he scrambled out to pull Scott out of the water. Scott's body was lifeless as Mr. Cantone dragged him across the ice back to shore.

While this was happening, an ambulance must have pulled up behind me. It was strange, I never heard any sirens. Two paramedics rolled Scott onto a stretcher then lifted him into the ambulance. They took all his clothes off and wrapped him in blankets. They had a hose that blew warm air. They stuck the end of it under the blankets to warm him up. I don't think it did any good, Scott looked like he was dead.

Sheriff Justice said to his deputy after reading Jacob's statement that the story pretty much matched Jim Cantone's story. He recalled the story of Sam Jenkins and Teddy Beesly two fifteen-year-olds, who had drowned in the lake in the summer 1950. It was the first day of summer 1950. Their bodies were never found, though.

Justice said, "That's why the townspeople believe the lake is bottomless."

"The two boys had to of gone for a swim, because their clothes were found lying on the shore next to the lake."

After the sheriff left, Mark asked Jacob, "Why didn't you tell them about the Game of Spirits?"

"Because, Mark, they wouldn't believe that story."

CHAPTER 2

The Game of Spirits

Jacob had been excited all day about the Spirit boardgame his best friend Mark told him he found in the attic of his grandmother's house. He and Scott were going to stay overnight at Mark's playing the new game. His overnight bag had a toothbrush, some toothpaste, and a stick of deodorant which he never used. He was going to throw a change of clothes into the bag, then decided the hell with it, he didn't need to bring anything to Mark's; after all Mark lived next door.

There was fifteen minutes to kill as he sat on his bed looking around the bedroom. The paint on the walls was fourteen years old. Dad had painted the room baby blue a week before Jacob was born. Denver Broncos posters plastered the walls. The posters dated back to 1960 when they played their first season. Dad bought a poster every year since. By now Jacob had collected quite a few of his own, so the room was papered with posters. He saved room on the ceiling for all his psychedelic blacklight posters. The guitar sitting in the corner had never been played.

He turned the blacklight on, laid back on the bed, and put his hands behind his head. He stared into his favorite poster on the ceiling. Staring down at him was the demon Zoavits from the Flat-Land tribe mythology. Jacob had bought the poster from a gypsy when the carnival was in town. The gypsy had told him that Zoavits was a cannibal, who kidnaped and ate children.

The eyes of the demon glowed blood orange from the light shining on the poster. They were shaped like a mountain lion's eyes, except the pupils were inverted. He had a crown molded into his head that wrapped around and turned into a mountain goat's horns. His face was shaped like a Flat-Landers, but it looked to be severely burned. The demon's body looked like it was muscle sculped in a perfect humanoid form with fire blazing from his upper arms and shoulders.

The wind was blowing hard that evening. It always was in Table Mesa, but tonight the shutters dad had placed over the west windows were rattling. Jacob lay there on the bed, he and the demon staring deep into each other's eyes when a loud knock came at the door, startling him.

Jacob's sister Leah was screaming, "Jacob! Mark's on the phone; he wants to know what's taking you so long."

"Shit," Jacob yelled as he looked over at the moonbeam alarm clock on the nightstand. Fifteen minutes had turned into half an hour.

Jacob jumped up and almost ripped the door off the hinges as he yanked it open. He stopped. Leah was standing there in the dark hallway blocking his path. She was a couple of years older than him and was very popular in school due to exceptional looks and an outgoing personality. She had long brown hair, blue eyes, often spending hours on doing her makeup. Even though everyone who knew Leah told her she looked better without make up. She was naturally beautiful, with the perfect body for a sweet sixteen.

That sweet sixteen, who was very popular at school, was Dr. Jekyll when it came to Jacob and his brother. She had a temper that would erupt on a second's notice. If you were the one who pissed her off, you better duck, because a knife may be flying your way.

Leah was standing there blocking the doorway as the bedroom door flew open for Jacob to make his escape to Mark's house. "Get out of the way, Leah, I don't have time to hear your shit," Jacob said.

Leah in a motherly smartass tone said, "You know, Jacob, you would probably have a girlfriend if you would do something about your looks and the way you dress." Leah stood there for a moment, observing him. "Shit, you have long brown shoulder-length oily hair, and French looking blue eyes with sharp facial features. If you cleaned up, you might actually look halfway decent." She was trying to be nice.

Jacob looked at her, "Since when did you start giving a shit about me?"

Leah continued, without any compassion now. "You look like a slob! Those old worn-out bell-bottom blue jeans have faded to almost bleach white. And Jacob, that old green plaid shirt has been hanging on you back for a year straight now," she continued to rip him. She looked down at his Keds sneakers. "And those shoes have got to go, Jacob," she said in a sarcastic voice.

Jacob pushed passed her in the dark hallway, then said, "Would you get lost, Leah."

Leah's temper flared. As he started to run through the living room, she was screaming, "You have zits, you only weigh a hundred pounds and you stink too, asshole."

As he bolted out the front door, he almost fell to the ground as he leaped over the three stairs leading off the porch.

When Jacob ran between the two houses, he was almost blown onto his ass. As he pulled open the front screen door to Mark's house the wind grabbed it, with a bang, it blew open hitting the wall next to the doorway. Jacob struggled to get the door shut and latched behind him as he entered the living room. Mark's grandmother was sitting in her rocker as Jacob ran by telling her hello." He could hear her yelling at him to be more respectful as he ran down the stairs.

Jacob entered the recreation room, sat at the table where Mark was setting up the game. The rec-room walls were covered in psychedelic posters of rock bands, with crates of rock and roll albums in one corner. Mark's drum set was sitting in the other corner of the room. He played the drums for the first year after his grandmother bought them for him, until discovering marijuana and peyote, they fell to the wayside as Mark went into his own world.

Mark was working on the game as Jacob sat down. Jacob observed his facial features as he worked on the game. They both had the same kind of hair, brown, shoulder-length, wavy. Mark had wide cheekbones, a semi-flat nose and dark almond-shaped eyes.

"Do you want a girlfriend, Mark?"

"Of course, I do." He looked perplexed about the question. "Why do you ask?" Mark stood there looking at him while he waited for Jacob to answer.

Jacob observed Mark as he stood there; Mark had a beaded necklace that hung down to his mid-chest. Mark found the necklace in the attic with the game. It looked like an old Native American medicine-man necklace they both had seen in the Old West Museum. He had a jean jacket with cut-off sleeves. The jean jacket was unbuttoned showing his bare chest. He wore striped bell-bottoms that frayed at the bottom. They both wore Keds sneakers.

He was thinking as they talked, about how much Mark had changed, since becoming a hippie.

"Leah says I could get a girlfriend if I cleaned up, but I'm not sure if I'm," Jacob stopped mid-sentence. Mark asked Jacob what wasn't he sure of.. Jacob turned his attention to the game, without answering the question.

"Where's Scott." Mark asked as Jacob observed the game.

"Dunno," Jacob said, he wasn't listening now that he was studying it. Mark could hear the front door slam against the outer wall as it blew open.

"Shit," Mark said as he could hear Scott running down the stairs. "You two assholes are going to bring the wrath of my grandmother down on us if you don't stop banging the door." As Scott entered the rec-room he said, "She already chased me through the living room swinging a broomstick."

Mark and Jacob observed Scott entering the room. Scott was the best-looking kid in school. The girls would hang around him talking and giggling for long periods of time. His jet-black hair was cut in the style of the Beatles' haircut. He had long dark eyelashes that would make any girl melt. Scott always wore buffalo plaid shirts, with bell-bottoms and worn-out leather boots. He had a furry of a temper, which could erupt on a second's notice.

Scott asked, "What are you two looking at?" as he walked into the room.

Jacob said, "Uh, nothing," thinking Scott was very good looking with those dark blue eyes.

Mark said, "Nothing, we were just wondering, who the ugly, smelly bastard is that can't open a door without banging it against a wall."

Scott looked at Mark, the rage starting to come up, he calmed down almost immediately saying, "At least I'm not a hippie."

"This isn't a new game," Jacob said, while studying the wooden box that held the contents.

Mark replied, "The game's over a hundred years old, the paint peeled away years before I found it."

It had to be the oldest game Jacob had ever seen. The only thing that remained on the wooden box were letters burned into the side of it. Jacob had to squint to make it out. He read aloud, "El Juego de Espiritus."

"What's that mean? Jacob asked.

Mark said, "It means 'The Game of Spirits.'"

Scott asked, "Where did the game come from?"

"I found it up in the attic."

Jacob asked, "How old is it?"

"I don't know, it's been passed down from one generation to the next on my dad's side of the family. When I asked grandma what it was, she told me not to ever touch the game. It's jinxed and whoever possess it can't dispose of it."

Scott asked, "Why did you take it out of the attic then?"

Mark said, "It couldn't be as bad as she says."

Jacob wasn't worried at all. "The game probably died eighty years ago."

"I don't think it will work anyway," Mark said. "My grandmother never goes in the attic, so she'll never know we borrowed it."

When Mark told them that, Scott said, "Whatever."

After Mark finished setting the game up, the three sat looking it over. The board was a round wooden plate with a flat surface-top bearing letters and numbers. The letters were A to Z with four additional letters ch, ll, rr, Ch. One side of the board had the word "Si" painted on it, and opposite that, the word "no" was painted. It had the numbers zero through five above the Si and no, the numbers six through nine under that.

The cursor looked like it had been hand carved out of pine wood. It had three legs attached to a flat surface with a hole in the middle. Each player was instructed by the directions to place their fingers lightly on each side of the cursor. The players were then to ask questions and wait for the cursor to slide along the board spelling out the answer. The letters or numbers would appear through the hole in the pointer.

Jacob asked, "How's the game played?"

Mark explained that two players lightly touch the cursor, but shouldn't try to move it, just wait and allow it to move on its own. Scott asked if he meant wait for the spirits to move it. Mark nodded. Mark volunteered to take notes in case they forgot the answers. He told Scott and Jacob to place their fingers on the cursor. Scott asked why was Mark making the decisions. They should discuss it first, then decide who does what. Mark said it was his game, so he'd decide.

Jacob said, "If your grandmother is right, you may wish you hadn't made claim to the game."

Scott and Jacob placed their fingers on the cursor, Jacob said, "Hello." For a long minute nothing happened. Suddenly the pointer slid to the "H" then it quickly moved to the "I." Scott immediately accused Jacob of moving the cursor. He called him an asshole. He told him not to do it again. Jacob denied moving the cursor at the same time he accused Scott of being the one who moved it. They argued for a couple of minutes until Mark interrupted to ask another question of the spirit.

He asked if it was a spirit that'd said hi. The cursor moved over the word si. Scott asked what si meant. Mark gave Scott a disgusted look then called him an idiot. Scott told Mark to get lost.

Scott said, "How the hell am I supposed to know what si means?"

Mark replied, "Si Scott is a dumb ass."

Scott asked Mark, "How do you want your knuckle sandwich served?"

Mark wrote, si = yes, F-O Scott, on a piece of paper then, showed it to him, asking him if he was able to read.

Jacob was getting tired of the other two playing their own games. He asked the spirit what its name was. The cursor moved much faster as it spelled, s-h-a-p-p-a. Mark and Jacob exchanged glances and shrugged their shoulders. Scott said the game didn't make any sense before asking what Shappa meant. The cursor moved around the board spelling Red Thunder. Mark said he got it. Shappa was the Native American word equivalent to Red Thunder in English.

Jacob asked if Shappa was a Native American. The pointer spelled the word, yes. Mark asked why it would spell the word yes. All it had to do was move the cursor over the si. Scott said, "I don't know, it's your game." Jacob did have to admit that he'd wondered the same thing.

"Are you an Indian warrior." Jacob asked.

Shappa said, "Yes, I'm an Indian warrior flower."

Scott asked Mark if that last word was flower. Mark said that it was. Scott asked Shappa, if he was a hippie like Mark. Jacob asked Shappa if he said Indian Warrior Flower. Shappa said si. Jacob said he had them confused. The pointer spelled out, "Ha, ha, ha, that was a joke." This pissed off Scott, who told Mark his game was all screwed up.

"Have you been in many battles?"

Shappa said his people were at war with another tribe. They were also, at war with the Europeans. He'd been in many battles and won most of them.

Jacob said, "You must be a great warrior then!"

Shappa said some people would say that.

"Have many of your people died in the wars?"

Shappa said a lot of his people had died, because of the Europeans. They didn't die in battle, though; they died from the sickness that was brought from Europe. Mark quickly claimed he wasn't responsible; his dad was Native American, and his mother was from Columbia.

Scott told Mark, "That is why you look like a stupid chipmunk with oily hair."

Mark told Scott to shut up.

"Are you married?"

"I'm married to a white woman."

"Is the sex better with a white woman than with Indian women?"

Shappa said he didn't know, he'd never had sex with an Indian woman, his wife was chosen for him by the Chief.

Mark asked if he had any kids. Shappa said he didn't have any baby goats. Scott told Mark that the spirit liked to mess with his head. Mark corrected his question and asked if he had any children. Shappa said he had a son. His name was White Foot.

Scott asked, "Why?"

Shappa said, "His mother is white and I'm of the Flat-Land tribe."

"Is White Foot a warrior like you are?"

Shappa said, "No, White Foot doesn't follow the warrior's path. White Foot is on a spiritual path."

"Does it bother you that your son doesn't follow in your foot-steps?"

"I love my son, but I have to accept that he doesn't have a warrior's heart."

"Do you still spend time with White Foot?"

"I spent time with him when he was a youth, now that he's grown, I don't see him much." Suddenly the connection to Shappa stopped as quickly as it started.

The three had become so involved in the game that a couple of months had passed, before they realized, it was the end of October. It was discussed how it was a great game for Halloween. Every night while playing the game, they'd meet a different spirit. To get in contact with a spirit previously encountered, they'd just concentrate on the name of the spirit while their hands were on the cursor.

One evening they were in contact with a spirit named Aiyana. She was a Native American woman who lived in a village right across the street from Jacob and Mark. They didn't believe her, because there was nothing out in the field except the bottomless lake. She was insistent that she lived there. She couldn't understand why they couldn't see the village; it was in plain sight.

Aiyana said she was born in the village right next to the lake. She was the daughter of the tribal medicine man. Mark asked her what she looked like. She had long brown hair with brown eyes. She'd seen fifteen summers, which meant it was time for her to find a man to settle down with and raise a family.

Jacob wanted to move on to meet other spirits. Mark told him no; he wanted to keep talking with Aiyana. As their conversations went on the two were starting to develop a bond. Mark told her everything about himself. Scott asked Jacob why it bothered him that Mark was getting to know her. Jacob didn't say anything was bothering him. He just wanted to move on.

Mark and Aiyana started talking about how they'd like to meet each other. Mark was hinting about having sex with her. The pointer spelled the word "giggle," then Mark giggled like a little girl. Aiyana said she was ready, all Mark had to do was come get it. They both giggled again. Jacob in an angry voice told Mark to go jack-off.

One evening they had a conversation with James and Mary Waddell, who had fallen in love and married in 1661 in Edinburgh, Scotland. Mary bore three children, two girls, and a boy. The oldest girl was six when Mary and James died from the plague in 1667. The couple suddenly dropped dead, while holding hands, when out for the evening walk after dinner. James was worried about their children. Mary said she was sure her sister would have taken custody of the them, because she was very close to them.

A few nights later they met a spirit from Honduras. They couldn't understand what he was saying. Jacob and Scott would ask questions in English. Jose would answer in Spanish. Mark decided he'd write the answers down, because they were spelled out anyway. He'd then take it to his grandmother, whose first spoken language was Spanish for interpretation. After she read it, she had the look in her eye as she stared at Mark. She yelled, "Marcus White Foot Hernandez, don't you ever think, write, or talk like that again!"

It was mid-December when they met Iktumi!

CHAPTER 3

The Demon

*I*t was Friday evening, December seventeenth. Scott and Jacob were going to stay at Mark's house overnight playing the Game of Spirits. Holiday break was starting. It started a little earlier that year, because Christmas fell on the following Saturday. The only drawback to the early start of the two-week holiday break was school would be back in session the Monday right after New Year's. They'd already had five days off from school, because of snow days. Luckily the school decided not to cut into the holiday break. Instead, it was decided to extend the school year into the summer break.

Zoe, Leah's best friend, was hanging out with Leah that evening. They decided to sit in and listen to all the excitement that they had been hearing about for months. Zoe was in hot pursuit of Scott anyway. That gave her two reasons to hang out with the guys. Zoe sat down next to Scott and said, "Hello." Scott glanced over at her. He was thinking to himself that he'd like to play with that dish. That jet-black hair she had hanging down to her ass was a total turn-on. I'd like to take that tie-dye tee shirt off her and get a look at those 32Gs and maybe some more.

He glanced down at her waist and said, "I like those bell-bottom pants."

She said, "Really."

"Oh, yeah," he said with a smile.

Jacob asked, "Can we play the game now?"

Scott looked over at Jacob and said, "We are."

Scott asked if there were any spirits out that evening. The pointer moved to the "si." Jacob said that was great, he was ready to start asking questions. Mark asked what the spirit's name was. The cursor spun around the board spelling the name Iktumi. Mark asked Iktumi if he was from Asia. Iktumi said he lived in North America. His ancestors were from Asia, though. He said his ancestors migrated over the land bridge a long time ago.

Scott asked if Iktumi knew how many years it'd been since his ancestors settled in North America. Iktumi said he didn't know; the family stories were told from one generation to the next. There had been so many generations living in the North America, that nobody knew how many years it had been. Iktumi said his ancestral story didn't matter anymore; it had ended when his family was killed by the Europeans.

Iktumi asked what the half-breed's name was. Jacob looked over at Mark and said that was the first time a spirit had asked them a question! Scott angrily asked Iktumi who he addressed the question to. The name m-a-r-k was spelled out. Mark started to get upset. Iktumi knew his name. Mark asked Iktumi why he'd asked his name, if he already knew what it was. There was no response.

Jacob in an angry and defensive voice asked Iktumi why he didn't answer Mark's question. Iktumi said he didn't like Mark. Mark, Zoe, and Leah started to freak out. Zoe said the three of them were fucking with their heads. Mark said they weren't messing with their heads. Jacob could tell that Mark was getting ready to freak out.

Zoe said to Leah, "The three amigos are moving the cursor on their own and they're trying to scare us."

Leah said, "It's working."

Jacob, who became angrier because Iktumi called Mark a half-breed, asked him why he called Mark a half breed. Iktumi said Mark's dad had mixed blood in him, he was half white and half Flat-Land. His mother was from the jungle in Columbia, that makes Mark a mutt. Jacob became pissed when Iktumi said it. He told Iktumi to fuck off. Iktumi told Jacob he should have more respect for his elders. Jacob told Iktumi he didn't have respect for idiots who insulted his friends.

Mark said he needed to smoke a joint in order to settle down. The cursor was flying around the board as it spelled out the next sentence.

"You do need a joint, Mark, you come from a long line of peyote heads, pot heads, drunks, and rapists."

"What's your problem, DICKTUMI?" Jacob yelled. "If you were a real person, I'd kick your ass."

"You're asking me what my problem is, Jacob?"

"Yeah, I am."

"Let me tell you something, Jacob; you're my fucking problem."

"You have any more stupid questions, Jacob?"

"Go to Hell, Iktumi!"

"I've been there, Jacob, and the next time I go, you're going with me."

"Oh, yeah, I forgot to mention that Zoe's a bitch."

Scott asked Iktumi, "Why are you calling Zoe names."

"I don't like her either."

"I'm in the room, Iktumi."

"You should address me instead, of saying things about me to Scott."

"I didn't know you were in the room, bitch."

Jacob pulled his fingers off the cursor causing the session to end.

"What the fuck did you do that for?" Scott was pissed when he asked.

"Iktumi's a freak. No other spirits know our names or insulted us."

"I'm not sure if I'm more pissed off at you, Jacob, or Iktumi for being a smart-ass."

Mark said he was glad that Jacob ended the game. "That spirit scared me."

"Why don't you stop being a pot-smoking weakling."

Jacob was getting sick of the insults being thrown Mark's way. He told Scott to lay off. Scott told Jacob even Iktumi knew Mark was weak. He said if Mark would stand up for himself, maybe he wouldn't get so much shit in life.

Mark said he had some dope. He asked everyone in the group if they wanted to get high. Jacob, who had smoked with Mark and Scott before, looked at Leah, not sure how he should answer. Leah had the same thought as she glanced over at him. She was thinking that Jacob wouldn't tell on her, he hadn't told on her for anything in the past, but he wasn't above blackmail.

In a soft voice, Leah asked Jacob if he'd tried smoking pot.

"I'm not admitting to anything."

Scott told Jacob and Leah to knock the bullshit off, he'd smoked with both before. Jacob and Leah decided it would be in their own best interest not to say anything about it.

Scott asked, "Is it okay for everyone to get high then?"

Mark said he didn't have a pipe to smoke from; he'd broke it. Scott said to Mark that he was the professional drug user in the group, shouldn't he have a stash of drug paraphernalia?

"What's drug paraphernalia?"

Scott looked over at Leah when she asked the question. He'd learned the term from his brothers, who smoked daily. He told her, "Drug paraphernalia is any tool a person uses to take their drugs."

Jacob told Leah that Mark's pipe was drug paraphernalia.

Leah asked, "What kind of bud is it?"

"It's Colombian Gold. That's the good stuff that's available."

Zoe said she had some rolling papers. She then complained about how smoking burned her throat when she smoked a joint. Leah said she could make a bong out of a Christmas wrapping paper tube.

Mark asked, "How do you make a bong out of a cardboard tube?"

Leah looked at Mark then said she took the wrapping paper off the roll tube.

"After that you drill a hole in the center of it. The hole can't be bigger than the joint, because the joint needs to fit snug in it. Two people put their lips on either side of the tube when the joint is lit. Then, both people suck through their lungs, until the joint burns down and falls through the hole. When that happens, it gives the smokers a big hit all at once, because the tube is full of pot smoke. It works just like a bong."

They all walked out of the house, across the street and to the field by the lake to smoke. As they walked through the field, snow crunched beneath their feet. Jacob complained about how his toes were already numb. Mark said his fingers were frozen.

"I don't know about you guys; I'm freezing my nuts off."

Zoe's pupils dilated when Scott said it. She thought she could see clearer for a moment. The five sat down on the log bench by the lake freezing their butts off. There were fifty-gallon cans set next to the benches. The cans were used during the day to warm the ice skaters, when fires were burning in them. The five decided they didn't have time to build a fire in the can' it was just too cold. Scott said they should make it fast, it was so fucking cold outside, they'd freeze, before they got the joint lit. They took turns smoking out of Leah's bong. Mark was the one who got the extra hit off the bong, there were five of them, so somebody had to get an extra turn. Besides, it was his dope.

Quietly sneaking back into the house, they tiptoed down the stairs to the recreation room. There was no reason to play the game, because Scott was paranoid. Leah said they should watch the ant races.

"What are the ant races?" Scott asked.

"After the television stations go off the air around midnight, there is nothing on but static. If you stare at the static on the TV screen long enough, it looks like ants racing around the screen."

Zoe said they should watch the ant races. She was thinking she wasn't going to get anywhere with Scott that evening anyway; he was worthless when he was high. After watching the ant races for about five minutes, Mark asked if anybody had any other ideas. Jacob said they could play the video game. Scott said that game was like the ant races after five minutes it was boring, also.

Zoe said Jacob could tell the story of how his great-grandparents met.

"I just love your stories."

Scott said he didn't like love stories.

"Tell the story, Jacob."

Jacob's eyes became distant as he started to tell his story.

Josh and Jackline Jericho had been married in July 1843 on Josh's sixteenth birthday. Jackline had turned sixteen a couple of months prior to the wedding. The couple originally planned a small wedding, but as more and more family members became involved in the planning, it turned into a big celebration.

Jackline had grown up in a large family. She had five sisters and four brothers. Their grandmother and grandfather lived in the farmhouse with the family. The whole family worked the land from sunup, until sundown during the summer months.

Because the kids were home schooled, winters weren't any easier than the summers. They'd spend long hours studying late into the evening, then wake up at four in the morning to feed the animals. Jackline's parents were determined to give the children the best education they could provide. They told them, if they worked hard and studied, they would have the opportunity in life to be whatever they wanted. Jackline wasn't interested in education. She wanted to raise a family of her own.

Josh was a dreamer his whole life. When he was eleven, he'd read about Alta California. In California there were endless opportunities; rumors that gold had been discovered along the Pacific Coast, and fertile farmland for thousands of miles just waiting to be homesteaded. Josh knew that was where he was going to live someday.

Josh was from a large family, also. The family owned thirteen hundred acres of farmland in the Missouri River bottoms. Farming provided a good life for his family, but he wasn't interested in taking over the family farm. Farming would be last on his list of opportunities in California. If he did, it would be a last resort.

Josh and Jackline met at the county farmers rally, the summer before they were married. The rally was a rodeo get together by the local farmers and ranchers in the county. Families would come from miles away for the annual get together to socialize, trade ideas, and simply have a good time. The scheduled event for the afternoon included a pork and beef roast, after which would be a dance later in the evening.

At the party Jackline kept moving in front of Josh, trying to get his attention so he'd ask her to dance. He had to be the one who asked her to dance; it would have been inappropriate for her to have asked him. He finally asked her to dance, and after that they dated once a week. Until, they were married.

Zoe had a dreamy look in her eyes when she said she just loved love stories. Scott was passed out as she looked over at him. She wondered what it was she saw in him. She thought about pursuing Jacob, then thought that would be a waste of time. She didn't think he liked girls anyway.

The next morning the three started playing the game as soon as they woke up. The Chinook Winds were blowing hard.

"What's that noise?" Jacob asked Mark.

Mark said he didn't know; his grandmother told him that when the wind was really blowing the demons were out.

Scott said, "It sounds like the seals around the doors are whistling from the wind."

Jacob agreed, "That's what it is."

Mark asked, "Are there any spirits who'd like to talk with us today?"

The cursor slid over to the "si." Mark asked who were they talking to. The cursor spelled Iktumi. Jacob told Iktumi to leave. He told him he wasn't welcome anymore.

Mark in a whiny voice begged the others to end the game. Scott was getting angry when he told Iktumi it was time for him to get lost. Iktumi said he wasn't going anywhere, after all, it was they who contacted him. Iktumi said to Scott he didn't understand why Mark and Jacob hung around with him; Scott was a total loser asshole.

Mark suggested again that they end the game. Scott told Mark to shut the fuck-up. He turned to Jacob and told him to leave his fingers on the cursor. Iktumi insulted him. There was no way he was going to end the game. Jacob said he was fine for now. Iktumi told Jacob, he and Mark were a couple of chicken shits. Scott agreed with him on that.

Iktumi told Scott not to side with him. He knew what kind of backstabbers Scott and his family were. Scott in an angry voice told Iktumi, his family line had ended because he was yellow. He asked Iktumi why he'd been spared. He then told him to never mind, it was probably because he ran away during the battle.

Scott continued with his attack on Iktumi. He said, "When the battle came to your front door, everyone in your family waved a white flag out the window, because your family's a bunch of chicken shits like you."

Jacob said he didn't think it was a good idea to insult Iktumi. "The spirit knows our names; there may be other things he knows."

Scott told Jacob to stop being so paranoid. Iktumi told Jacob he shouldn't be so forgiving of Scott. Jacob asked Iktumi what he meant by "forgiving of Scott."

"Do you remember when, Scott kicked the shit out of you the morning you were walking your little brother to school?"

Jacob said he did remember that.

Iktumi said, "When you came back to pick your brother up, Scott got down on his knees and started kissing your ass."

Scott yelled, "Fuck off, Iktumi!"

"Scott then begged you to be friends with him."

Scott was yelling again, "You don't know anything about our friendship!"

Iktumi said Jacob always told his stories, so why couldn't he tell his?

"Let's hear the story, Iktumi; it'll be a lie anyway."

"Okay, you decide, Jacob, whether it's true or not."

As Iktumi started the story the cursor was flying around the board. Mark could barely keep up while trying to write everything down. This was Iktumi's story.

Jacob's younger brother Timmy was born with part of the pupil missing in his right eye. The vision in the left was 20/20, which was great. The right eye, on the other hand, was 20/200, because the pupil hadn't developed properly before he was born. The doctor, along with his mother, decided that he would wear a patch over the good eye for a couple of years, that would strengthen the weaker eye.

A few years ago, Jacob was in a huge fight with his mother. She told him he'd be walking his brother to the elementary school every morning that year. After getting Timmy to school, Jacob would then have to walk to his school, which was in the opposite direction. After Jacob finished with his classes in the afternoon, he'd have to walk to the elementary school to meet Timmy, so he could walk him home.

Jacob was furious with his mother when she told him. He had tried to talk her out of it, but her mind was made up. Jacob was so angry that he stood face to face with her and yelled, "This whole fucking thing is bullshit!" She was pissed off, because he yelled in her face. She told him he'd be walking Timmy to school the following year as well. Jacob screamed as he stormed off, it pissed him off that there was no compromise on her part.

He knew when the argument escalated to that level his dad would get involved meaning the fight was lost. Really, the fight was over from the first time he was told he'd be walking Timmy to school every day.

His mother's mind was made up. He screamed that he'd love to kick the shit out of Timmy but didn't because his younger brother was too small.

Jacob hadn't given any thought to befriending Scott. The first day back from the summer break, Jacob was walking Timmy to his school. About halfway there, Scott met up with them. He started to follow them. Scott wasn't welcome as far as Jacob was concerned, but it was a free sidewalk. Scott would walk along with them doing the line skip along the sidewalk, while doing that, he'd say, "Step on a crack, break your mother's back." Jacob thought Scott was a little old for that saying, but whatever.

Scott started ragging on Jacob about how skinny he was. He was calling him names as Jacob and Timmy walked. Jacob was trying to ignore Scott, who just became angry and more verbally abusive. Jacob hadn't given any thought to fighting Scott in the past, but it could turn that way easily. Scott continued to call Jacob names as they walked. He told Jacob he dressed like a loser. Jacob asked him why he was following them to the elementary school. After all Scott was in the same grade as he, so why didn't he turn around and walk the other direction?

Scott not getting the reaction he wanted from Jacob asked why Jacob was walking the cyclops to school, referring to the patch over Timmy's eye. Before Jacob realized what, he was doing he'd hit Scott with three jabs, then nailed him in the nose with a right. Scott backed off into the street as Jacob kept swinging. Jacob saw Scott's facial expressions change from complete surprise to anger. He asked himself, "What the fuck did you do that for, Jacob?" It was too late; he knew he'd better keep throwing punches, which he did.

Scott started swinging fists at Jacob. Jacob was now on the defensive as he backed up. Scott was throwing punches so fast that Jacob couldn't block them. He started backing up more as Scott punched him in the side of the face. Scott then nailed him with a hard right in the eye. Jacob couldn't see, so much blood had run down into his eyes. Scott hit him again in the side of the face. Jacob was starting to go down; he was so dizzy. Scott continued to punch him as he fell to the ground. When

Jacob was on the ground, Scott started kicking him as he yelled at him calling him every name in the book. He gave Jacob one last kick in the side as he yelled at him to fuck off.

The fight stopped just as fast as it started. Jacob sat up and looked around as the crosswalk lady came up to him and asked if he was okay. Jacob said he was fucking fine. He got up and started walking across the street away from the school. He turned to see if his brother was there, he saw Timmy running into the school building. Jacob thought to himself, *Thanks, Timmy, the least you could have done was picked up a rock and hit Scott in the head with it.*

That afternoon Jacob sat outside the school building waiting for his little brother to come out, so he could walk him home. Scott walked up and asked how he was doing. Jacob asked why he gave a fuck. He then asked Scott if he was back to finish the job he started earlier in the morning. Scott said the fight wasn't personal. He then asked Jacob if he'd be friends. Jacob asked him if kicking the shit out of somebody was his way of making friends.

Scott said, "You put up a good fight, Jacob, I didn't take it personally, so why should you?"

Scott tried to do the shake with Jacob, who had no idea how to do it. Scott then explained the shake to Jacob. "The shake is where two people grab hands to do the traditional handshake. Instead of shaking hands, they hooked all four fingers, then each person drops their thumb to the right, then to the left."

They then smacked knuckles. After that, they shake hands with one shake.

As they did the shake, Jacob asked why Scott wanted to be friends. Scott said that his three older brothers beat the shit out of him like all the time. He said he was sorry. He then said he understood what it was like to be treated like that.

Iktumi asked Jacob if he thought the story was true. Jacob thought about if for a moment then said, "That was the way the fight happened."

He asked Mark how Iktumi knew about the fight. Mark just looked at Jacob then shook his head. He couldn't think of anything to say. When Jacob looked at Scott, he saw the rage in his eyes. Scott accused Jacob of siding with Iktumi. Jacob said he wasn't siding with Iktumi, the fight did happen that way.

"Fuck off, Jacob, you son of a bitch, you sided with Iktumi!" Scott yelled.

"Fuck you, Scott, he told the story word for word, you just can't handle the truth."

Mark told them both that Iktumi was trying to divide the three of them. Jacob and Scott yelled at Mark to shut the fuck up at the same time.

"Put your goddamn fingers back on the cursor, Jacob; I have something I want to tell Iktumi." Scott was enraged.

They both put their fingers back on the cursor.

"Iktumi, are you still there?" Scott asked in an angry voice.

The cursor slid over the word "si."

"If you were standing in front of me, I'd kick the fuck out of you," Scott yelled.

"Is that an invitation, Scott?" Iktumi asked.

"Yes," Scott replied.

Jacob became fearful and told Scott to be careful; Iktumi wasn't like other spirits they had encountered. Scott told Jacob that Iktumi was just a spirit, so he couldn't hurt him.

Iktumi said, "Okay, Scott, I accept your invitation."

CHAPTER 4

The Antagonist Adversary

*I*t had been over a week since Jacob and Mark heard anything from Scott. It was New Year's Eve. Jacob and Mark were hanging out looking for something to do. Mark kept bugging Jacob to call Scott, so they could play the spirit game. Zoe had been over to Jacob's house the day before, blaming him for the fight. She complained about how Jacob shouldn't have sided with Iktumi. Jacob's ego was getting in the way of calling Scott. He felt he was right; Iktumi told the story word for word.

Mark was relentless when Jacob wouldn't give in and call. Jacob told Mark they could have Zoe or Leah sit in and play. Mark said it wouldn't be the same with one of the girls playing, besides he was tired of the two asking him masturbation questions. Mark was right about Zoe and Leah's intrusive questions. He knew they did it to embarrass them. The two were pretty good at entrapment questions, also.

Scott had been pissed off all week about the last time they'd played the spirit game. He knew Jacob was right about Iktumi telling the story of the fight. Iktumi did tell the story word for word. Scott wanted to call

Jacob to see if he and Mark would play again, but his ego was in the way. Every time he thought about Jacob siding with Iktumi, he became angrier. What pissed him off about the fight was Jacob started it. Scott admitted to himself that he did get a little carried away with the insults, but Jacob did throw the first punches.

Scott's sister came down the stairs and told him Jacob was on the phone. As Scott walked up the stairs to take the call, his sister followed him. She asked why he hung out with Jacob.

"The only thing he has going for him is his blue eyes and his brown wavy shoulder-length hair. His body is a total turnoff. He only weighs a hundred pounds; he must have nothing in his pants."

Scott told her she should start hanging out with Leah and Zoe.

"Why would I hang out with those two losers?"

"Because you think like they do."

Scott picked up the phone and said hello. Jacob didn't waste any time, when he asked if he was still pissed at him.

"I'm still pissed off about Iktumi."

"I hate Iktumi."

"I don't like him either."

"I'm sorry I sided with Iktumi; he did tell the story word for word, though. It wasn't my intention to side with him."

"Would you like to play the game again with Mark and I?"

Scott was there in five minutes eager to play.

Before the game started, Mark had a big smile on his face as he pulled a bottle of whiskey out of his backpack. Jacob asked where he'd found it. Mark said he'd taken an empty whiskey bottle out of the trash, raided his grandmother's liquor cabinet, poured a little out of each bottle into his whiskey bottle.

"I had to be careful, grandma marks the level of each bottle in the cabinet with a piece of tape." He looked quite proud of himself, when he said, "I moved the tape down to the new level, Happy New Year."

Mark asked, "Are there any spirits who want to speak with us, tonight?" The cursor moved to the "si." Jacob could tell by the energy from the cursor, it was Iktumi. Scott looked at Jacob, he could see, Jacob was about to take his fingers off the cursor.

"If you take your fingers off the cursor, I'll kick your ass."

Iktumi asked Scott if he always settled his differences with violence.

"Fuck off, Iktumi, you're all talk no action. If you were a person, I'd love to meet you, so I could kick his teeth in."

Iktumi told Scott that Jacob wasn't going to end the game. He said, "Jacob won't end the game because he's loyal to you."

"I don't understand why he's loyal to you, after all, you're a prick." Jacob complained about how he wanted to end the game. Scott told him to quit complaining. He said Iktumi couldn't hurt them; he's was just a lost and angry spirit.

Scott told Jacob he needed to get his shit together, Iktumi was a piece of crap that nobody liked. Mark was concerned about Jacob when he told him, if he wanted to end the game he should. Jacob said he wanted to end it but wouldn't because he knew Iktumi was messing with his head. Iktumi told Jacob he was a good sport. He said he was just getting started messing with his head.

Iktumi told Scott if he cared about Jacob, he'd let him end the game. "Jacob, you need to be brave, and Mark needs to grow a pair of balls."

Scott told Iktumi his statement was coming from a spirit that didn't have any balls. "I don't think insulting Iktumi is the right thing to do."

"There you go siding with Iktumi again."

"I'm not siding with him; I just don't think you should mess with him."

Iktumi told Scott he understands how he feels. He didn't give a fuck about Jacob or his feelings, either. Iktumi said that he had killed many men, women, and children in his day, so he certainly wasn't going to give a fuck when he killed hundred-pound boy. Jacob told Iktumi to kiss his ass.

Iktumi said, "In time, Jacob, in time."

Iktumi asked Scott if he was trying to learn anything, while they played the spirit game. "I've nothing to learn from a loser spirit."

"You're right, Scott, you don't have anything to learn from me. In fact, I don't think you have anything to learn from life at all."

"What do you mean by that?"

"Don't worry, Scott; you're too stupid to understand."

Scott was angry when he asked Iktumi to give him an example.

Iktumi said, "You're messing with a demon, Scott; I'm probably going to kill you very soon."

Scott said, "Whatever."

"Scott, do you know Mark carries a Bible in his backpack?"

Scott a little surprised by the question asked, why it mattered if Mark had a Bible in his backpack.

"Don't you find it a little odd that Mark would carry a Bible around with him?"

"It doesn't matter to me."

"Mark's a lost soul searching for meaning in his life."

"The difference between you and Mark is he's on a spiritual search."

"You're just a soulless person walking around empty."

Jacob looked at Mark, he didn't say anything. Mark knew what Jacob was thinking. He was thinking Iktumi knew everything about them.

Jacob pulled his fingers away from the cursor ending the game.

Scott blew up. He yelled, "I want to know why you ended the session." Jacob said, "We're not playing the game anymore."

"That fucker Iktumi knows everything about us and he's playing us."

"Why can't you see that? Scott said, "Iktumi's just a stupid fucking spirit; he's not smart enough to play us."

"He's not stupid, Scott. He knows everything about us, he knew about the fight, word for word."

Scott turned his attention to Mark and asked him what he thought.

"Since when do you give a shit about what Mark thinks?"

"I asked Mark because you're a chicken shit, Jacob."

Mark told Scott he thought Iktumi did know too much about them. Jacob said maybe they should stay away from him. Scott said they were both needed to grow a pair. Scott wasn't backing down he was ready for the fight.

It was four-thirty in the afternoon, the sun had just gone down. The wind had been blowing hard all day. There was a huge long gust of wind that howled, so loud the seals around the doors screeched a loud scream.

"That sounded like a Red Fox screaming," Jacob said.

Mark said, "The demons are out this afternoon."

Scott said, "That sounded more like a person being attacked."

The shutters on all the west facing windows began to rattle. The lights flickered then, went out.

"Marky, are you downstairs?" a shrill voice came from the top of the stairs.

"Fuck," Mark said, he whispered, "Hide the game in case she comes downstairs."

Mark stood up and ran to the bottom of the staircase. When he looked up at the top of the stairs, he could only see a silhouette of an old lady standing there, the only light coming into the kitchen was the twilight coming through the window behind her.

"Marky, you and the guys need to walk down to Joyce's Supermarket and pick up some candles, it looks like the power will be out all night."

"Oh, grandma, it's almost a mile down to the store," Mark said it in his whiny voice.

"Marcus White Foot, you three get off your asses and get to the store, before it closes, NOW!"

Shit, Mark thought to himself, *the NOW means, I'm going, period.*

When Mark turned around Scott was flipping him off. "Fuck you, Scott."

"Okay, Marky."

The three walked up the stairs, then through the dining room into the living room. Jacob said, "Hello, grandma." She was sitting in here rocking chair wearing her blue nightgown with her pink rabbit slippers. As Jacob observed her in the dark room, he realized that Mark had the same facial features as she.

"Hello, Jacob, dear," she said it in a motherly voice. He and Mark had been best friends all their lives; she was his surrogate mother.

Mark opened the door, hanging onto it tightly, so it wouldn't get away from him. Grandma told Jacob she was going to call his dad to let him know he was staying overnight. Jacob told her not to bother, he worked the second shift, he wouldn't be home until after midnight. Scott was the last one out the door. When he went to grab the door-knob, a gust of wind blew it up against the wall.

Mark turned around and said, "You just fucking had to do it, didn't you?"

After they left, Grandma sat in her chair thinking about the evening a couple of years ago, when Jacob was spending the night with Mark. She began to cry when she remembered the call from Jacob's dad that evening, telling her Jacob's mother was killed in a car accident.

When they returned with the candles, they set them up on the table around the spirit board game. When the new session started in candle-light, Jacob could feel a difference in the energy when Iktumi was present. Iktumi told Jacob he liked the story of how his great-grandparents Josh and Jackline met and fell in love.

"Why don't you tell us the story of the wagon train that brought Josh and Jackline to this part of the country?"

"Apparently you already know the story, Iktumi."

Iktumi asked Jacob if he knew Josh had helped build the new town of Table Mesa. Jacob said he knew the story. Iktumi said he thought Jacob didn't know the real story. Jacob said Josh was part of the Table Mesa Colony that discovered the town.

Iktumi asked Jacob if he was interested in hearing the real story of how the Table Mesa Colony was a band of murderers. Jacob said go ahead and tell the story. It would be lie, anyway. Jacob thought to himself, he had said the same thing to Iktumi about the fight.

It was 1852, Leroy Abrahamson had been working on his scheme for some time now. There was good farmland thirty miles northwest of the Denver camp. Leroy had to find a way to get a small Indian settlement cleared out of the way, so he could establish a township in that area. He had given up on the prospects of gold. If he could establish a township, he could sell parcels of land for farming and ranching which in turn would make himself enough money to last a lifetime. That would also allow him to govern the township, which was his ambition in life.

He had five men he could depend on to take part in the attack. He'd been working on recruitment for weeks when six wagons rolled into camp. There had been rumors of a wagon train that had been attacked by Indians just west of the Julesburg outpost a few days earlier. Captain Joe was the lead of the train. Leroy knew there was no way Joe would be interested in joining him on his endeavor. He knew Joe was honest and had a great deal of integrity. There would probably be a good chance though, that some of the survivors of the attack would be interested in joining him.

As the six wagons rolled into camp, Leroy along with everyone else in camp greeted the survivors. After all, news of that type of attack spread fast in those parts. Leroy was already spreading the news about the gold prospects in a canyon thirty miles away. He met Josh and Jackline Jericho a couple that had two children, one of their boys had been killed in the attack. Then he met a half breed name White Foot, who was rumored to speak English and the Flat-Land language. He talked with a few more men, then left before Joe saw him, Joe didn't like Leroy at all.

A few months prior, Leroy had been talking with a gold prospector named William Harris, who said that he'd been up in the area thirty miles northwest of the Denver Camp. The prospector had searched for gold in that area and had given up. The only thing out in that area was good farmland. Williams said he was going to California, the chances of discovering gold was much better there. Before, leaving Leroy asked him for the directions to the area.

The prospector's directions which Leroy followed making his discovery, was to ride out of the camp heading northwest for twenty-seven miles, at the twenty-fifth mile turn due west. At that point, he'd be heading in the direction of the mountain range. Look for the biggest mountain. Keep heading west in the direction of that mountain, until you come to a watering hole that is located a mile east of it. You'll know you're there by a view that nobody can see, except when standing at the top of the east hill overlooking the watering hole.

The watering hole is surrounded by three hills, one hill is part of the foothills that leads up to the mountain, the second hill is south of the watering hole, the third is to the east. Together the three hills form a bowl, where the water runs down forming the small lake at the bottom. When you are standing on the hill above the watering hole looking west, you'll see a silhouette image of a sleeping man formed by the large mountain and the smaller one to the right of it. The Flat-Land tribe calls the landmark image "The Sleeping Shet."

Leroy started his trek to the area to discover whether William Harris knew what the hell he was talking about. It took him a day to get to the area. He wandered around for half a day trying to find the watering hole. On the afternoon of the second day, he rode to the top of a hill and came upon a watering hole to the west of him. He had to be careful, because there was a village just to the right of the small lake. He backed off just enough, so the people in the settlement wouldn't see him.

Leroy dropped down off his horse and stood looking at the mountain. He peered up at the peak of the mountain. Using that as a starting point and the blue sky as the backdrop he followed with his eye the outline of the mountain to the right. He continued to scan the silhouette down to the small mountain just to the right of it. Sure enough,, the smaller mountain formed a head with a nose; it did appear to resemble

THE DEMON OF TABLE MESA

a demon's face profile. Scanning back to the left, his eye followed the outline back up over the peak which appeared to be the chest, as he continued to follow the line against the sky, it appeared to look like a stomach, then a leg that led to a rock, which resembled a toe. So, the whole image, looked like the side view of a demon from head to toe laying on his back sleeping. He then said to himself, "The goddamn son of a bitching gold prospector was right."

A few days later when Leroy return to the Denver camp, he looked for White Foot. He approached him in his camp near the river. He asked him if he'd be interested in a job interpreting a conversation that he wanted to have with a settlement of Flat-Landers about thirty miles away. White Foot said he would be interested in taking the job, but wanted to know what the conversation would be about. He also, wasn't sure what language the people in the settlement spoke.

Leroy explained to him that it looked like a small clan, he didn't know for sure what language they spoke. He wanted to see if they'd be interested in moving a little further to the south where there was a larger tribal settlement. White Foot said the people who live in the village may not be the same tribe as the people in the settlement. Asking them to move there would be a waste of time. Leroy was quite insistent they have the conversation, there was quite a bit of money at stake.

Leroy asked White Foot if he knew where Mr. and Mrs. Jericho and the two children were. White Foot pointed Leroy in the direction of their burned-out wagon.

Leroy made his way over to the Jericho's wagon and started a conversation with Josh. He wanted to know if Josh would be interested in homesteading land northwest of there that would be good for farming. He continued with the conversation saying he needed to move a settlement of Indians off the land in the area, so he could establish a township which in turn would allow the sale of parcels of land.

Josh told Leroy he needed a couple of days to think about it; he said he would discuss it with his wife. Farming wasn't part of the plan, but since they had lost everything, it wasn't out of the question. Josh did want to know the terms of the agreement. Leroy told him he'd give him fifty acres of farmland, but the Indians needed to be removed one way or another. Josh angry about the death of his son said he didn't care how it was done. If he and his wife agreed to make the trip out there to start a new life, he didn't care how the people living there were removed.

Leroy asked Josh if he would keep that part of the conversation between them. Josh agreed and returned to the wagon to have a conversation with his wife. Leroy left and continued seeking out more recruits to start his new town.

Iktumi asked Jacob if he enjoyed the story. "I thought you may want to hear the truth for once."

"You're a liar, Iktumi."

"Maybe it's Josh who's the liar. After all, he started all the bullshit stories you believe, Jacob."

Scott told Jacob not to listen to Iktumi. He said he was trying to twist lies into the truth.

"Oh, Scott, I almost forgot your invitation in our last encounter."

"Are you up for the challenge?"

"I'm ready; you're not a physical being so, you can't hurt me."

Jacob reminded Scott that Iktumi wasn't like any other spirit they had encountered and maybe, it wasn't safe. Scott told him to shut up and stop whining. Scott then told Iktumi to bring it on.

"The last time we talked, I told you about the Bible that Mark carried in his backpack."

Iktumi suggested Mark and Scott switch places. Scott told Mark to get up off his ass and come over and take his place. Mark didn't think it was a good idea for them to switch places. Scott told him to shut up and get over there and put his fingers on the cursor. He told Mark there wasn't anything to be afraid of. It was obvious Mark was frightened by the idea; he hadn't played that role yet. He then complied with Scott's demands.

"Scott, reach into the pack and pull out the Bible."

Scott then looked at Mark for his permission. Jacob thought it strange for Scott to ask for Mark's permission. It wasn't like he respected anybody's privacy, anyway. Scott looked at Jacob and asked if he had something to say.

Jacob said, "Uh, no."

Mark, after putting his fingers on the cursor said he didn't realize how much power the cursor had as it moved around the board.

Iktumi told him to hold the book up in the air. The cursor stopped moving from letter to letter and started spinning around the board. Jacob told Mark he must have broken the game; the cursor had never spun like that before. Mark didn't argue about it. He thought it was better that it didn't work anyway. Scott told them both to be quiet. Scott said okay, he had the Bible in his hand. He asked, "What next?"

As Scott held the Bible in the air, the cursor started to spin faster and faster. As it sped up, Scott started to feel a burning sensation in the hand that was holding the book. He thought it was weird, the burning feeling in his hand felt like it was spinning at the same speed as the cursor on the board. The feeling started to move up his arm from his hand. The sensation moved from his arm into his chest.

Scott was beginning to freak out, he could feel the sensation in his chest. The cursor began to slow, so did the spinning sensation in his chest. The pointer slowed to a stop. Scott didn't have the same feeling anymore.

Then he heard a voice in his head. "Hi, Scott, it's me, Iktumi, were going to have some fun now."

Scott burst into tears as he freaked out. "He's in me, he's in me!" he screamed.

Mark then freaked out. He just started yelling and carrying on about how Scott shouldn't have fucked with Iktumi. Iktumi told Scott he should have listened to his friends. Scott danced around the room screaming that the weirdo was in him. As Mark and Scott were freaking out, Jacob tried to stay calm even though he was about to go into hysterics himself. Jacob knew it was useless to try to get them both to calm down.

Scott stopped crying and looked at Jacob, then said he had another story for him.

Jacob looked at Scott and said, "That didn't sound like you at all."

"What should I sound like, a Native American, an Indian that's been scalped?" He turned and stared right through Mark. "What do you think; tell me what you think, little brother."

Mark couldn't talk, he was completely pale in the face with fear

Scott's demeanor changed as he started crying again, "He's in me, he's in me, what do I do?"

Scott stood up and ran for the stairs. Jacob was worried about him when he asked where he was going. Scott ran up the stairs, out of the house and was gone.

Mark and Jacob sat there for a while, trying to figure out what had just happened.

Mark finally broke the silence and asked, "Do you think that maybe, Scott was just messing with our heads?"

"I don't know."

"Do you think Iktumi is really in Scott."

"I don't know," Mark continued to whine. "If Iktumi's in Scott, what do you think he's planning to do?"

"I don't fucking know, Mark."

"Give me a minute to think," Jacob said, as he tried to control his fear.

If Scott was messing with them, he would probably let them know in a few days, Jacob thought. Jacob continued to think. If Scott was possessed by Iktumi, then Iktumi would make the next move. "I mean, it's not like we know what Iktumi wants. If he wants anything at all," Jacob continued his line of thinking. "Iktumi may just be a crazy spirit. On the other hand, he knows a lot about us. He's probably been listening in on our conversations for a long time."

"If that's the case, he probably does have a plan, why else would he wait so long to introduce himself to us?"

A few days later Jacob called Scott to ask him if he was planning to walk to school with him when they returned to school after the winter break. Scott sounded more like himself when he told Jacob he'd walk with him to school. He told him he'd be there to pick him up at the usual time. Jacob asked if he was okay. Scott said yeah, he was but he could still hear Iktumi telling him to do things. They said goodbye and would see each other in a couple of days.

The morning Scott died, Sheriff Justice sat down with Jacob to get his statement of what led up to Scott's death.

CHAPTER 5

The Dream

Six months later. Jacob set the ladder against the back of the house to climb up on to the roof. The back of the house faced west, which was the perfect angel to get a tan from the afternoon sun. The temperature for the day was predicted to be over one hundred degrees. He sat down on the roof, then applied coconut oil to his body to intensify the tanning effect of the sun.

The personal ritual usually started earlier in the summer when school let out for the break. This year that didn't happen, until the third week of June, because there had been so many snow days from the previous winter. It was great having a lot of days off from school during the winter, but it had to be made up at the end of the school year. That cut into the summer break by two weeks.

Jacob had been lying there tanning, when Leah and Zoe climbed up the ladder onto the roof. They were talking about boys, of course. Jacob wondered to himself if they talked like that around him just to get a reaction out of him.

Zoe was telling Leah about two brothers who had just moved into the neighborhood. Their names were John and Joey. She described them both as having wavy blond hair, brown eyes, black eyebrows and black eyelashes. She said the older brother John was already growing a beard.

"They dress in the latest fashion," she said it in a turned-on voice. "John has a shirt that has 'God bless Jim Morrison' printed on the front of it. He has short shorts and tube socks with red and gold stripes to go with his Nike Blazers." She was talking about how good he was at everything he did, including kissing girls.

Jacob laid there with his eyes closed thinking to himself that she was saying it to get under his skin.

Jacob was dosing off as the two started down the ladder, chattering away about the different boys in the neighborhood. He laid there for about half an hour bored, when Susie from the house behind his came out her back door. Susie was a beautiful blond with dark blue eyes, she already had a dark summer tan. Jacob watched her as she pruned the rose bushes that were planted around their yard. As he watched her in her bikini, he was thinking she was probably a cheerleader from the private charter school.

Susie's backyard had the greenest grass of all the homes in the neighborhood. There were rose bushes that lined the backyard. The flowers on the bushes were in full bloom with bright red, yellow, and pink flowers. Jacob laid there for a while, watching her. He was thinking to himself, it was like being in the perfect dream.

Susie looked up at Jacob and said, "You could say hi instead of just staring at me, Jacob Jericho."

Jacob was startled when she said it. "Hi, Susie, are you having a good time trimming the bush?" He said it with a smile without making eye contact.

Susie gave Jacob's body the onceover. After checking him out she said, "You probably don't like girls."

"Why are you hanging out on the roof?"

"I'm working on a good tan for the summer."

"You must only weigh a hundred and ten pounds."

"You should work on developing your body into something more promising, then maybe work on your tan."

Jacob asked her if that was a joke.

Jacob sat up to get a better view. "I'm bored."

"I'd be out at the Boulder Reservoir today, but I don't have any way to get out there."

Susie looked at him with a big smile and said, "I have the keys to my dad's car."

Jacob wasn't sure if she was serious, "Let's go for it."

As Jacob climbed down the ladder, he asked her what kind of car was it. He thought it was probably a Chevy Nova or maybe a Chevy Impala. She said she didn't have any idea what kind of car it was, it was just a yellow car. Jacob followed her through the backyard and around the house. As they came around to the front of the house, there was a brand new 1974 yellow Oldsmobile 442 convertible sitting in the driveway.

Jacob said, "Shit, yeah," as he walked around to the passenger side.

Jacob was still climbing into the passenger seat when, Susie fired the engine up. Jacob told Susie about his dad's mustang. "My Dad's car is a 1966 Mustang. It's fire-engine red with a 289-V8 engine. It had air conditioning but, my dad took it out because, he doesn't think a convertible should have air conditioning. My mother's car, before she wrecked it was 1968 Chevy Camaro. It was powder blue with a white vinyl top. That car had a 327-V8 engine under the hood." Jacob thought he was impressing Susie, after all he read all the muscle car magazines. "Both cars are faster than shit."

Suzie laughed.

Jacob's mouth was running as he told Susie, "Before mom died, she was always giving dad crap about how fast he drove the Mustang." He was excited as he continued to talk. "Yeah, mom was always telling him that a married man in his thirties shouldn't be driving around in a hot rod."

"We have a 1954 Willys-Jeep Station Wagon out front of the house."

"Dad took me into to the mountains a couple of years ago in the Willys for the ritual, but I screwed it up."

"What's the ritual?"

"It's a tradition in the family. When a person in the family starts puberty in their twelfth year, dad takes them out hunting for their first animal. After killing, gutting, and skinning the dear, I was supposed to eat the heart. That marks the start of my journey to adulthood. Dad would've then painted my face with the blood of the animal."

Suzie just looked at Jacob, "Your family's a bunch of savages, Jacob; why would your dad paint your face with blood?"

Jacob shrugged his shoulders, "Dunno, I've never thought about it."

Susie took it easy as they drove through the neighborhood. She also took it easy as they cruised through town. As they turned onto the highway, Susie punch the accelerator to the floor. The engine howled when the four-barrel carburetor kick it. Jacob sunk into the seat as Susie banged through the gears. He looked over at the speedometer to see they were doing over a hundred miles an hour.

As they cruised down the highway the stereo was blasting the song "Susie Q" by "Creedence Clearwater Revival." Jacob looked over at Susie; she had a big smile of total freedom on her face. Her long blond hair flowed freely in the hundred mile an hour wind. She looked at Jacob and smiled.

They exited the highway then rounded onto the service road that led to the reservoir. Susie payed for the two of them at the gate, Jacob didn't have any money on him. When they were pulling into their parking spot, the guys were already starting to pay attention to Susie. The two of them stepped out of the car and walked over to the beach.

The water on the lake was turquoise blue as Jacob looked out over it. There were motorboats on the water pulling skiers. There were also, sail boats out on the water. Jacob wondered, why they were out there, because there wasn't a breeze blowing. The day was very hot now.

Susie and Jacob's feet burned as they walked on the sandy beach. They hadn't had a chance to sit down, they were swarmed by guys introducing themselves to Susie. There was a group of guys playing football on the grass just above the beach. One of them came over and asked Jacob if he'd be interested in the playing, their team was short a person. Jacob said sure, the two of them walked off to play.

He'd been playing ball for about an hour when Susie called to him. She said they needed to go home. As Jacob walked up to her, she explained they should leave for home before her parents came home and found she had taken the brand-new car out for a ride.

She asked him why his lip was bleeding.

"Eddy had tackled me."

"I thought you guys were playing touch football."

"We were."

The ride home wasn't as fun. Susie didn't have the same carefree look about her as they drove down 28th Street past the Shakey's Pizza Parlor, past the Oasis Diner, then past the Cross Roads Mall. Jacob continued to talk her ear off about everything except sex. She didn't hear a word he was saying. As they rounded the corner to her house, she became relieved to see her parents hadn't been home yet. She looked at Jacob and told him to keep his mouth shut about the trip to the lake. He agreed to keep his mouth shut, after all it wouldn't have gone over well with his Dad either.

He suddenly awoke on the roof, sweating badly. Zoe was coming back up the ladder when she saw him wake up. She told him he needed to get out of the sun.

Jacob was talking to himself when he said, "Shit, Susie was just a dream."

Zoe asked, "What are you talking about?"

He looked at the yard behind theirs, there was no rose bushes, no flowers, not even grass, it was only dirt.

Zoe said she was going up to John and Joey's house to visit John. She asked him if he'd like to go along, since he wasn't doing anything anyway. He thought to himself that Zoe always had to get the first jab.

"Why isn't Leah going with you, after all you two never go anywhere without each other?"

"Leah's grounded for throwing a dart at Timmy." Jacob looked again at the backyard behind theirs then thought Zoe was right, he wasn't doing anything. After thinking about it he said, "Yeah, I'll join you."

The two climbed down the ladder, walked around his house, then started up the street with Zoe leading the way. Jacob asked her where their house was as they walked along. Zoe pointed across the field, past the bottomless lake, up the hill, to a green-colored house that sat next to the high school. The high school and middle school were built on top of the hill next to each other.

As the two walked down the sidewalk Jacob asked what direction Zoe was taking to get to the house. Zoe said they were going to take the road. The road wound around the outskirts of the lake, then climbed the hill past the green house to the high school.

Jacob said taking the road would take too long. He grabbed Zoe's hand and led her across the street to the trailhead. The trail went straight through the field that surrounded the lake. At the lake the trail split into two trails, one trail led north around the lake and up the hill to the middle school. The other trail went around the lake to the south, then up the hill to the high school parking lot.

Zoe complained when Jacob changed her plans. She didn't want to walk by the lake, it frightened her. She always had a sick feeling when passing it.

Jacob said, "I walk by the lake every day going to school. I get that sick feeling every time I walked by it."

Zoe said, "I take the road around, so I don't have to walk pass it."

"You should start walking the trail every day, you need to confront your fears."

"I don't know about that, Jacob."

As the trail passed the bottomless pond, Jacob pointed to the area where the first stake was driven into the ground establishing the town of Table Mesa. "That's where the first stake was driven into the ground marking the start of Table Mesa."

Zoe asked what was the first stake.

"The first stake is driven into the ground to mark construction of the first building to be built in a new township."

"How come there's no stake there now?"

"The stake rotted away years ago."

"Who drove the first stake into the ground?"

"In the old days there was a bunch of bush-whackers, who called themselves the Table Mesa Colony. They were led by Leroy Abrahamsen. Leroy Abrahamsen wrote on the stake: 'This is the first stake driven into the ground, for the ground break of the first building by the Table Mesa Colony for the new township of Table Mesa, June 1852.'"

Zoe asked him how he knew that part of the town history, she had never heard about it.

"Great-Grandpa Josh was one of the men who belonged to the colony. The story's been passed from generation to generation."

Zoe said Leroy wasn't in any of the town history books. "What happened to him?"

"I don't know; Leroy just disappeared."

As they approached the lake Zoe complained about how hot the day was. She said even the breeze was hot. Jacob was watching the weeds wave in the breeze as his gaze became distant. He looked passed the weeds out over the water. He said he could see seaweed floating on top of the water through the ripples in it.

Jacob stopped and stared into the lake when they reached it. Zoe grabbed his hand, then asked if he was okay. Jacob said he felt like it was his fault that Scott had fallen through the ice. Zoe told him to stop blaming himself, after all everyone knew how stubborn Scott was when he made his mind up about something.

They turned and walked up the hill to the high school parking lot. From there it was an easy walk over to John and Joey's house. They walked up onto the porch and rang the doorbell. When John opened the door, he didn't have a chance to say anything, before Zoe said hi in an excited voice. Jacob was surprised by John's facial features. *He's strikingly good looking,* Jacob thought to himself. *He's probably letting the stragglers grow on his chin, so everyone will know how far along he is, in his physical development.*

John turned around and walked into the living room, signaling them to follow. He pointed to his brother, who was sitting on the couch with a package of half-eaten cookies lying next to him.

John yelled, "Hey, dumb-ass, come over here and meet Zoe and Jacob."

Joey stood up from the couch kicking a can of grape Shasta off the coffee table onto the floor.

As Joey walked over to introduce himself, Jacob was thinking to himself that Joey was a clumsy dork with big feet. Joey reached out and did "the shake" with a Jacob, who was surprised he knew it. Joey said hello to Zoe as he turned to retake his place on the couch.

Zoe sat down on the recliner next to the couch. John sat in in the middle of the couch, then leaned over toward Zoe. Jacob sat down next to Joey, there wasn't any other place to sit. Joey grabbed the package of cookies and handed them to Jacob. He ate the cookies as he and Joey sat looking at an old rerun of *I Love Lucy* on the television.

"So, where are your parents, Joey?"

Joey didn't look away from the television when he said, "Dad's at work. John and I live with him."

"My parents are divorced." He sounded relieved when he said it.

Zoe was telling John about how her friend drowned last winter in the lake at the bottom of the hill. John was leaning over closer to her listening with intrigue. She had this suspenseful look on her face as she told him, how Scott was walking across the ice in twenty-below-zero temperatures, then he fell through into icy water. Jacob couldn't tell if John was listening with sincerity or just making it appear that way. John leaned over and whispered in Zoe's ear. They both stood up and walked out of the house.

Jacob shrugged his shoulders then turned to Joey and asked if there was anything to drink in the house. Joey said there was more Shasta in the fridge as he pointed to the doorway that led into the kitchen. Jacob stood up, went into the kitchen to grab a soda pop. When he returned to the living room, Joey wasn't sitting on the couch anymore. He was looking out the front window. Jacob asked, what he was looking at. Joey said he was watching John and Zoe. That got Jacob's attention as he walked over to the window to look.

Zoe and John were walking through the parking lot of the school holding hands. Joey's house was at an angle to the school, so as Zoe and John walked closer to the school building, they moved out of sight.

Joey suggested they go to he and John's bedroom where they'd have a better view. They darted into the bedroom and looked out the window. From that window they had a good view of the school building. John and Zoe walked over to the building, sat down on one of the windowsills, then started to make out. John then started to reach up her shirt.

Jacob and Joey were becoming aroused by watching them. John stopped kissing her, then whispered something in her ear. They both jumped off the sill and walked around the building. Jacob turned to say something to Joey, then stopped when he saw that he was rubbing his crouch. Jacob told him not to masturbate, while he was there. Joey asked him what that meant, he'd never heard the word before.

Jacob said, "It's that thing your brother does at night in bed when he thinks you're asleep."

Joey just shrugged his shoulders. Jacob thought to himself that Joey should have figured it out by now. Jacob asked him if he knew what jacking-off was. Joey said no, then asked what was it. Jacob asked him if he had a burning feeling down there when he watched Zoe getting kissed. Joey said yes, he did.

Jacob said, "The next time you get that feeling, go into your dad's bathroom and grab the petroleum jelly. Slap some of that jelly on your hand then, grab your dick." Jacob stopped mid-sentence, then told him he'd figure it out from there.

Jacob told Joey not to grab the Vapo Rub, if he slapped that on his dick, it'd burn like hell. He said, "If you do that, you'll be sitting there with a burning dick trying to figure out how you going to explain it to the doctor."

Joey sat there trying to figure out the joke, he said he had the strongest bladder in the world. Jacob just stared at him not saying anything, he didn't know where Joey was going with it. "I can piss ten feet in the air."

Jacob said, "Fuck, dude, nobody can piss ten feet in the air."

Joey said, "I can."

Jacob was thinking to himself that he wasn't going to ask him to prove it, he decided the conversation should just move on to another subject.

Looking for something to do, he asked Joey if he had the video game "Pong." Joey said no. He didn't even know what it was. Jacob said it was an electronic video game that hooked up to the television. He asked Joey, if he'd heard of the Wizard Game. Joey said he had played it with some of his friends in Colorado Springs. Jacob asked if that was where he lived, before moving to Table Mesa. Joey said yes, that was where his mother lived. He said he and John would go back there after the summer break.

Jacob said he and some of his friends had been playing the Wizard Game for a couple of years, until Mark found an old spirit game in his attic. Joey asked who Mark was. Jacob said Mark was his best friend. They'd been friends, since they were born.

"What's the spirit game?"

"It's a game where players communicate with spirits. We met spirits from all over the world."

Joey's curiosity was growing when he asked Jacob how the game worked. Jacob said the players put their fingers on the pointer then, ask questions. He said the pointer spells out the answers. Joey asked if the spirit had the right answers. Jacob said sometimes it did, sometimes the answer made no sense at all.

"We were in contact with a spirit named Iktumi."

Joey said, "I know what the name Iktumi means."

Jacob asked him, "What?"

"Iktumi's the trickster spirit."

"How do you know that?"

"I learned a lot of Indian words, when I was in the 'Indian guides' with my dad. Are you and Mark still playing the game?"

"We stopped after Scott died last winter. I don't think Iktumi liked Scott. After Scott died, Mark and I couldn't find a third person to play the game."

"I'd be interested in playing with you."

Jacob thought about it for a moment, then said, "That's a great idea. Let's call Mark and see if he wants to play."

When Jacob called, Mark was a little hesitant, he then agreed to play. Jacob said they should go outside where he could point out where he and Mark's houses were located.

The two walked across the street to the high school parking lot. Jacob said he wanted to show Joey the Sleeping Demon, before he showed where his house was located. Joey asked what the Sleeping Demon was. Jacob said the Sleeping Demon is an image of a demon lying on his back sleeping. As they stood in the parking lot looking west, Jacob pointed to Bear Mountain and gave his explanation of the Sleeping Demon.

The Sleeping Demon is a mountain that appears to look like the devil lying on his back sleeping from a side view angle. The Sleeping Demon can only be seen in full at two locations. Those locations are either viewed from the high school parking lot or from the bottomless pond at the bottom of the hill.

Jacob told Joey to look at the peak of Bear Mountain and imagine that's the top of the chest. Using the sky as a back-drop silhouette, follow the line of the mountain to the right. Continue to follow the line down to the smaller mountain to the right. The valley in-between the two mountains appears to look like a neck. Continue to follow the line up and over the second mountain. That image appears to be the head. The image of the face will appear as the line goes up and over the head of the smaller mountain. The rock sticking up at the top of the smaller mountain looks like his nose. Jacob asked if he could see it. Joey said yes, he could.

Jacob told Joey to look back at the top of the peak which is the chest. Follow the line against the sky to the left. That line against the blue sky appears to show the stomach. As the line continues down the stomach it appears to lead to the leg. The rock standing up at the bottom of the leg looks like a toe. The whole image put together looks like the devil lying on his back from a side view angle.

Jacob was rather proud of his explanation of the Sleeping Demon, he asked Joey if he could see the whole image. Joey said he could see it. He then in an excited voice said again, he could see the image, he really could see it.

Jacob pointed to the toe and told him, "That's called Devil's Thumb." Joey said, "It looks more like his dick than his thumb."

Jacob laughed then thought to himself, Joey had a sense of humor after all.

Jacob said the Flat-Landers that lived there before, called Devil's Thumb the Shet. Joey asked Jacob if he meant the to say the word shit. Jacob said no, it was pronounced S.h.e.t, the shet. Joey thought about it for a moment then said, "Shet is the word the Flat-Land people call, the demon."

Jacob asked how he knew about the Flat-Land people. Joey said he'd been taught that the Flat-Landers were the people who lived on the plains, before the white man lived there.

"Oh," Jacob said, as he lost interest in the conversation, "let's go play the game." He then started down the hill toward Mark's house.

CHAPTER 6

The Vision Quest

*J*acob and Joey started the walk to Mark's around five-thirty. Joey could see from the top of the hill that the road went all the way around the lake to Mark's house. He asked why they weren't taking the road. Jacob said it would take longer to take the road, maybe five minutes longer.

As they walked down the hill toward the lake, Joey was feeling depressed. As they approached the lake, he told Jacob he had a sick feeling in his stomach. Jacob said that everyone who walks by the bottomless pond gets that sick feeling. Joey wondered what was wrong with him, he had the same feeling, he felt when he'd go with his mother to the cemetery to visit grandma in Colorado Springs. He didn't want to go to the cemetery, his mother would make him feel guilty, when he told her he didn't want to go.

"It's the same feeling I get when I visit my grandmother at the cemetery," Joey said.

"Were you close to your grandmother?" Jacob asked while thinking how close Mark was to his grandmother.

Joey said, "Yeah," then began to think back to when his grandmother had died. That's when he and his brother started to notice the change in their mother. His mother and grandmother were very close. They used to have big dinners for the family on the weekends. His mother was a nurse, she worked Monday through Thursday on twelve-hour shifts. Grandma would be at their house when he and John came home from school. She'd stay with them, until dad arrived home around five.

Grandma smoked a lot of cigarettes, maybe five a day, well that's what she said she smoked. There was a gallon jug stashed under the kitchen sink at their house. Also, there was one stashed under the kitchen sink at her house. It took him a long time, before he figured out it was a bottle of whiskey, she kept stashed under there. Before he figured it out, he had wondered, why she was senile in the evening's, then the next morning she had her mental faculties back.

Jacob turned to look at Joey as they approached the bottom of the hill. He could see Joey was in deep thought.

"What are you thinking about, Joey?" he asked with concern.

"John and I once sneaked a couple of snorts from grandma's whiskey stash to see what it would do to us."

"Did you like it?" Jacob asked, while smiling.

"Yeah, one time when we were getting tipsy, grandma caught us dipping into the stash. We knew when she told dad that we were sneaking drinks from her stash, he'd take the razor strap to us," Joey had a worried look on his face as he said it. He then looked confused at Jacob when he said, "Grandma never said a word to dad, she just told us to keep our mouths shut about the jug. She then dropped the conversation and never said another word about it."

Joey thought about his dad. "My dad is too strict on me and John," Joey said changing the subject. He remembered when his dad had whipped John for ringing "crab grasses" doorbell. He and John called the family down the street, the crab grasses. "If you walked in their yard, they'd come out of the house screaming to get off their grass."

54

John and a friend ding-dong-ditched them one evening, walking home from a baseball game. Crab Grass's twenty-three-year-old son chased John and his friend, until he caught them. He dragged them back to the house, he then called the police. John said the police were nice, when they came to the house, but they had to take them to the police station where their parents would have to come pick them up. Joey remembered how pissed off his dad was when he received the call from the police.

"Does he whip you?" Jacob asked. The concerned tone in the Jacob's voice showed that he was bonding with Joey.

"Yeah."

"I'd never seen my parents get into an argument, until grandma died. After she died, mom and dad were fighting all the time. When they told us, they were getting divorced, we were glad. We're tired of my mother's bullshit," Joey said it again with relief.

His mother had tried to turn he and John against their father. She'd tell them everything he'd done to her. She told them he was having an affair with a woman at work. He and John had discussed it, then decided it wasn't any of their business if he had an affair.

After his parents split up, she continued to use them to hurt Pa. He moved into an apartment. It was agreed that Joey and John would go over to the apartment on the weekends. Sometimes, he'd show up just to have her tell him, they didn't want to go to his apartment for the weekend. Joey was pissed about that, because she lied. He wanted to go spend time with him. Joey felt it was he and John, who were punished by not being allowed to see him.

"Mom accused Dad one evening of smashing the rearview mirror on her car. It was a Friday night; he'd stopped by to pick us up for the weekend. She was screaming at him, calling him an asshole for breaking her mirror. The argument was so loud the neighbors called the police. When the police showed up at the house, they asked him to leave. I was pissed again, because I couldn't spend the weekend with him.

"The following weekend when John and I were at the apartment, John confronted him and asked him if he broke the mirror. He only said he wasn't that kind of man. I believed him, he isn't that kind of man. He can be an asshole about some things, but it's usually, when me or John broke his set of rules. John once told me, 'If you don't break his rules and stay out of his way, he'll leave you alone,' which I learned was true. That's why I don't believe anything mom says about him."

He hadn't realized they stopped at the bottom of the hill. He was angry about everything that had happened in Colorado Springs before they moved to Table Mesa. He was so pissed off, he didn't want to go to his mother's house at the end of summer. He'd had enough shit to last him a lifetime. As far as he was concerned, he'd never go there to live. He remembered when he told his dad that he didn't want to live with his mother. Pa told him he didn't have a choice; it was court ordered. Joey was angry, he was fed up with her lies and deception.

Jacob was becoming concerned about Joey as they stood by the lake. Joey looked at Jacob, then said, "I like living in Table Mesa. The house is quiet all the time. John and I are getting along great with Pa; he isn't stressed out. I met you today, Jacob, we've already become friends. You're comfortable talking about anything with me and I feel comfortable talking to you. I don't feel like you'll put me down for saying stupid things."

Jacob grabbed Joey by the arm then said, "Come on, Joey, let's get away from the lake."

As Joey stood there thinking, he noticed a wolf spider standing in the middle of the trail looking at him. He kicked at the spider, then yelled scram as it ran into its hole. He noticed there were a lot of spider holes around them. There must be hundreds of spiders along the trail. He thought to himself, he may want to be more careful, there were probably rattlesnakes in the field, also.

As Jacob led him down the trail, Joey was almost in a trance. "Dad told me, he'd almost been bitten in the balls by a rattler when he was ten. He'd been out hunting rabbits with a friend. They were walking along the trail carrying their dinner for the night, when he almost stepped on the snake. Grandpa had told him that a snake wouldn't launch at you, unless it was curled up and rattling. That's not true, Jacob, the snake was laying across the trail. When he almost stepped on it, it jumped up and bit him on the jeans just to the right of his dick. He then jokingly told us, we were lucky the snake bit him in the jeans, otherwise we wouldn't be here." Jacob was becoming more concerned as they rounded the lake.

Joey continued to babble. "He taught us how to use guns. We know how to handle handguns and long guns. During my ritual to adulthood, Pa taught me how to set up. As I aimed at the whitetail, he told me to slowly squeeze the trigger. I hesitated, Jacob. Pa asked me if I was having a second thoughts. I said yes. He leaned over and whispered in my ear. When he stood up and back away, I squeezed the trigger. The animal's legs buckled, then it collapsed on the ground."

Joey was taught that handling guns came with responsibility. One of the responsibilities was gun safety. He would drill safety into he and John's heads every chance he had, while they were handling the guns. They had to wear eye protection when shooting. He also taught them how to disassemble the guns to clean them, then reassemble them.

Joey looked at Jacob, who was leading him down the trail. "I think I'm drunk, Jacob."

"No, Joey, it's the lake, it can have a bad effect on people."

"When I was younger, I fired the .22 handgun. Do you know how to handle guns, Jacob?"

"Yes."

"As I became better at handling the .22, I was allowed to fire the 9mm. John got to fire the .38, that gun was a little too big for me at the time." He thought back to when John fired the double-barrel twelve-gauge. When he fired both barrels, the kick threw him onto the ground on his back. Joey started laughing.

"What are you laughing about, Joey."

"Nothing, John's a dork."

There had been guns inherited as family members aged and died. Great-Grandpa Joe, who Joey was named after, had a couple of guns that had been passed down through the generations to his father. One of the guns was an 1847 Walker Colt, John would inherit that gun. Joey was going to get the Mississippi Rifle.

The Mississippi rifle was an old Mussel-loader from Harper's Ferry. Joey didn't know what Harper's ferry was, but he knew the mussel-loader was old. When his dad explained to him how to clean it, he stressed to Joey that there shouldn't be any oil residue left on the gun.

Joey still had the steps to loading the gun memorized. "Measure the powder charge in the powder measure. Pour measured powder down the barrel of the gun. Place the patch and ball on the muzzle. Push the ball into barrel with the starter. Remove the ramrod. Ram ball down the barrel. Place cap on nipple." He and John would Joke about the directions for months, that's how they memorized them.

Before Joey realized it, Jacob had led him around the lake where they were approaching the road. When they arrived at the road they turned right, walked up to the blue house. As they stepped up onto the porch, Mark came out of the house. Mark stepped down onto the porch and introduced himself. Joey reached his hand out; the two did the shake.

"You look like you have seen a ghost," Mark said as they shook hands.

Joey looked confused; he couldn't remember the walk from his house to Mark's.

Jacob said, "I think the lake got to him."

Mark looked Joey over then said, "It will do that to you."

When Joey first looked at Mark, his first impression was that he was a hippie. He had long brown hair that flowed into pigtails, which draped down on either side of his head. As Mark stepped onto the porch, Joey could see Mark's piercing almond-shaped eyes. Mark was wearing a blue jean vest with the sleeves cut off. The vest was open exposing his chest. He had a colorful beaded necklace that draped down to his midsection. As Joey observed Mark's features, he thought Mark was very handsome. He reminded him of portrait he'd seen in the museum of a Native American Chief. Joey concluded Mark was Native American or at least, he had Native American blood in him.

Mark reached out to open the screen door, but didn't get a chance, Leah was running across the front yards to introduce herself to Joey. She introduced herself to him, she immediately started asking questions about his brother John. Jacob knew she was trying to get as much information about John as she could for Zoe. Joey was doing a good job of giving her as little information as possible.

The three walked down the stairs into the recreation room where Mark had the game set up. As Joey was studying the board, Jacob and Mark were explaining the game to him, both at the same time. Joey had a full understanding of what was being explained to him. He took the information in fast. Mark launched into their experience with the game. At the same time Jacob was telling his own version of the experiences they had. It didn't bother Joey that Mark and Jacob were talking to him at the same time. He wasn't confused either, he just absorbed the information and asked questions. After about twenty minutes of being blasted with information, Jacob asked him if he'd gotten it. Joey said yes, he did.

Joey told Mark, he had learned some Indian words when he was in the "Indian Guides," with his dad. Mark said he knew some of the Flat-Land language. He said he could form a simple sentence. Jacob asked Mark how he knew about the Flat-Landers.

Mark said he had Flat-Land blood in him. He looked at Jacob and said, "You know that." Mark said he knew how to shoot arrows from the bow and arrow. Joey said he knew how to shoot arrows from a crossbow.

Jacob started to tell Joey the story of how he almost died one night when he and Mark, and some friends had taken peyote. As Jacob started his story, Mark interrupted to tell Joey that Jacob exaggerates his stories.

"I don't exaggerate my stories. My stories are true."

"Jacob's going to tell you the story of how his family ended up living along the front range."

Mark asked Jacob if he was going to tell the story of the wagon train.

"Of course, that's how my family ended up here in Table Mesa."

"Let's hear both stories," Joey demanded.

Mark told Joey, he better be ready for an X-rated story from Jacob, he was going to tell him how he was almost raped the night they were taking the peyote. Joey looked confused when Mark said it. He asked how a guy could get raped, he only thought women were raped.

Mark looked at Joey, then asked, "Where the hell have you been living?"

Jacob's eyes became distant as he started to tell his story. "Mark has a friend who lives on the reservation just south of here. His friend had stolen some peyote from the reservation spiritual leader and medicine man. It was a Friday night when we decided to take the peyote.

"It was in October, so it wasn't cold outside yet. We went over to the field next to the lake across the street. I laid on the ground next to the lake as the drug began to kick-in."

Joey could see as Jacob continued with the story; he became more distant. It was like he was reliving it.

"At first, I thought it was in a dream but, it seemed real. Indian ghosts swirled and danced around my head showing me a story of a massacre. There was a Native American village that sat next to the lake. A group of soldiers had ridden over the south hill on horseback. They opened fire on the village people, killing most of the them with gun shots. Then they rode into the village with bayonets and swords butchering everyone, who hadn't been killed by gunfire.

"There were bodies of people laying all around the village. They had killed every man, women, and child. The soldiers piled the bodies on top of each other and burned them down to their bones. After they were done burning the bodies, they threw all the bones into the lake.

The leader, whose name I think was Leroy, ordered his men to take down the burial ground that was north of the village."

Joey asked with wide eyes, "Did they rape all the women after the attack?"

"I didn't see anything like that, there were a lot of people screaming, though."

"How were you almost raped?"

"I freaked out and started screaming as I witnessed the massacre. My friends were yelling at me to shut the hell up. They held me down on the ground face down, because I was totally freaking out. They were holding my hands and feet, so I wouldn't run away. The way they were holding me, I thought they were going to butt-rape me."

Joey was startled when Jacob said it. "Do guys really do it with other guys in the butt?"

"Some guys do."

Mark asked Joey if he'd ever smoked pot.

"I've never smoked pot, but John and I drank whiskey from grandma's stash when she was alive."

Jacob said he and Mark had drunk whiskey several times, also. Mark told Jacob he could admit to smoking occasionally, the conversation was between friends. Jacob said he tried pot, but he didn't smoke as much as Mark did.

Jacob asked Joey if he'd like to hear the story of the wagon train that brought his kin to the Front Range. Joey said, "Yeah." Mark said he'd heard the story a hundred times, he still enjoyed listening to it. Mark told him to go ahead then.

There was a wagon train leaving Independence, Missouri, on March 15th, 1852. The planned route to California was to leave at dawn on the Santa Fe trail. The Santa Fe trail would lead to the California-Oregon trail. At Fort Hall in the southern Washington Territory, they'd meet the California Trail. The California Trail would lead them to the new city of Sacramento, California.

Twenty-one wagons assembled on the west side of town starting a few days before the planned departure. Captain Joe was to lead. Marcus White Foot Swanson was assigned to the train as guide and scout. There were a variety of families who made up the rest of the train. The total for the group were sixty-five people. There were thirty-six adults and twenty-nine children, some as young as two.

Captain Joe had worked for his family ranch in his early teens, leading cattle drives to and from the ranch. Joe volunteered with the cavalry when he came of age. He rapidly advanced through the ranks to captain, because of his leadership capabilities. Joe had an exceptional reputation as a commander, he was fiercely loyal to his friends and subordinates. His men would follow him into battle with confidence, because he made sound command decisions. When he retired from the army, he took the job as captain of wagon trains.

White Foot was raised in an Indian tribal community in the Nebraska Territory. His mother, who was white had survived an Indian attack that killed her family when she was fourteen. She was taken to the tribal leader by the warriors. He decided his best warrior would marry her. As Marcus grew up, he showed little interest in the warrior's path to the disappointment of his father. He did learn the ways of the tracker and scout, though.

Josh and Jackline Jericho had saved their money for the trip across the west to California. They had three children, two twin boys, Toby and Tyler and a baby girl, Tina. The boys, who were five years old, rode in the wagon with their sister. Josh and Jackline walked the trail leading the horses, because there wasn't enough room in the wagon, due to all the supplies. Josh had done his homework months before the planned departure. He had written a list of supplies:

- Six-hundred pounds of flour.

- Four hundred pounds of beacon.
- One hundred pounds of sugar.
- Sixty pounds of coffee.
- Burlap sacks of beans and rice.
- Two hundred pounds of lard.
- Two hundred pounds of dried pork.
- Ten gallons of whiskey.
- A cow.
- Dried beef.

Josh brought the ten gallons of whiskey for medicinal purposes at Jackline's disapproval. They weren't big drinkers, but they were known to have a few in a social setting. It would also, come in handy if there wasn't a good source of water. When mixing the spirits with water, the alcohol would kill the bacteria. That was Josh's argument, anyway.

The rest of the group of pioneers in the newly formed wagon train were a variety of single people and families from different parts of the country and different backgrounds. There were people making their way to California looking for gold. Some were settlers looking for land to homestead. Mr. and Mrs. Jones were a young newlywed couple in search of farmland in California. Most of the people were leaving the Missouri sickness and bad weather. They all had one thing in common. They were searching for better lives.

Captain Joe had meetings with the heads of households in the evenings a few days before departing. He explained the trail routes they'd be taking. He also said there were hazards that could be encountered along the way. Parents would have to be creative with children to help them in dealing with boredom. He told the group they needed to practice gun safety, most of the accidents and deaths on wagon trains were due to people mishandling guns.

Joe told the group that Indian attacks were rare when traveling through the plains, occasionally it did happen. The wagons would be circled at the end of the day when they were finished traveling. Circling the wagons offered protection in case they were attacked; it also kept the animals from wondering.

The first ten days on the trail were difficult, it was raining all day through the night. Pulling wagons and walking on muddy roads made life difficult. The meals consisted of mush, there was little meat to eat, unless it had been packed. Occasionally White Foot would trap a rabbit. It wasn't enough to feed the entire group, though.

The last week of May the pioneers were a couple of months into their journey. The wagon train was about fifty miles from the Julesburg Out Post. White Foot had been scouting all day as he always did. He was reporting to Captain Joe every couple of hours. He'd reported to Joe there was a party of Flat-Land warriors that had been following them most of the day.

When White Foot returned from the field to update Joe on the movement of the warrior party for the fourth time. Joe decided it was time to set up camp. It was late afternoon when he gave the order to circle the wagons. He told White Foot he needed to stay in the camp for the night. He ordered White Foot to relay the massage to the adults in the train, they needed to arm themselves just in case of an attack.

The pioneers were still in the process of circling the wagons, when the war party of Flat-Landers attacked. The warriors launched flaming arrows into the group of disorganized wagons. Captain Joe was yelling orders to the settlers to start fighting. Men and women were firing their weapons as the warriors charged. Fire arrows rained down on the frenzied group of settlers killing the unlucky ones, who hadn't had time to hide behind a wagon for protection.

Horses and oxen were killed by the flaming arrows as they rained down. Some of the animals were shot by the settlers by mistake as the animals ran around in a panic. The horses and oxen were trampling pioneers and warriors as the panic continued.

The first wave of warriors retreated, just to have a second wave attack. They came at the settlers on foot swinging tomahawks. The settlers started swinging axes as they ran out of ammunition for the guns. As the two groups swung their axes and tomahawks at each other the battlefield became a blood bath. After a few minutes of hand-to-hand combat the fight ended. The warriors then retreated from the battlefield.

It was getting dark; Joe knew the battle was over for the night. There were probably a hundred bodies lying around the area. Josh and a group of angry men went around killing the remaining wounded warriors with axes.

During the battle Captain Joe had seen White Foot get hit by an arrow in the shoulder. He went over to the area where he'd seen him drop to the ground. Sure enough, there was White Foot lying on his back with an arrow sticking out of him. Joe walked over to him to check if he was alive. As Joe walked up to him, White Foot asked if he was still living. Joe laughed then said he'd have to remove the arrow from his shoulder.

White Foot knew what that meant. Captain Joe handed him a bottle of whiskey. He told him to get started drinking, because it was going to hurt when he pulled the arrow out. Joe walked over to his wagon and grabbed the fireplace poker that he used for stirring campfires. He didn't have to start a fire, because almost all the wagons were on fire. He heated the poker, until it was red hot.

White Foot was starting to feel the buzz from the drink, when Joe knelt beside him. Joe grabbed the arrow sticking out of the front of the shoulder and broke it off. He turned White Foot over then pulled the remaining part of the arrow out the back side of the shoulder. White Foot screamed when Joe pulled it out. Joe walked over to get the red-hot fireplace poker. White Foot was trying to argue with Joe, when he rammed the poker into the wound on the back side of his shoulder. White Foot didn't scream, he just passed out. Joe place the poker back in the fire and waited for it to become red hot again. He rolled White

Foot onto his back then jammed the poker into the wound on the front side of the shoulder.

Josh returned to his wagon after killing the wounded warriors. As he walked up to the sight, he saw Jackline sitting on the ground crying. She was holding Toby in her arms. He could see Toby was dead. An arrow had entered his body from his left side. It had almost exited his right side. The direction the arrow traveled through his body had hit him in the heart, killing him instantly.

The following morning Captain Joe had a meeting with the survivors. He explained to the group that it was pointless to go on to California after the attack. He said he was going to divert to the Denver Camp by way of the Cheyenne Trail. He asked the survivors if they'd be interested in riding with him to the Camp. When arriving in the Denver Camp he was going to resign his commission. Nobody in the group argued about the planned diversion.

It took a couple of days for the surviving pioneers to bury their dead. After the dead were buried, the pioneers collected everything salvageable from the fires, then loaded it into the charred wagons. They then set out for the Denver Camp.

Jacob asked Joey if he liked the story. Joey said, "Yes, I did like it. What had happened to Scott?"

Jacob asked, "What does Scott have to do with the story of the wagon train?"

"Nothing that I know of."

"Why'd you ask me then? I told you how Scott died, he drowned in the lake last winter."

"I know you told me he drowned in the lake. You also told me that you didn't think Iktumi liked him."

Mark's right leg started to shake; Mark's right leg always shook when he was hiding something.

Trying to change the subject, Jacob said, "It's time we explain what the plan is for the game."

Mark said, "We're going to try to contact Shappa again, we know we can trust him."

Joey asked, "Why do you want to talk to Shappa?"

Jacob said. "Shappa has information we need."

Joey said, "I feel you're being vague in your answers. If playing the game with me is going to work, you two have to be honest with me."

Jacob asked, "What is it you feel we're not being honest about?"

"Did Iktumi have anything to do with Scott's death?"

Mark looked over at Jacob for direction. Jacob paused for a moment, before he answered the question.

"Mark and I decided not to tell anybody, how Iktumi killed Scott. We don't think anybody would believe our story."

Jacob asked Joey if the answer was honest and straight forward enough for him.

Joey said, "Yes, thank you for being up front about what kind of spirit we'll be dealing with. Would you tell me the story of how Iktumi killed Scott?"

Jacob said, "I don't think you'd believe the story."

"I'll believe the story."

"Okay, Joey, I'll tell you Scott's story then."

CHAPTER 7

The Spirit Guide

*J*acob told Joey where to touch the cursor. He didn't need to apply pressure, just to rest his fingers on it. Mark said when it moves, he needed to leave his fingers on it, or they'd lose the connection to the spirit. Joey asked how do the spirits communicate. Jacob said they thought the spirits channeled through the two players, whose fingers were on the cursor. Mark said they couldn't scientifically prove that was how the spirits communicated.

They concentrated on Shappa's name, so they could contact him. The three concentrated for a few moments, then Mark asked if Shappa was near. The cursor slid across the board to the "si." Joey was surprised by the power in the cursor as it slid across the board. Jacob told Shappa they were happy to contact him. Shappa asked where they had been; he enjoyed talking to them.

Jacob asked Shappa if he'd heard of a spirit named Iktumi.

"I know of him."

"Did you guys meet him?"

"Yes, we met him," Jacob sounded angry. "I warned you three about being careful, who you come in contact with."

"Who's your new friend, Jacob?"

"This is Joey, Scott's not playing anymore, Iktumi killed him."

"I'm sorry to hear that, Jacob."

"We need to find out as much information as we can about Iktumi."

"What's your plan, Jacob?"

"We don't know yet."

"I'll find out what I can about Iktumi, then I'll pass it on to you."

"It's going take a couple of hours, though."

The cursor stopped moving.

Mark asked Joey if he'd like to meet Aiyana. Joey said yes, he did want to talk with another spirit. Joey said he could feel the power in the cursor as it moved around the board. Jacob told him as he played more, he'd find that the energy is different with each spirit. Jacob asked Mark if they had to contact Aiyana. Mark asked Jacob why he didn't like her, he said she was his favorite spirit. Jacob said he didn't dislike her; he just didn't understand Mark's attraction to her.

The three concentrated on Aiyana's name, Mark asked if she was near. The cursor moved to the si.

"Is this Aiyana?"

"Yes, what happened to you, Mark?"

"It's been so long, since you came into my dreams, I missed you."

"I miss you too."

"I wish we could be together."

"I've been praying for you to come back into my dreams, Mark."

"I'm in love with you, Aiyana."

Jacob couldn't believe what he was hearing. How could he have fallen in love without meeting her?

"We haven't met, but for some reason I'm in love with you also, Mark."

"We've gotten to know each other in our dreams."

"I didn't think people could fall in love without meeting."

"Me either," Jacob said it in an angry voice.

"What was that, Jacob?"

"Oh, nothing."

"Mark, I had a dream you and I were married. Then we raised a big family in the village."

Mark thought to himself that it wasn't possible to meet her. He then said, "Maybe, someday we'll meet."

They talked for a while, then said goodnight.

A while later when they contacted Shappa again, Shappa asked Jacob if he knew anything about a massacre that took place on a village just east of the Sleeping Demon by the watering hole. Jacob said there was no massacre east of the Sleeping Demon, because there wasn't a village by the watering hole. Shappa asked if there was ever a village in that location, his sources told him there was. Jacob said he didn't think so, because the first stake for Table Mesa was driven into the ground next to the lake and there wasn't anything there before the township was created. Jacob said the only thing that's out there now, is the lake and a field of weeds. He said when the city raises enough money, they plan to put a city park out there.

Shappa asked if he was sure there wasn't a Native American village that stood there before the town was created. Mark said there was an Indian reservation on the other side of the south hill about five miles away. Shappa said his source told him, there was a village just east of the Sleeping Demon, right next to the watering hole that was wiped out during the wars in the 1800s. There was a bigger tribal community south of that location, but they're sure there had been a village community by the watering hole.

Jacob told Shappa about the night he and some friends had been out by the lake tripping on peyote. He swore he had a vision of an Indian massacre. Everyone tried to tell him it was a bad dream.

Jacob said, "I didn't think it was a dream, it seemed real."

Shappa asked him if he saw soldiers attack the village from the south hill.

"Yes, yes," Jacob said, "I did see that, they killed everyone in the village. How do you know all this, Shappa?" Jacob asked.

"I talk with spirits in my dreams."

"Jacob, are the three of you spirits."

"No, we're not."

"Shappa, are you a spirit or a living person?"

"I'm a living spirit."

Mark didn't understand what Shappa was saying.

Joey said, "We're in our reality and Shappa's in his reality, so we communicate with him through the board and he communicates with us through his dreams."

"Why does it make a difference if there was a village there or not?" Jacob asked. "For that matter, why do we care about a massacre over a hundred years ago?"

Shappa told him that during the Indian wars, there were many injustices that took place on both sides. He agreed with Jacob that in this case it was long ago forgotten, except there was one person who hadn't forgotten.

Jacob asked, "Who hadn't forgotten?"

Shappa said it was Iktumi. Mark and Jacob said Iktumi at the same time. Shappa asked Jacob if he saw how the massacre ended. Jacob said everyone in the village was killed, then the soldiers burned all the bodies.

"After they burned the bodies of the dead, they threw their bones in the lake."

Mark and Jacob exchanged glances then asked Shappa, who was Iktumi.

"Iktumi was the spiritual leader of the village."

"So, what does he want with us?"

Jacob and Mark didn't want to know the answer to the question. Jacob recalled when they first encountered Iktumi, he'd had asked him what was his problem. Iktumi replied Jacob was the problem.

Joey yelled, "Iktumi's getting revenge for something."

"That's right, Joey," Shappa said, "he's been getting revenge on every person's family involved in the killing of his family for over a hundred years. There were four people left or somebody in their family line, who he wanted to get even with, until your friend Scott fell through the ice and died. Now, there's only three left."

Mark asked if it was, he, Jacob and Joey. Shappa said Joey's family had nothing to do with the massacre, so no, it wasn't him. Jacob asked who was the third person. Shappa said he didn't know. Mark asked how he and Jacob's families were involved. Shappa said he didn't know that either. He said he'd get back to them. The cursor didn't stop moving when Shappa left.

Jacob could feel the energy change in the cursor when Shappa left and Iktumi appeared. Mark was overwhelmed by fear as soon as he knew it was Iktumi. Iktumi directed his attention to Joey. He called him Little Joe, then asked why he was getting involved in something that had nothing to do with him. Jacob looked at Joey, then signaled him to not respond. Jacob told Iktumi it was rude to interrupt. He asked Iktumi what he wanted. Iktumi said he was listening to their conversation with Shappa. He said he wanted to be the one to tell them he was going to kill them.

Jacob could feel the angry energy emanating from the cursor as it spun around the board. Mark told Iktumi in a shaky voice, they were going to get him, before he got them. Iktumi told Mark not to be afraid, he was going to make it as painless as he could for him. He told Jacob he wasn't going to get off that easily, he said when he killed him, it was going to be a very painful death.

"You're also, going to suffer before I kill you Jacob."

Iktumi told Joey he'd only give him one warning about staying out of it, it had nothing to do with him. Jacob told Iktumi to fuck off, as he took his fingers off the cursor, breaking the connection.

When Jacob and Joey started the game again, Shappa reappeared wanting to know where they had gone. Jacob explained to him, when he had left the last time, Iktumi appeared.

Shappa told them they need not provoke Iktumi, "He is an evil spirit. Jacob, I need to explain to the three of you what is going on here.

Iktumi was the spiritual leader and medicine man of the village that was destroyed before, the town of Table Mesa was created by Leroy Abrahamsen. Leroy wanted all the land around the watering hole to create a town, so he could sell parcels of land. Some of the parcels would be in the town limits and some were in the surrounding country, good for farming and ranching. The Flat-Landers who lived in the village were unwilling to move. Their only option was to move to the tribal community to the south, which was out of the question.

"Leroy being very greedy and wanting the land, didn't care if he killed everyone in the village to get what he wanted. He made a deal with his friend George McCabe to massacre the people in the village. McCabe and his small army of men patrolled the front range of the Rocky Mountains for the federal government. He made money on the side from farmers and ranchers who wanted Flat-Land renegades killed for crimes they committed against their property. Most of the Flat-Landers McCabe and his men lynched were innocent of any wrongdoing."

"What does that have to do with Mark and I? Why are we the target of Iktumi?"

"Josh and Jackline Jericho were your kin, Jacob. Josh made a deal with Leroy right after they arrived in the Denver Camp."

Jacob interrupted Shappa to tell him, "I know the story of why they moved to the front range, because the wagon train Josh and his family were a part of, had been attacked near the Julesburg outpost." Jacob said, "One of their sons was killed in the attack. They diverted to the Denver Camp instead of continuing to California. Josh joined the Table Mesa Colony, while they were staying in the Denver Camp."

Shappa told Jacob that was all true but, the story that Josh passed on to the next generation didn't include the fact that the Table Mesa Colony massacred the people in the village.

Jacob said, "Fuck, Iktumi was right, then."

Mark asked what he had to do with it, nobody in his family was involved in any agreement with Leroy.

"Your family line goes as far back as Jacob's."

Mark was confused, he knew he had Flat-Land blood in him, nobody ever told him where it came from. It was never talked about in the family, it was taboo to talk about it.

"White Foot is your great-grandfather, Mark. He was translating for Leroy, while in negotiations with the Chief of the village."

Mark said, "At least I now know where my middle name comes from."

Mark still didn't understand what it had to do with him. Shappa said his family line came down from White Foot, who helped discover and build the town of Table Mesa.

Mark said, "If I'm a descendant of White Foot, that means I'm a descendant of yours."

Shappa said, "It does appear that way."

"Jacob, do you know the name of the leader of the wagon train that was attacked?"

"I know his name was Captain Joe, but I don't know any more about him."

"According to the story, after the wagon train arrived and disbanded in the Denver Camp, he moved south somewhere."

Shappa said his last name was Fracks. Joey was in disbelief when he said that was his last name. Shappa said he knew that.

Jacob and Mark looked over at Joey as the same time then said, "Joe Fracks, what the fuck."

Joey had a confused look on his face as he thought to himself, *What the fuck did I get myself into?* He asked if Mark and Jacob were messing with his head. Shappa said he had to leave again but would get back to them with more information.

Jacob could hear Leah and Zoe coming down the stairs talking. When they reached the bottom of the stairs, they walked into the room and immediately started their interrogation of the guys.

Leah asked, "Why are you guys playing that stupid game all the time?"

Zoe started asking Joey questions. She wanted to know more about his brother John. Jacob had queued Joey earlier in the day about not saying anything, especially to Zoe and Leah.

He gave Joey the "zipper over the lips" sign as they started to question him about what he and Jacob had seen earlier. Joey stayed silent thinking for a moment, then he said they'd just sat around watching TV most of the afternoon.

"Were you and Jacob looking at the skin magazines John has hidden in his bedroom?"

Joey not taking the bait said, "I don't know anything about skin magazines."

"John told me about the magazines."

"I know what guys do when they looked at skin magazines."

Joey looked at Jacob, then said, "I don't know anything."

"About what?" Zoe asked drilling into Joey.

Joey held his cool then said, "I don't know what other guys do."

Leah turned her attention to Zoe and said Joey was kind of cute.

Joey blushed when Zoe said, "Yeah, he's not as cute as John, though." Zoe said, "I wonder if he kisses as good as his brother. Do you want to try kissing me, Joey?"

As his blush turn to a full red embarrassment he said, "Uh, no."

Mark knew that trap all too well.

Zoe asked, "Are you gay, Joey?"

Joey looked at Jacob for help to get out of it.

Jacob said, "He seemed excited when John was kissing you on the windowsill earlier today." He thought to himself, he'd just blown it.

Zoe ripped into Jacob. "Joey just told me you were watching TV." She accused them of watching her and John on the windowsill earlier in the day.

Joey gave Jacob the "You just fucked up look" as Jacob said they'd notice it from the bedroom window.

"Yeah, from the bedroom window," Joey said.

Zoe wasn't backing off. "What were you doing in the bedroom?"

Joey jumped in fast and explained he was just showing Jacob, his and John's room.

The girls left saying as they were walking out of the room, they'd take it up with them later. Mark looked a little confused when he asked Jacob what was that all about. Jacob said he'd no idea, he couldn't figure them out anyway.

Mark said, "The next time they come into the house, I'll have my grandmother stop them at the front door."

Jacob said, "You should hear the way they talk around me, sometimes you'd think I was one of the girls."

Joey thought to himself, *Oh, shit, I left the jar out.*

Joey turned to Jacob and said, "Fuck, I left the jar open in the bedroom."

"You mean the petroleum jelly jar."

"Yeah." Mark burst out laughing.

When they reached Shappa again they had more questions. Shappa said he'd acquired more information. Jacob asked what Scott's family connection was to the people, who committed the massacre. Shappa said Scott Abrahamsen was the great-grandson of Leroy Abrahamsen.

Jacob looked at Mark then said, "That's why Iktumi killed Scott."

"That means meeting Iktumi wasn't a coincidence."

"Iktumi been planning it all along." Jacob had thought Iktumi wasn't anything serious when they first met him, he realized Iktumi was planning to kill he and Mark after all.

Jacob said, "I can't believe Josh would willingly take part in murder."

Shappa said Leroy took advantage of the loss of his son.

"How did Leroy take advantage of him?"

"Leroy knew Josh was angry about his son's death. When somebody is mourning the loss of somebody close to them, they don't always make rational decisions. With that knowledge Leroy was able to manipulate Josh into joining the Table Mesa Colony."

"What was White Foot like?" Mark asked in a wondering tone.

"I don't understand the question. Are you asking if White Foot was capable of murder?"

"Was he?"

Shappa said, "No, Mark, White Foot was a womanizer, not a murderer."

"What was his son, who was my dad like?"

"Let's just say he passed a lot of his traits down the family line."

Jacob asked, "What was the deal that Leroy and Josh made?"

"Jacob, you need to understand that the deal made didn't necessarily happen the way it's been told."

"What do you mean?"

"I have visions of things that will happen. I also, have visions of things that have happened, but that could change if something happens in the past to change the course of the future."

"I have no idea what you just said, Shappa."

"I'll explain it to you in the future, Jacob. Let's just say that the future or the past may change."

"Okay, Shappa, what was the deal Leroy made with Josh, before events changed, if they changed?"

"Leroy had offered Josh one hundred acres of land on the other side of the south hill from the village. The land sat between the south hill and the tribal community further south."

"That's not where Josh and Jackline's farm was built."

"It was built on the top of the east hill where the high school is located."

"That's what I've been trying to tell you, Jacob, stories change."

"Are you sure they told you the farmland offered to Josh was to the south?"

"I can only pass on the information given to me."

Jacob said there were stories passed down through the generations about how the house Josh built shook like crazy when the Chinook winds blew during the winter.

78

"Josh and Jackline wouldn't move though, the house had one hell of a view of the Sleeping Demon."

Mark asked Shappa if he'd tell him more about White Foot. He said he didn't know much about his family on his dad's side.

"I don't want to hurt your feelings, Mark, by telling you what your great-grandfather was like."

"Iktumi wants to kill me, so I'm not concerned about getting my feelings hurt."

"Some things are better off untold."

Mark said, "We've gone this far, I want to hear the truth."

"There had been a lot of resentment on the part of the Flat-Landers as the Europeans encroached on the land in North America. For many years the Flat-Landers tolerated the invasion, because there was enough land to share. As more and more pioneers moved west, it began to cause scuffles between the two cultures. For the most part both sides kept it to a minimum, after all the two groups of people did trade with each other. They had also signed peace treaties.

"Both peoples were guilty of atrocities that took place during the Indian wars of the eighteen-hundreds. Flat-Landers would be attacked by white settlers. Pioneers would be attack by Flat-Landers. The Indian community that White Foot was born into, had attacked his mother's family ranch in retaliation for an attack, her father participated in."

"I didn't take part in that attack, I was hunting bison that day."

"They killed everybody in the family except her. The warriors took her to the Chief, who gave her to his best warrior, me. I never forced myself on her. Over a period of three months, she and I slowly bonded, then married. Nine months later a baby boy was born. His right foot was the color beige, his left foot was white. White Foot just seemed like the appropriate name for him."

Mark looked at Jacob and said, "That's weird you have the same color variation."

Jacob said, "So what, that doesn't mean anything."

"When White Foot turned thirteen, he left the community looking to find meaning in his life. He drifted in and out of the two cultures trying to find a place where he'd fit in. I didn't know if he was a lost soul or a free spirit. He didn't know himself as he started doing peyote trips hoping to get some direction in life.

"My son took odd jobs in the white man's culture. He was an excellent guide and tracker. He'd once taken a job with a bounty hunter tracking an outlaw. He was good at taking beginner fur traders out in the wild hunting bear, buffalo, raccoon, you name it. White Foot had taken a job guiding for wagon trains when he met Joe Fracks.

"Joe Fracks who was well respected in the cavalry had retired. After he retired, he took the job as Captain of wagon trains. White Foot and Joe had become very good friends over the couple of years they rode together. When Joe put together planned routes for wagon trains to California, he always requested White Foot be his guide and scout.

"He and Joe would have long conversations along the trail about how they wanted to someday find wives, then settle down and raise families. Joe said one of his dreams was to homestead land in a small community called Colorado Springs. It wasn't established as a city or town yet, but it was up and coming. White Foot, who always felt lost said he'd like to raise a family of his own, but he didn't know where he wanted to live, he hadn't found any place that felt like home to him.

"Captain Joe and White Foot had spent time in camp after traveling all day with Josh and Jackline. Josh had quite a stash of whiskey that he had brought along. Joe had a little of his own, so they'd go over and spend the evenings with the Jericho's, before calling it a night. They'd become good friends with Josh, Jackline and the kids. White Foot had become close to the kids, that's when he came to the realization that he was going to find a way to raise a family of his own.

"Toby and Tyler had bonded with Joe. He let them ride with him on the lead team as they traveled through the plains. They would listen to his stories for hours never getting bored. He became their hero, because most of his stories were about him, while he was in the cavalry. Jackline was thankful to Joe for allowing them to ride with him. It gave her a chance to spend time with Tina in their wagon, not to mention she didn't have to walk.

"After the wagon train was attacked, Joe told White Foot he'd just had enough of all the injustices he'd seen over the years during the wars. He couldn't stomach seeing children murdered like he saw with Josh and Jackline's son. He said that was the last straw. He was moving south to find his dream in life.

"When the burned-out wagon train arrived in the Denver Camp, Josh and White Foot were easy targets for Leroy. Leroy was a predator. He'd tell a person everything they wanted to hear. Leroy knew White Foot longed to find a wife and settle down to raise a family. Leroy offered him the job of interpreting the conversations, between the Chief of the village and himself.

"White Foot asked what the job paid. Leroy said he'd give him fifty acres of good farmland. Leroy told him he was going to build a town near the watering hole. He was going to be the mayor of the new city of Table Mesa. He said with the position of mayor he'd be able to introduce him to plenty of good women who would be interested in marriage."

Mark asked if White Foot had any idea what Leroy was planning.

Shappa said, "I don't know, Mark, White Foot did have a dark side. Iktumi and his family were killed in the attack on the village over land that Leroy wanted. Land Iktumi's ancestors had live on for hundreds of years."

"It's irrational for Iktumi to kill Jacob and I over something we hadn't done."

"Mark, there's nothing rational about a demon; you guys made the mistake of meeting him."

Jacob said jokingly, "I wanted to get revenge on Iktumi, now it looks like we must go after Leroy Abrahamsen and George McCabe."

"If you are serious, Jacob, I can help you with that."

"I'm just kidding, Shappa."

"Why do you want to go after Leroy and George McCabe, Jacob?"

"Justice would be one reason, I guess. Maybe I could undo the injustices that Josh committed."

"If I had a way for you to bring Leroy and McCabe to justice would you be interested? You'd have to be sincere in your belief, you're doing the right thing."

"I am, Shappa, but how would I do it?"

"You have to pass through 'The Portal to When' to the time after the massacre. You'd have to be placed after the massacre, that's when Leroy and McCabe will be building the town of Table Mesa. Once you capture Leroy and McCabe, you'll take them to the tribal council for trail."

"I have to leave again. I'll contact you in a few minutes."

Joey without hesitation said, "I'm going with you, Jacob."

"Thanks Joey." He looked at Mark and asked if he wanted to go. Mark said he'd have to think about it.

CHAPTER 8

The Portal To When

When they contacted Shappa, Jacob asked, "How are we going to catch Leroy and George?"

"All I can do is tell you where and how to access the portal, Jacob. It's up to you guys to figure out how to catch Leroy and McCabe."

"Can you give us some ideas on how to catch them?"

"There are things in life, you'll have to figure out for yourself, Jacob."

Mark said, "What you're telling us, Shappa, is once we're in 1852, we'll have to wing it."

"Not quite in those words, Mark."

Joe said, "I think we can handle it."

Jacob asked Shappa to tell them about the portal.

"The portal is kind of like a worm hole in space. The worm hole is a shortcut that connects one place to another. The portal can take you from one place in time to another place in a different time."

Joe said he understood, "We'll enter the portal here in our time in Table Mesa, then exit the portal in 1852 in the same location."

"You have the right idea, Joe. You could also, exit the portal in any location you asked the Shet to place you."

Jacob asked, "So, how do we access the portal?"

"The portal can only be accessed once a year."

"Why is the portal only allowed to be accessed once a year?"

"It's not a rule that it can only be accessed once a year. It's because, there is only one day out of the year the shadow of the Shet falls on the lake."

Mark asked, "What day is that?"

Shappa said the longest day of the year was the first day of summer. "When the sun goes down behind the Shet, it casts the longest shadow of the year. The tip of the shadow touches the lake causing the portal to open."

Jacob said, "The first day of summer always falls on the twentieth of June, that's tomorrow."

Joe asked, "How do you know that?"

"I know it's the first day of summer, because my watch told me."

"I've never seen a watch that has a calendar. Can I see it?"

Jacob took his fingers off the pointer and ran around the table to show Joe the watch. He knelt next to Joe and started to show it to him.

Jacob said, "Joe, check this out, it has three dials, this one sets the time. See this dial, Joe, it sets the month."

Joe with wide eyes open said, "Cool."

"Yeah, and check this out, the third dial sets the day," Jacob was getting pretty wound up as he showed off the waterproof watch. "I saw a digital watch in the watch store that sold for over two thousand dollars."

"Wow, two thousand dollars."

"Yeah, my dad wouldn't buy it, though."

"Where's the dial that winds the watch up?"

"I don't have to wind it up, it has a battery."

Mark asked, "Hum, Jacob, did you forget something?"

"Would you guys put your fingers back on the pointer?"

As soon as they laid their fingers back on the pointer, Shappa asked where they had gone.

Jacob apologized, "We were having technical difficulties," as he smiled at Joe.

Joe said, "Yeah, technical difficulties."

Shappa asked, "Do you want to know how to access the portal or should we sit around and talk about magic?"

"Sorry, Shappa, so how do we access the portal?"

"The way to access the portal is by way of peyote."

"I'M IN."

"I knew you'd be the first to volunteer as soon as you heard the conditions, Mark. You'll need to take the peyote an hour before the sun goes down. You want it to kick in around the same time the shadow reaches the lake. You'll have to be sitting on the west shore of the lake when the shadow passes over."

Jacob said it sounded easy enough. Just take the peyote an hour before sundown, then wait for the shadow to take them away.

Shappa said, "There's more to it than that. You guys have to memorize a prayer, asking the Shet where and when you want to be placed in time."

"What's the prayer going to say?"

"I don't know, Jacob, it's up to you three to create the prayer that will be used."

Jacob asked Shappa if he could tell them what it would be like traveling through the portal.

"When the shadow passes over, you will feel a powerful lurch in your stomach area. Don't let that scare you, it's just the force grabbing hold, to keep you stable, while traveling through the portal. Don't eat anything before passing through, the portal. You're going to barf anyway, when the peyote wears off. If there's food in your stomach, it will make the nausea much worse.

"Starting fifteen minutes before the sun goes down, start the prayer asking for permission to use the portal. In the prayer ask the Shet to place you in the location and time of the Indian massacre that took place a couple of miles from the Sleeping Demon in the direction of the sun rise. Under no circumstance are you to use the day, month or year on your watch calendar, because the Shet won't understand it. You'll have to join hands during the prayer otherwise you could be drop off separately in different locations."

Jacob asked, "Is there anything else, we need to know?"

Shappa said, he wanted to give them more information about Leroy Abrahamson and George McCabe before they left, so they'd understand what kind of men they were dealing with.

"I think we already know, Shappa."

"I'm going tell you the story anyway, so you won't have any misunderstandings what these men are like."

"Okay, Shappa, go ahead and tell us then."

Leroy Abrahamson and Colonel George McCabe had known each other for over twenty-five years. They hung out in the Hansen Gang from their late teens, until their late twenties. The gang was known for rustling cattle along the open prairies on the edge of rancher's lands in the Nebraska Territory during the 1830s. They were known by the law as a group that rob banks, kidnaped people for ransom, and murder. For some reason they were considered heroes among the common folk, who lived in that part of the country.

Leroy had been living in the Denver Camp for about a year. The camp sat just east of the Rockies on the Platte River. Leroy had an idea that he would discover gold in the canyon just west of the camp. He'd gone up into the canyon several times in the last few months with no luck in finding gold. He was beginning to realize that gold prospecting wasn't his thing. After all it was to honest a living for him. Land was where the money was as far as he was concerned. A person could deal in land the same as cash.

George McCabe had just ridden into camp with his twenty-man cavalry force. McCabe and his men had been patrolling up and down the front range of the Rockies for a couple of months looking for Flat-Land out laws. Not necessarily under orders, McCabe and his men had been known to kill groups of Flat-Landers that were rumored to be attacking wagon trains and were also known for not moving to reservations when ordered.

As soon as McCabe's men set up camp on the out skirts of the Denver Camp, they started drinking and raising hell. Leroy was already in search of McCabe; he wanted to make a deal with him as soon as possible. He was already starting to put together his colony for the building of the new city of Table Mesa, but he needed to get a problem out of the way first. McCabe was the man, who would help solve his problem.

A big jug of whiskey was going along with Leroy for this deal. He approached the camp around six pm. As he walked into the camp, he asked a couple guards where he would find old man McCabe. The two told him, he couldn't just walk into their camp and ask to talk to the boss without them knowing who he was. Leroy told them to let McCabe know that his friend Leroy was there to visit with him.

George came out of his tent to greet Leroy as soon as he heard that he was there. George asked what was he doing in that part of the country. Leroy said he was looking for gold, but he'd given up. He said he had a deal if he was interested in hearing it. George signaled Leroy to follow him into his tent where they could speak privately.

When the two sat down, Leroy pulled out the bottle of whiskey. George knew there was going to be a deal made as he pulled out two cups to fill with the drink. Leroy said he had a deal for him that would make them both rich. George told him he was making a good living roaming the Front Range with his men. The pay from the federal government wasn't that good, but he made deals on the side with ranchers and farmers, which made him some good money. Leroy said he should quit while he was ahead, if he was caught killing Flat-Landers, he'd be tried and hanged for killing innocent people.

George asked what was the deal. Leroy said rumor had it there was gold in the canyon about thirty miles, northwest of there. Ten miles south of that canyon was another canyon that may possible have gold, also. If they were to acquire all the land between the two canyons and all the land miles to the east, they could sell parcels to farmers and ranchers. They could also take over the mining supply camp at the mouth of the north canyon. The land to the east was good for farming and ranching, with that land they could sell farmland to newcomers to the area.

What's the catch George asked, knowing Leroy wouldn't be there, unless he had a problem that needed to be dealt with. Leroy leaned over to pour more whiskey into both cups. The catch was, there was a village of Flat-Landers sitting next to the watering hole between the two canyons. It sits just east of the Sleeping Demon which Leroy then explained to George. George knowing what direction the conversation was headed asked, how many people were in the village. Leroy said roughly one-hundred people give or take.

George asked what was his take going to be on the deal. Leroy said he wanted seventy-five percent of everything for himself. George said he wasn't going to risk everything he'd worked for his entire life for twenty-five percent of the take. Leroy said take it or leave it. George said he'd fucking leave it; he wasn't going to do the dirty work for twenty-five percent. George said fifty, fifty. Leroy said it was his idea, but he'd be willing go sixty, forty.

George told him to take his bottle of whiskey and get lost, he pulled his gun and stuck it in Leroy's face. He said he should put a lead ball in his head for insulting him with that kind of offer. He laughed and said he'd take forty-five percent. Leroy said he'd be willing to settle on forty-five, fifty-five.

There was one catch though. Leroy asked what would that be. Leroy was going to have to invest some of himself in the dirty work; that meant he'd have to ride with the group, while they attacked the village. Leroy said he had a deal.

The following evening Jacob, Joe, and Mark sat on the west shore of the lake getting ready. Jacob asked Mark if he had any problems getting the peyote from his friend on the reservation. Mark said he had no problems. Jacob looked over at Joe, who was memorizing the words to the prayer. He asked him if he was ready for the trip. Joe said yes. He said they should take the peyote; it was seven-thirty. Jacob and Mark agreed, all three took their hits.

As they took the peyote Mark said he was having second thoughts about going through the portal. Jacob asked, "What's the problem?"

"I've never known you to hesitate. Jacob, you're no hero, so why are you going?"

"I'm being drawn to it. I know in my heart it's the right thing to do."

"That's not a good reason, Jacob."

"Mark, you're the one who always says to take a leap of faith, so why are you trying to back out?"

Mark turned to Joe and asked him why he wanted to go. Iktumi told him to stay out of the situation, he had nothing to do with it.

"I asked myself the same question. I then asked myself what Captain Joe would have done."

Jacob asked if he believed Captain Joe would have gone.

Joe said, "Of course he would've gone, he was loyal to his friends."

"Both of you are my friends, therefore I'm going."

Joe looked at Mark with empathy. He could see Mark was frightened by the idea. He asked Mark what was he afraid of. Mark didn't take his eyes off the water as it lapped up onto the shore.

"I'm next to die. I know it."

"Joe, your kin had nothing to do with the massacre."

"Captain Joe rode off south and started a new life when he left the Denver Camp."

"I understand why Jacob wants to go. He wants to fix the injustice Josh committed. Iktumi wants to kill me."

"I don't know what crimes White Foot committed against his family, if he committed any at all."

Jacob wanting to move on told Mark they needed to start the prayer. He said this time he was telling Mark he was going. Joe agreed with Jacob, he said they were going, and Mark was going with them. He then said they needed to start their prayer. Mark conceded to the other two. They joined hands and started the prayer.

"Dear Shet, please allow us access to the portal. It's necessary for us to go to the area and time of the massacre before, it took place east of the Sleeping Demon by the lake."

They continued to chant the prayer for a few minutes when Jacob could feel the peyote taking effect. Their chanting continued not letting anything distract them. They continued to chant the location and time where they wanted to go.

Jacob kept thinking to himself that if Mark and Joe weren't concentrating on the goal, he'd end up going through the portal alone. He couldn't get it out of his mind. If they screwed it up, he'd end up in 1852 alone. He thought he'd never forgive them for that. He then told himself to concentrate on the prayer and not the negative thoughts.

Jacob became confused as the peyote kicked in. It felt like something reached into his midsection and grabbed his spine. He screamed in pain as he felt this powerful force wrench him forward. He could hear Mark and Joe screaming also. They took off at a fast acceleration into space. Mark had no idea where they were headed as they passed stars, still rapidly accelerating even faster. He was thinking to himself as they traveled through the portal that he was finally going home.

They continued to accelerate faster, and faster, then all three heard a voice say, "It's not time yet."

As soon as they heard it, the three splashed into the water of the lake. They were in waist deep water when Jacob stood up, he walked over to the shore and threw up. Mark followed right behind him. He crawled up on the shore and threw up. Joe walked up onto the shore and lied down on his stomach then throw up.

Jacob stood up, looked at Mark and Joe lying on the ground next to the lake and said, "Shit, you guys don't have any fucking clothes on." He then looked down and realized he didn't either. Joe sat up and started to look around the shoreline for his clothes.

Mark sat there saying, "Oh, fuck." Jacob looked around to see they were in the exact same place as before, except it was morning, the sun was over the east hill.

Joe asked why were they back in the same place. He remembered they were hauling ass through space. Yeah, Mark said they were moving like a bat out of hell. Jacob said he heard a voice say, "It's not time yet." Joe said that must be why they were back at the lake.

Mark said, "If that's true, then where are our clothes?"

Jacob said, "Our clothes must have blown off from the force of the Shet when it grabbed us. You guys know what I mean, it's like the clothes get blown off people when they're in an airplane crash."

Mark looked at Jacob and shook his head, he had no idea what he talking about.

Jacob turned to see eight warriors standing there with bows drawn on them. Shit, he thought to himself, that wasn't the only problem they had. He could see past the warriors to where his and Mark's homes had been. There was nothing there, but field all the way up the foothills that led to the Sleeping Demon. Mark said he didn't remember an Indian village between the lake and the road. Joe asked what road. Mark asked the other two if they could speak the Flat-Land language. Jacob told Mark that it wasn't the time to joke around.

The men signaled them to follow them into the village. They were led through the village to the longhouse in the village center. They followed the men into the council room where they were greeted by the tribal elders. The elders were three men sitting at a table with at least ten additional men gathered around the room. Joe said it must be the clan leaders. Yeah, Mark agreed they were going to be judged.

Sitting in front them was Chief White Lightning. On his right was his best warrior and Counselor, Roaring Fire. Sitting to his left was his spiritual counselor and medicine man Iktumi. The three men sat observing the strangers standing before them. Roaring Fire reported to the Chief that some of his men had seen the three just appeared on the edge of the village out of nowhere. Roaring Fire asked if they should put them to death, they were ghosts from the spiritual realm. White Lightning told Roaring Fire not to be so quick to judge. The Chief knew enough English to ask their names.

After he learned their names White Lightning asked Iktumi for his opinion. Jacob realized it was Iktumi sitting to White Lightning's left.

Man, that's the biggest nose I've ever seen, Jacob thought as he observed Iktumi sitting before him. Iktumi's nose took up a quarter of his face. He didn't look like any Flat-Lander he'd ever seen. Iktumi had a big square head with slanting eyebrow ridges that sloped down an inch from the middle of the top of his big bulge for a nose. His mouth sloped down at the same angle from the center as his eyebrows. He had long dried out stringy hair that frayed like an out of control Afro. And that medicine man necklace looks like the one Mark found, Jacob thought.

Joe looked at Jacob and said, "That is the ugliest fucker I've ever seen."

"No shit," Jacob said as he couldn't take his eyes off how ugly Iktumi was.

Iktumi said he thought maybe, they were white slaves except, for Mark. He looked to have Flat-Land blood in him. Roaring Fire continued to observe the guys, when he turned to Chief White Lightning and said, "Poor Jacob looks like the runt of the litter."

White Lightning said, "Looks don't always tell you everything about a person."

Iktumi said he'd heard stories of the white man holding slaves in the direction of the sunrise, but he'd never heard of them holding boys as slaves.

Mark turned to Jacob and said, "That's Chief White Lightning sitting between Iktumi and Roaring Fire."

"At least I can tolerate the Chief's looks."

"Fuck, when I look at Iktumi I want to barf again," Jacob said.

"Yeah, at least he looks to be a Flat-Lander with his round face, almond-shaped eyes, and flat nose," Mark said as they observed him.

"I like the peacock feathers coming out from behind his head," Joe said.

Mark said the feathers were a part of his war bonnet.

Roaring Fire suggested, maybe they'd come into the world on Ship Rock. The Chief said he had conversations in the past with tribal leaders who lived near there. There hadn't been any legends of slaves coming into their world on Ship Rock that he'd heard. Iktumi said maybe the people who live near Ship Rock wanted to keep it secret after all, that's how the people who live there, come into the world. Maybe, they feel it's disgraceful for slaves to use the rock to access our world.

Jacob said to Mark, "Check out that scar Roaring Fire has on the side of his face."

"Yeah, it looks like somebody sunk a tomahawk in his head."

Joe said, "I'll bet White Lightning and Roaring Fire are brothers; they look just alike."

Mark said, "Except Roaring Fire has a tomahawk print down the side of his face."

Jacob said, "I bet he's been shot by ten arrows at least."

Joe said, "Yeah, ten arrows."

Iktumi said to White Lightning the whole thing of them appearing out of thin air was unnatural. He agreed with Roaring Fire they should kill them. White Lightning told Iktumi they weren't going to put them to death. He asked Iktumi what kind of people would they be if they killed them. Roaring Fire asked the Chief what were they going to do with them then. White Lightning said he felt the spiritual realm had entrusted him with their souls.

Mark turned to Jacob and said, "I think they're going to butt rape us."

Jacob said, "They're not going to do anything of the sort."

Joe said, "Shit, I just became a man yesterday, now I'm going to have to take it like a man."

Mark burst out laughing.

Jacob turned to Joe and said, "For Christ's sake, Joe, you're starting to sound like Mark."

Mark asked Jacob, "Why are they looking at our dicks?"

Roaring Fire asked the Chief, "Why would all three have their foreskin removed?"

The Chief said it must have been some form of punishment performed on the slaves when they didn't behave. Iktumi said it may be some form of religious ritual.

Roaring Fire said, "Maybe, they were punished for messing around with one of the slave owner's daughters."

"That must be it then," Iktumi said.

Roaring Fire said, "If I caught any of them messing with one of my daughters, I'd cut more than their foreskin off."

Everybody in the longhouse erupted in laughter.

Joe looked around at the laughing men then asked Jacob in an angry voice, what he thought they were laughing at.

Mark turned and looked down at Joe's dick and said, "They're laughing at your little bearded monkey."

Mark started laughing right before Joe punched him in the forehead. That crossed the line with Mark, he was passive, until someone punched him. The fists went up and Joe and Mark started punching each other. The Chief signaled two of his men to grab the two and separate them before somebody was hurt. Mark and Joe then returned to each side of Jacob.

Iktumi asked the Chief what he thought Mark said to Joe.

"I don't know. He probably told him he had a little dick."

The whole house erupted in laughter again. Joe stood there red faced with anger. He didn't speak the native language, but he knew what the Chief had just said.

Before he thought about it, he blurted out, "Keep it up, chief, and I'll come over there and punch you in the head too."

The Chief rose to his feet staring through Joe. Joe could feel the power and strength emulating from his eyes. The Chief didn't speak Joe's language, he also knew exactly what Joe said.

White Lightning said in a firm voice that he would get away with that once with him. He told him not to do it again. Joe knew he had crossed the line. The Chief stared through him. Joe dropped his eyes to the floor. He could feel the power and the strength of the man.

Chief White Lightning sat back down; he continued to think as he looked them over. He turned to Iktumi and asked if he agreed with him that they were sent to them for a reason. Iktumi acknowledged that it was a pretty good chance of that. "What if," he paused before he spoke, "what if they were starting their 'rites to pathway' to adulthood?"

The Chief said, "We know there are three stages of the 'rites' the youth must go through to become an adult. The first stage is the 'initiate must experience a methodical death.'"

Roaring Fire was starting to understand what White Lightning was saying.

"If they've left their past lives behind, then they're already started the transformation."

"I think they've been sent to us by the spiritual realm to finish their 'rites.'"

The Chief told Roaring Fire, "Joe has the heart of a mountain lion."

Roaring Fire said, "He also has the fury of the warrior in his eyes."

"Do you think Joe could be trained to be a warrior? Joe's close to the same age as my son Fire Foot."

"I could put him in the same warrior training class with him."

"Fire Foot and Joe will make a good training combination; they both are fierce."

"Roaring Fire, you and your family will adopt Joe. He'll become your son and your Fire Foot and Little Fire's brother."

The Chief turned to Iktumi and asked what he thought of Mark. Iktumi said he needed a moment to read Mark's soul to form an answer. Iktumi studied Mark's aura. As he analyzed the energy from Mark's soul, he said Mark was on a spiritual search for meaning in his life. Iktumi continued to gaze at the energy around Mark's body. He said Mark was disconnected from his physical self. He found it interesting, though, Mark's soul felt a connection to their village. He said Mark feels in his heart he belongs here, but his mind won't accept what he's feeling.

White Lightning told Iktumi he wanted him to adopt Mark and be his "rites to pathway" guide and counselor. He said Iktumi would train him in the ways of the healer. If what Iktumi said about Mark being on a spiritual search, then learning the ways of the healer would lead him to a higher spiritual path. White Lightning told Iktumi he would adopt Mark and make him a member of his family.

Roaring Fire asked the Chief what were they going to do with Jacob. White Lightning asked Iktumi if he could do a reading on Jacob. Iktumi started analyzing Jacob's aura, then he became angry as he tried to read Jacob's soul. He turned to White Lightning and said he couldn't get a reading from Jacob. Jacob was able to block it or there was nothing there.

White Lightning observed Jacob, then said, "I think he has leadership qualities."

Iktumi said, "I don't think there is much hope for the runt of the litter."

"You're misjudging Jacob, Iktumi. In the short period of time we've spent with him, I can see Joe and Mark look up to him for direction."

White Lightning said, "I'll adopt him."

The Chief had made his decision and it was to be carried out by the council elders. Roaring fire told some of his men to go find some clothes for the new members of the village. Iktumi said he hoped the Chief's conclusion was the right one. White Lightning asked Iktumi if he was questioning his decision.

Iktumi said no he wasn't. He then, looked at Jacob and mumbled under his breath, "Jacob, the blue-eyed demon."

CHAPTER 9

The Bonding

The Chief had made his decision. Jacob would be living with him. Joe was going to live with Roaring Fire and his family. Mark was going to live with Iktumi and his family.

One of the men left the chamber. He returned with clothes for the three to wear. As they dressed, Mark was complaining about having to live with Iktumi. Jacob told him to stop complaining at least he knew, who he was going to be living with.

Mark continued to complain about the arrangements, he said, "Yeah, I know Iktumi. I also, know he wants to kill me."

Jacob and Joe reassured Mark he was safe for the moment, because Iktumi didn't know who they were, yet.

The clothes each of the three were given were a pair a pants, a shirt, and moccasins made of deer skin. Joe was the one who recognized the type of material in which the clothes were made. Jacob and Mark joked about how the pants didn't fit. They decided to switch pants to see if that would work. That was worse, Mark was a little shorter than Jacob. Jacob looked like he was waiting for a flash flood with Mark's pants on him. Mark looked like he was going to trip over the pant legs when he tried to walk.

Mark was laughing as they exchanged clothes back. Jacob said it reminded him of when they were smaller. Mom would bitch at them, because they were always exchanging clothes. When they were finished getting dressed, Joe asked the duo, if they were finished horsing around.

The Chief came into the room where the three were getting dressed. He signaled Jacob to follow him. Jacob said goodbye to Joe and Mark. Joe said hopefully they'd get to see each other again. Jacob told him they'd be okay.

The Chief gave Jacob a tour of the village. Jacob didn't understand anything he was saying as they walked. He understood the Chief was trying to teach him words in The Flat-Land language as they toured the village. He showed him the village center where people were going about their daily lives. As they walked through White Lightning would introduce Jacob to the people.

White Lightning led Jacob back to the longhouse where he showed him the inside of the house. They entered a room where there was warrior gear hanging on a wall next to the fireplace. White Lightning showed Jacob the ceremonial costume he wore during the village ceremonies. He pointed at the war paint he wore when going into battle. Jacob liked the headdress White Lightning showed him. Jacob could see White Lightning had a great deal of pride as he showed Jacob the battle headdress. The headdress had peacock feathers surrounding the headband. Jacob wondered where he would've found Peacock feathers.

On the other side of the room there was an area that appeared to be women's clothing. Jacob assumed White Lightning was married. There was also a child's clothing in the same area as the women's clothing. Jacob though they were standing in the family quarters. As he observed the room, he realized there was no furniture. White Lightning walked over to the other side of the room with Jacob following behind.

White Lightning was explaining something to Jacob as they viewed the clothes. Jacob couldn't understand what it was he was telling him.

White Lightning led Jacob out of the longhouse. They walked a trail that led out of the village going north. They walked for a mile, then came to the burial ground. Jacob was uncomfortable there; he'd never seen bodies laying out in the open before. White Lightning led Jacob to a structure where the skeletal remains of a women and child lay. Jacob understood it was a woman, the remains were dressed in a women's clothing.

The Chief began to weep as the two stood looking at the decomposing bodies. Jacob understood the women was White Lightning's wife. He also understood the child was his son. White Lightning then gave Jacob a tour of the burial ground.

Chief White Lightning signaled Jacob to follow him as he led him back to the village. When they returned to the village, they walked to a teepee. He and Jacob entered. Jacob understood it was White Lightning's sleeping quarters. Jacob wondered to himself, why he didn't sleep in the room in the longhouse. He figured it was probably too painful for him to stay in the room he'd shared with his wife and son.

When they left the teepee, they walked to a smaller teepee about twenty-five yards away. White Lightning pointed to the teepee. He then pointed to Jacob. Jacob understood that was where he'd be staying. Jacob went over to the teepee to get a look at it.

A few weeks had passed Jacob and the Chief had begun to communicate. Jacob was picking the Flat-Land Language up fast; White Lightning had a tutor teaching him the language. It was a couple of weeks into Jacob's stay when White Lightning told Jacob he had been entrusted by the spiritual realm to guide him through his "Rites to Pathway."

Jacob asked, "Can you explain the 'rites to pathway,' I have no idea what it means."

"You have started the process of transitioning from your old self to a man. You'll need a counselor, who will guide you through the process."

"I'm concerned about what you are telling me, White Lightning. I don't need any help to make the transition to a man. I'm already a man."

"Where you come from don't you have a ceremony celebrating the transition from a child to an adult?" the Chief asked.

"Yeah, it's more of a family thing, though."

"What does the 'rites' entail?"

"There are three stages of the process. The first phase of the ritual is called the 'separation phase.' The second phase is called the transition phase. The third phase is called the reintroduction phase."

"Can you explain the first stage to me?"

"That's the stage of separation from your old self. That phase is where you separated from your previous world."

"That makes sense to me, since I've been removed from the world in which I came."

"It's more figuratively speaking that you were removed from your previous world. I meant, it was more like your old self is detached from the person you'd been, so now you can go through the transformation to the new person you will become."

"What's the second phase?"

"The second phase is the transition phase. In that phase you no longer hold your past role in life, but you haven't become the new person yet. You'll be in transition. Phase two will follow a strict agenda. That's where you'll need a counselor who must teach and guide you through the process. I'll explain the exact sequence of the phase as we go through it. There will be no misunderstandings on your part on what you'll be learning. That part of the pathway must be done under 'A Master of Ceremonies,' which is me."

"What is the third stage of the rites ceremony?"

"That will be your reintroduction phase. I'm going to give you the tools that you need to develop you into a leadership role."

"I don't think I have it in me to be a leader."

"It doesn't matter what your mind thinks, Jacob. What matters is what your soul knows, you're going to become. Once a year the village has a ceremony for the graduates who successfully achieved their goals, while passing through their 'rites to pathway.' During the ceremony I'll announce the graduates who have accomplished their goals. Their success in achieving their goals will lead them to their new status in society. I'll then give them their new names. After receiving their names, they'll be welcomed back as new adult members of society. The conclusion of the ceremony marks the beginning of the pathway to adulthood for the graduate. Jacob, you are welcome to attend the ceremony, but you won't attend as a graduate."

"Why not?"

"My intentions are to reach the goals set for me. I'll give you the tools to help you become a leader, but you're not going to be one."

"What's the point, if I don't achieve success?"

"You'll know you're a successful leader when the time comes."

"Why will I not be rewarded for achieving leadership goals at the ceremony?"

"Leaders have to make difficult decisions that affect people's lives. Sometimes people die, because of those decisions. There is no reward in leadership decisions, Jacob."

Jacob said, "I like how this sounds; I feel the 'rites' give me some meaning. I want to do this, Chief White Lightning, I really do. This gives me a feeling of purpose in my life. I feel in my heart, this is the right direction for me."

"Jacob, you have to earn your 'rites.' It's not going to be handed to you."

"Okay, I'm willing to work hard to achieve the set goals."

Iktumi entered the room where Mark and Joe were waiting. He signaled Mark to follow him. Mark said goodbye to Joe telling him that was the end. Joe reassured him again, he'd be fine. As Mark left with Iktumi he had a worried look on his face.

Iktumi led Mark out the front entrance of the long house. They walked around to the side and re-entered through another door. When they entered the side of the house, they went into an area that was sectioned off for Iktumi's family. In that area there were three beds with mattresses made of hay. There were deer and buffalo skins stored above the beds on shelves that Mark thought were probably used for blankets in winter.

In the corner of the room was a small fireplace. To the left of the fireplace were ceremonial costumes hanging on the wall. There were shelves with dried herbs, roots and powders sitting in bowls. As Iktumi showed Mark the different herbs, he'd name them for him in the Flat-Land Language.

Iktumi was speaking to Mark in the native language. Mark already knew some of the new words, Iktumi was trying to teach him. He remembered when his Grandmother had told him how his mother learned English. She started to pick up the language within a couple of weeks, because she was submerged in it.

When she and Mark's dad were married, neither one spoke the others language. She spoke Spanish, because she was native Colombian. She was an exchange student going to school at the university when they met. Mark's Grandmother had always told him that she and dad had fallen in love and married, before they could verbally communicate with each other.

Mark was born six months later. She told him that he was born prematurely. That tale worked for several years, until Mark was thinking about the birds and the bees story. That's when he realized the math didn't add up.

Mark was having to pick up the information fast. Iktumi gave Mark a tour around the family quarters. He showed him with a proud look, his ceremonial costumes. Mark could tell Iktumi was the medicine man of the village. As they did the walking tour, Mark started to realize Iktumi was the spiritual leader of the people. He remembered Shappa had told him that when they were playing the spirit game.

Iktumi continued to walk around the area with Mark. He was pointing out different items and naming them for him. Mark was observing the quarters as they walked. Iktumi pointed to his and his wife's bed. Then pointed to the two other beds in a sectioned off space from theirs. Mark thought it strange that he could figure out, the two other beds were for Iktumi's children. He thought to himself in his world, and in this one, the cultures were completely different, but you could still figure out what was the parents' room, which was the children's rooms.

As Mark continued to make his observation, he thought to himself he could tell Iktumi's two children were girls. One was probably a teenager and one was probably preteen. Iktumi told Mark to follow him over to the other side of the family space. They walked to a door just to the right of the fireplace that led to a small room. Mark poke his head in the room and saw a small bed made of hay. He knew that was going to be his bedroom.

The only thing in the room was the bed. Mark was looking the bed over trying to compare it to his bed at home. The bed, he was looking at was about half the width of his twin-size bed and probably five feet in length. Shit, he thought to himself, he'd have to make it work.

When he turned around Iktumi signaled him to follow him. They walked out of the building and across the open space in the middle of the village. The open space in the center of the village reminded Mark of the small park in the middle of his neighborhood. There were people working in the center of the village. Some were cooking the evening meal. Others were grinding grains. Some were doing laundry. They continued through the village center, then approached a round building with a mud and grass roof.

As they walked up to the building, Iktumi pointed and said the word "Kiva." Mark knew what a kiva was. He had taken a field trip to Chaco Canyon in northern New Mexico a couple of years earlier. The kiva was where the village ceremonies were held. Mark followed Iktumi into the kiva, inside he gave him a tour of the of the ceremonial room.

Mark looked around and was impressed with the red plaster that covered the walls on the inside of the kiva. While he stood there observing the wall, he realized, the walls weren't like the walls in the ruins. Those walls were made of stacked rock. The walls in this kiva had plaster on them. He just assumed the way the walls were built in the ruins was the way the people had originally built them. He didn't realize the walls from the ruins originally had plaster on them.

Iktumi led Mark out of the kiva. They walked back across the village center heading back to the long house. They walked by Joe, who was standing with a group of boys. The boys were showing him their hunting bows as they talked. Mark said hello, as he and Iktumi walked by the group. Everybody in the group turned and said hello all at once. Mark thought to himself that they were a friendly bunch.

Joe said hello with a big smile on his face. He told Mark he liked the people in the village.

Mark said, "Yeah, it's not a bad place at all."

Mark asked Joe if he had seen Jacob.

Joe said, "I saw him and the Chief about an hour ago. They were returning from the burial grounds. Jacob is lucky, he gets his own teepee. I have to share a bed with my two new brothers in a teepee where the whole family lives."

Mark laughed and said, "You still have it better than I do."

Mark followed Iktumi back into the side entrance of the house. As they walked into their quarters, Wakanda was starting preparations for the evening meal. Iktumi introduced Mark to Wakanda, his wife and the two girls helping her prepare the meal. He pointed to the younger girl and said her name was Amitola. Amitola looked like a smaller version of her mother. She smiled at Mark and said hello.

Amitola appeared to look ten or eleven years old. She stared at Mark as she was mashing corn into meal. When she thought Mark wasn't paying attention, she turned and whispered in her sister's ear. Both sisters started to giggle.

The older girl looked to be about fifteen years old. Mark was thinking how beautiful she was as he viewed her with a glazed look in his eyes. Iktumi was a little irritated by the way Mark was looking at his oldest daughter. He introduced her anyway. Iktumi told Mark his oldest daughter's name was Aiyana. Mark repeated after him the name "Aiyana," he then said, "Oh, Aiyana from the spirit game." She was as she described herself to him, while he and Jacob played the Spirit Board Game. Mark looked back and forth between Aiyana and her mother, he thought she looked just like her mother also. He couldn't understand how she could have Iktumi's genes, though. Iktumi was an ugly Mud Head.

Aiyana took a closer look at Mark, she recognized him, she said, "Mark."

Iktumi asked her how she knew him. She, thinking quickly, said, there were rumors about how Mark and his friends had just appeared out of thin air on the edge of the village. Some of the warriors told her Mark looked like a Flat-Lander.

The following day Iktumi started teaching Mark the Flat-Land language. Within a month Mark had picked up on the spoken language so fast, he was starting to have conversations with Aiyana and the people in the village. He was able to understand Iktumi when he started setting goals for him. Mark asked why was he setting goals for him. Iktumi told him he was going through his "Rites to Pathway."

Mark asked Iktumi, "What's the 'Rites to Pathway'?"

Iktumi explained it to Mark. He said he'd be his guide through the process.

Iktumi said, "I'm going to teach you the healing herbs."

Mark asked why.

"When White Lightning asked me to do a reading on your aura, it was communicated to me that you are a healer."

"Are you able to read minds?"

"No, I don't read minds; I read souls. I can read anybody's soul."

Over the next several months Mark learned the Herbs. When mixed correctly, some had healing powers that helped with different illnesses. Mark became Iktumi's assistant. He would mix the different herbs for Iktumi when a patient came to visit. He became so good with the herbs that when Iktumi diagnosed an ailment for a patient, he'd give Mark the diagnosis. Mark automatically knew what herbs to mix for treatment.

Mark worked with Iktumi during the day and spent his evenings with Aiyana. Iktumi at first didn't like him spending so much time with Aiyana, as he grew closer to Mark, he began to respect their relationship. He knew their relationship was getting serious, he decided to stay out of it. He was starting to like Mark, he also thought Mark would make a good son-in-law.

Aiyana and Mark's relationship did develop into something more than friendship within a week of meeting each other. In a way they had already met and fallen in love before Mark appeared out of thin air. Aiyana told Mark she knew they were going to meet; she'd prayed every night to the higher powers to bring him from her dreams into the world.

It wasn't a couple of weeks after Mark moved in with the family, that Wakanda was getting worried about Aiyana and Mark's relationship. Wakanda was uncomfortable with Mark sleeping in the same space where Aiyana was sleeping. Iktumi told her he felt, Mark was a respectful person and could be trusted not to make the moves on Aiyana.

Wakanda said, "Mark's not the one I'm worried about."

Iktumi leaned over and kiss her on the lips, then said Aiyana was like her mother. He seemed to remember she made the first moves on him. Wakanda said she thought Mark and Aiyana were way past that stage. Iktumi said he was sure they were.

"It'll be fine, though, Mark is going to make a good son-in-law."

Wakanda said she felt he was already their son-in-law. They both loved Mark and thought he was the best thing to happen to Aiyana.

Wakanda asked Iktumi how Mark was doing with his training.

"He's a very good student. He's picked up on the Flat-Land language fast. As soon as he started to understand the language, he learned the medicinal herbs quickly. Mark will be ready for the 'rites' ceremony soon. The only thing he has left to do is his retreat."

"What's the retreat entail?"

"Mark has to spend a week in the wild alone meditating under the Shet."

Wakanda said, "I hear Joe and Jacob are learning fast, also. All three seemed to have assimilated into our society."

Iktumi agreed with her on that assessment. All three had integrated into the Flat-Land culture with ease. Wakanda asked Iktumi if he was uncomfortable with the three.

He said, "I really love Mark, in fact I feel he's family. I actually feel Mark is our son, Wakanda."

Wakanda and Iktumi had always wanted a son. They had Aiyana and Amitola. After Amitola was born they couldn't have any more children. Iktumi and Wakanda looked at each other and laughed when Iktumi said, "God knows we've tried for ten summers to have another child."

"And the other three seasons, also."

"Then Mark appears out of thin air. With his Flat-Land looks, he fits right in as a family member."

"I can tell you don't like Jacob or Joe."

"I don't have a problem with Joe. Joe's soul is a true warrior's spirit. I have to admit, I don't like the idea of a warrior's spirit being in a white skin body, but I do respect Joe. It's the blue-eyed demon Jacob that I don't like." He said it with anger in his voice.

Wakanda asked what was it he didn't like about Jacob. She said he hadn't done anything to hurt or deceived anybody.

"I can't read Jacob's soul. When a spiritual leader can't read the soul of the person who carries it, it's because the soul is a demon."

"Maybe, Jacob's soul is able to block you from getting a reading."

Iktumi said, "Jacob has blue eyes, bluer than the sky."

"Why do you feel blue eyes makes Jacob a demon?"

"Up north in the direction of the swirling lights, there are rumors of dogs, who pull sleds for the native people. Those dogs have blue eyes, bluer than the sky. Legend has it, those dogs have evil demons for souls. That's how I feel about Jacob."

"Are you suspicious of the Jacob's reasons for coming to our village?"

"I have no doubt in my mind Jacob knows why they're here. I also, know he's up to no good."

"What do you think it is?"

"I don't know yet. I'm going to get to the bottom of what he's up to, though."

"Do you think Mark and Joe are aware of Jacob's intentions?"

"There's no doubt in my mind the other two know as tight as those three are. There's no way they will tell anybody, though. As far as I'm concerned Jacob is leading Mark and Joe down the wrong path."

"Why are all three going through the 'rites of passage' if they have ill intentions? I don't think their coming of age and their intentions are related."

"The spiritual realm is taking them through their 'rites' without them having any understanding of what is happening to them. Their minds think there for one reason; their souls are here for another reason."

"Mark's ready for his 'incorporation phase' celebration," Iktumi said. "I better start planning the festivities. At the ceremony, White Lightning will elevate Mark to healer, then he'll give Mark his new name. That will start him on his path to spiritual healer. It looks like Fire Foot, Mark, and Joe will graduate with a couple of other warriors at the 'rites' ceremony."

Roaring Fire came into the room where Joe was waiting after Mark and Jacob left. He had Joe's new brothers Little Fire and Fire Foot with him. Roaring Fire introduced the two brothers. They gave him a bow, then they left for the hunting grounds to teach him how to hunt.

Both brothers looked like their dad. The older brother Fire Foot was the same age as Joe. When the older brother shook Joe's hand. He shook with a limp hand. Joe thought that was odd. As Joe observed Fire Foot, he realized that he had feminine physical traits. Fire Foot's hair was very long; it hung down to his ass. His hair was clean and perfectly combed all the way down. Joe at first thought that maybe, Fire Foot was a girl. As he observed his body though, he could see it was square like a male's body.

The younger brother Little Fire, who looked to be eleven was on the other hand very male even for his age. He had a piercing stare as he looked into Joe's eyes. As Little Fire pierced Joe's eyes, Joe could feel him reading his soul. As Joe left himself open to Little Fire's intrusive reading of his soul, Joe felt a strong bond forming between the two of them. Little Fire was naked, except for his loincloth. His stance was very masculine. When he and Joe shook hands, Little Fire knew the shake.

"How the hell does he know the shake?" Joe asked himself.

When they arrived at the hunting grounds. They didn't have to teach Joe anything. He was already experience in taking an animal down with a bow and arrow. Joe killed the whitetail deer with one arrow. Roaring Fire was impressed with him, he knew right where to aim the arrow to kill the animal with one shot.

When Roaring Fire tried to show Joe how to gut the animal, it was obvious Joe already had been trained. Joe without any coaching rolled the animal onto it's back and went to work gutting it. Roaring Fire could see somebody had taught him the process of gutting.

When Roaring Fire hung the carcass for skinning, Joe went to work removing the hide without any coaching. As Roaring Fire, Fire Foot, and Little Fire watched him working on removing the coat, it was obvious to them, somebody had taught him the proper way to use the knife when cutting the hide of the animal.

CHAPTER 10

The Schooled Hunter

*I*t was late September. Jacob, Mark, and Joe adapted to their new homes. Mark and Aiyana started spending a great deal of time together. Jacob was jealous of their relationship. He didn't know whether he was jealous of Mark having a woman to spend time with. Or if he was just angry that he didn't get to see him anymore. Toward the end of summer, he and Joe had bonded stronger as they spend more time together.

Jacob and Joe had been hanging out one evening in Jacob's teepee when he asked Joe if he'd teach him how to hunt with a bow and arrow. Joe was kind of surprised by the request. He just assumed that Jacob already knew how. Jacob was very adamant about wanting to learn to hunt with a bow. He said a few years earlier, his dad had taken him into the mountains for the ritual, but they didn't get a chance to finish.

Joe said, "Sure, I'll teach you, but first you have to learn how to use the bow. I find it much easier to hunt with a gun."

"I don't know, Joe; I just don't feel right shooting an animal with a gun."

Joe said, "It's much easier to take the animal down from a distance with a gun. We wouldn't have to sneak up on it."

Jacob said, "I feel It's more sportsmen like to use a bow. Do you agree with me, Joe?"

"Well, no, I prefer using a gun. I think it's much easier."

After Jacob mastered the bow it was time to go on his first hunt. The two set out west in the direction of the Sleeping Demon. Joe knew there was plenty of game up against the mountain in the hunting grounds. As they walked, they talked how much they'd developed relationships with the people in the village.

It took them an hour to get to the hunting grounds.

"Okay, Jacob, when we arrived at the top of the hill, we're going to see whitetail down in the valley. As we stocked them, we need to make sure we're downwind from the dear. If the animal picks up our scent, it'll run. It's not like home where the deer are domesticated and protected. At home they have no fear of man."

The two hunters moved down the hill to the creek. When they arrived at the water's edge, they started to crawl along the bank. They had to move slowly, so they could sneak up on the buck.

When they were within twenty-five yards of the animal, Joe quietly whispered in Jacob's ear, "Jacob, you need to set up for the kill. The sound of the stream will muffle any sounds we make."

Jacob set the arrow in the bow and pulled back. Joe kind of took pride in the stance Jacob had taken. It was very graceful watching him standing like an archer with perfect form. He must have had a good teacher he thought to himself.

Joe continued to whisper. "Do you have the back of the shoulder in sight?"

"Yes."

"Whenever you're ready, let the arrow fly."

Jacob was hesitant as he stood there in the swaying weeds that were up to his chest. Joe waited patiently for Jacob to let the arrow go.

Joe understood from Jacob's hesitation that he was having second thoughts about killing the buck. They continued to whisper the conversation.

"Why are you hesitating, Jacob?"

"I don't feel right about killing the animal."

"I felt the same way the first time I was going to shoot a deer."

"How did you get over it?"

"I hesitated; dad knew I was having second thoughts."

"What did he say to you?" Jacob continued to aim the arrow right behind the shoulder.

"He told me it's wrong to shoot an animal for sport, if you're shooting it for food, you're killing it with a clear conscience."

Jacob let go of the arrow, with a swish it flew a perfect path just above the weeds hitting the young buck right behind the shoulder. The buck started to run, then dropped to the ground and didn't move.

Joe yelled, "All right, great job, Jacob."

Jacob turned to Joe and they gave each other a high-five.

Joe said, "Come on, Jacob, I'll show you how to field process the animal."

They ran over to the buck as it lay dead in the weeds. Joe coached Jacob on the gutting process. Jacob had to do all the work, because it was his kill.

While Jacob was gutting the carcass, Joe went to collect firewood. When he returned, he showed Jacob where the heart was inside the guts.

"We're going to eat the heart in celebration of your first kill, Jacob." Joe then explained the skinning process to Jacob.

After eating the heart, Jacob finished skinning the carcass. When he was finished, Joe had him sit down on the ground. Joe sat in front of him and drew lines on his face with the blood of the buck.

Jacob asked, "Why are you drawing lines on my face with blood?"

Joe said, "It's your blooding rite, Jacob, you earned it with your first kill."

They cooked and ate meat, until they were stuffed full. During their dinner Joe was telling Jacob stories about his family.

"Dad taught John and I how to shoot guns. He taught us how to use the crossbow too. Dad taught us how to clean and take care of the guns." Joe became excited as he talked, "I miss my brother John. I've really missed him, since we came here." Joe burst into tears.

Jacob scooted next to him and put his arm around his shoulders as he cried. "I know how you feel; I miss my family too."

In-between sobs Joe asked if he thought they'd ever see their families again.

"I don't know. One thing I do know is we found a way here, so I don't see why we can't find a way home."

"I'm not sure I want to go home, Jacob."

"Why?"

"I don't want to live with my mother."

"Why do you have to live with her?"

"Living with mom is the court's order."

"Is she really that bad?"

"Ever since grandma died, mom changed into somebody I don't know. She completely lost her mind after the divorce."

It was too dark to hike back to the village.

"There's no moon tonight, Jacob; we're not going to be able to find our way back to the village."

Jacob said, "Let's camp here tonight."

"Okay, we should cook as much meat as we can, then carry it back with us in the morning."

Joe was looking over the fur; he was thinking it would make a good blanket for the two if them to sleep under.

Jacob said, "It would have been nice to have some whiskey to celebrate my first kill."

"That's funny you should mention that; I have some whiskey stashed in a cave."

"What are you talking about, Joe?"

"It'll take a while to explain. Let me tell you a story, Jacob."

Jacob liked the sound of that.

It was dark as they lay under the fur blanket by the fire. Joe started his story.

"The first time Little Fire and Fire Foot took me out hunting by ourselves, we killed a buffalo. Little Fire and Fire Foot know a little English. Did you know that?"

Jacob said, "I had no idea."

"Neither did I." Joe continued, "The three of us killed the buffalo and skinned it. We did the same thing you and I did today. We ate as much meat as we could. Fire Foot and Little Fire got into an argument about whether they should tell me that they know English. When they decided they could trust me not to say anything to Roaring Fire, they started speaking to me in broken English.

"I asked them where they learned English. They told me from the people at the trading post. Little Fire told me, 'We're going to trade the buffalo hide at the post.' I asked where was it located. I wanted to check it out. As we hiked there with the hide, I taught Little Fire and Fire Foot every swear word in the English language."

Jacob asked, "How come swear words are always the first words to learn when learning a new language?"

"I don't know, Jacob; I've never thought about it."

They spent the next ten minutes telling jokes about swear words before Joe returned to his story.

As the two laid on their backs gazing up at the stars, Joe continued. "There's a small mining supply camp at the mouth of the canyon about two miles north of here. There's a gold rush going on in the hills to the west of the camp. The only access to the gold fields is through the canyon. Everyone in the camp buys, sells, and trades with gold prospectors, who must pass through the canyon, on their way to the gold fields.

"Little Fire and Fire Foot explained to me they could take the buffalo hide to the trading post in the mining supply camp and trade it."

"What do they trade the hide for?"

"They like the taste of dried pork, that's what they buy with the hides they trade."

"Little Fire and Fire Foot really like dried pork?"

"Yeah, I guess the people that came across the plains in the wagon trains carry loads of it."

"That's true, it's on the list."

"What list?"

"My family saved the original list of supplies Josh had written, before leaving on the wagon train."

"Yeah, dried pork was on the list, along with ten gallons of whiskey."

"How's that lead us to your whiskey, Joe?"

"We took the hide to the trading post. Mr. and Mrs. Chong are the owners. They're a Chinese couple who are willing to trade anything for pretty much anything to anyone. When we first walked in with the hide, Mr. and Mrs. Chong just stared at me. I spoke up to tell them my name was Joe. I asked them if they had ever seen a white Indian before. The Chongs burst out laughing, then said, 'You're funny, White Indian Joe.'

"The Chongs addressed Fire Foot and Little Fire. Mrs. Chong said, 'Sorry, no dried pork today.' She asked Little Fire what else did he want. We looked around the trading post and to my amazement there was anything you could think of in there. I guess people trade anything, when they have the gold fever.

"I walked around the trading post, until I came across a couple of bottles of whiskey. Mrs. Chong asked me if I wanted them. Sure, I said not thinking she'd let me have it. She handed me the two bottles, then walked over and took the hide. She said, 'Thank you, White Indian Joe.' Then she told the three of us to leave."

"Where are the bottles of whiskey?"

"I have them stashed in a cave. I was waiting for a reason to drink."

"Today would have been a good reason to drink."

"I was waiting for the three of us to drink it."

"The three of who?"

"I wanted Mark to join us."

Jacob said in an angry voice, "Mark too busy eating peyote and smoking the peace pipe."

Joe said, "Mark has changed, hasn't he?"

"You must admit, though, he has taken to learning the ways of the healer."

"Yeah, he's taken to Aiyana too."

Joe turned his head to ask Jacob if he was jealous of her. When he looked at Jacob's face in the light of the fire, he realized he didn't have to ask.

The next morning when Joe awoke, Jacob was already up and cooking more meat for breakfast.

Joe crawled out from under the skin and said, "Jesus Christ, I have to take a piss."

He walked over to the edge of the small cliff next to the camp and whipped his dick out. He aimed it straight up in the air and started to pee. Jacob looked over and saw Joe standing there pissing at least ten feet in the air. Joe was smiling at Jacob with pride as he shot the stream high off the cliff. Jacob was laughing so hard his stomach hurt.

As he laughed, he said, "Oh my God, that fucker wasn't lying."

From beneath where Joe was pissing, Jacob heard someone yelling, "You Goddamn, fucking son of a bitch, you're pissing on my head," in perfect English.

Joe backed up as a naked teenager with jet-black greased hair came charging over the hill with a buck-knife in his hand. As he came up over the edge, he was still yelling at Joe calling him a fucking son of a bitch. Joe continued to back up as he charged him with the knife. Joe tripped and fell backward. Jacob was thinking to himself that the guy with the knife looked like he was straight out of the movie *I Was a Teenage Were-wolf* from 1957, except he didn't have any clothes on.

Jacob picked up a rock and started running toward the guy, as he was getting ready to throw it at him, he tripped and fell into the knife. The knife cut through the inside of his right shoulder and came out the back side under the shoulder blade. As he fell, the knife cut downward completely slashing his armpit open. As he continued the fall to the ground, the knife cut a gash six inches down his rib cage under his arm. Jacob screamed in pain as he hit the ground.

Joe had fallen right next to his bow. He loaded it while still laying on his back. There was another teen coming up over the edge yelling at his friend Ted, wanting to know what he'd done. Ted was going after Joe with the bloody knife in hand. Joe had the arrow drawn back. Ted was yelling in hysterics as he charged. Joe let the arrow go without hesitation. The arrow passed through his nose at an upward angel. When the arrow pierced his brain, he stopped, then stood there for a moment then dropped to the ground dead. Joe instinctively loaded another arrow within a second.

The second guy came running up and looked at Jacob rolling around in a pool of blood screaming. He could see Jacob had lost a lot of blood already. He looked at his friend lying on his back with an arrow in his head. He yelled at Joe wanting to know why he'd killed his friend. Joe asked who he was as he pointed the arrow at his heart. Joe was thinking to himself, *What are these two freaks that look like they're right out of a movie from the 1950s doing running around naked?* He said his name was Sam, Sam Jenkins.

Joe started to ask him another question, then said fuck it. He adjusted his aim from Sam's heart to his side. As he let the arrow fly, he said he didn't have time for conversation. Sam dropped to the ground and laid there.

Joe ran over to Jacob and removed his shirt. He stuffed the shirt into the wound. Jacob screamed as Joe shoved the shirt into the gash.

As Joe worked on the wound, he could hear Fire Foot and Little Fire calling to him. He yelled back that they were up on top of the small flat. Fire Foot and Little Fire ran up and asked what had happened. Joe told them he didn't have time to explain.

He told Fire Foot, while he was gone, he needed to collect tree branches and start building a sled to carry Jacob. He had Little Fire take over applying pressure to Jacob's wound. Joe took off down the trail running. He could hear Fire Foot calling to him asking where was he going. Joe yelled he was going to the trading post. He yelled back to Little Fire to keep the pressure on Jacob's wound, until he returned. He told them, "If the fucking idiot with the arrow in him tries anything, you kill him." He did a double take at Little Fire then asked if he understood.

Little Fire said, "Yes, I understand."

As Joe ran the trail, he was thinking to himself, the trading post was two miles away at the pace he was moving he could get there and back in an hour. He thought shit, Jacob could die in an hour. Joe was doubting his decision when he asked himself if he was making the right decision. He thought what would his dad tell him, if he'd asked him. He'd say, "Joe, you made the decision, now go through with it right or wrong, you live with your decisions in life."

When Joe entered the trading post, he was breathing heavy from running.

Mr. Chong said, "Ah, it's the White Indian Joe," as Joe barged in with the fur in hand. "You look like you seen a ghost, ha, ha, ha," Mr. Chong laughed, then he said, "you always looked like you've seen a ghost."

Mrs. Chong told him to slow down and get his breath. Joe looked around the trading post, until he found the items he was looking for.

He brought the items over to Mr. Chong. "Will you take the buck skin for these items?"

Mr. Chong looked at Joe with concern and asked, "Why do you need a needle and thread?"

"My dog had a run-in with a black bear. I need to sew him up."

Mrs. Chong said, "You don't have the right needle and thread to sew your dog." Mrs. Chong said, "I'll show you the right needle and thread. See, Joe, silk thread. Do you see how smooth it is?"

"Thanks, Mrs. Chong, I really need to go."

"No, no, wait, you need the right needle." She handed him some upholstery needles. "See how the needles curve?" she asked.

Joe said, "Okay, I'll take 'em."

As Joe ran out the door with his merchandise, he could hear Mr. Chong yelling at him to return, "Yes, White Indian Joe, I have more whiskey. I also, have a Colt baby Dragoon. It's the perfect size for you."

As Joe ran back up the trail, he was thinking to himself, *A Colt might come in handy in these parts.* He thought he'd have to go back to the trading post to see what Mr. Chong would want to trade for it. He'll probably want a lot of buffalo skins. It would be worth it, though.

Joe knelt next to Jacob, who was lying on his left side moaning. Little Fire was still applying pressure to the wound. Joe took the needle and threaded it. He decided to start sewing the inside of the shoulder, then work his way around to the underarm. When finished with that he'd stitch closed the gash running down Jacob's side.

"JACOB! I'm going to roll you over on your back."

As he rolled him onto his back, Jacob screamed in pain. Joe took the needle and shoved it under the start of the gash. He forced the needle all the way under the wound then brought it back out the other side. Jacob let out an agonizing scream. Fire Foot almost freaked out from the sounds of Jacob's screams.

Jacob clinch the fist in his left hand and with everything he had, he nailed Joe in the eye with a hook shot. Joe went straight back and landed on his back. He sat up and bellowed at Little Fire and Fire Foot to "FUCKING HOLD HIM DOWN!" Fire Foot moved away from building the sled and immediately ran over to help hold Jacob down.

As he ran over to help, he was thinking Joe sounded like one of those women giving birth, then screams how she'd going to kill the father for doing it to her.

"NO, NO, NOO," Jacob screamed when Joe dug the needle in again. Jacob went into convulsions. He threw up his breakfast. Joe yelled at the two brothers to roll him over onto his left side. He continued to sew around the front inside of the shoulder as Jacob barfed. Jacob continued in convulsions, until he passed out.

Little Fire said, "I think Jacob died."

Joe said, "I don't think so, little brother. He's still breathing."

Joe spent the next half-hour sewing the back side of the shoulder. When he was finished sewing the shoulder, he told Fire Foot to roll Jacob onto his back and raise his right arm up over his head.

"I'll have to sew his armpit back together." Joe took a deep breath and started to stitch again.

When he was finished sewing the underarm together. He walked over to Sam and knelt beside him. There was a huge pool of blood around him. He couldn't decide which of the two Jacob or Sam had lost more blood. Sam had passed out.

Joe slapped him, "Wake the fuck up, dumb ass." Joe shook Sam's head then said, "You're not dead yet so, wake up."

Sam slowly awoke, looked at Joe then said, "Shit, I'm still here."

"Yeah, Sam, you're still here."

"So, Sam, tell me yours and Ted's story before you die."

"Do you want it from the beginning?"

"Yeah, I do, you better hurry, though, because you don't have much time left."

"A couple of days ago, Ted and I were hanging out at his house. We were bored out of their minds, when he came up with the Idea of stealing his dad's car, so we could drive out to the Indian reservation just south of town. Do you know where the reservation is located?"

"Yes, I do."

"Ted had the idea we'd steal a bottle of his dad's whiskey and take it out to the reservation and trade for some peyote. I sat there for a minute thinking about it, then I said, 'I'm game.' Ted has a friend who lives on the reservation. His name is Tender Foot. He likes whiskey. Tender Foot has access to peyote, so, the trade is mutual. Even though I wouldn't recommend he get drunk, because he can't handle his liquor. But you know that's his problem.

"We made the transaction. On the drive back, we were having a conversation about where we should trip on the drug. Ted came up with the idea to turn left onto the dirt road at the top of the south hill as we came back into town. If you follow the road around and down the hill, it takes you to the lake, where you can park in the field by the water's edge.

"It's the perfect place to trip, because there's nothing around there."

Joe looked a little confused, he asked, "What are you talking about, there are houses all around the lake and up on the hill."

"No, there isn't, there's nothing out there, but the lake and an old farmhouse on top of the hill. Anyway, it was getting late in the evening probably around seven-thirty or so, we decided to take the peyote while we still had some light."

Joe interrupted, "Did it just happened to be the first day of summer?"

"Yeah."

"What year?"

"1950."

Joe looked deep into Sam's eyes and repeated 1950.

"Yeah, 1950."

"I know you like to play cowboys and Indians, but the year still doesn't change until January 1st."

"The peyote hadn't kick in after forty minutes, so we thought maybe, we'd wait another half-hour, then say fuck it and write it off as a rip-off. About fifteen minutes had passed, all the sudden we were flying through space then appeared here butt naked running around like monkeys in the jungle."

Joe asked, "Where did you find the knife?"

"About a quarter mile back, we'd came across a dead man in his camp. It looked like he had died in his sleep. It must have been last night, because he hadn't been eaten yet. There was a shit ton of flies and gnats buzzing around him. The fucker had already started to stink too. We looked around the camp for clothes and a gun but didn't find anything. The only thing we found was the buck-knife Ted carved your friend up with.

"We could smell the food you guys were cooking, so Ted thought we'd come up and see if you'd be willing to share some of it with us. Instead, we crossed paths with a crazy white boy playing Indian, pissing off the rocks onto his head."

"Well, I didn't piss on him on purpose."

"You're lucky you knew how to use that bow, because if Ted had caught you, he would have cut your little pecker off for pissing on him. By the way, Indian boy, what's your name?"

"Joe Fracks."

Sam looked deep into Joe's eyes then said, "That's odd, that's the name of the captain of the wagon train that brought Ted's kin folk out to this part of the country back in 1852."

Joe was looking straight into Sam's eyes as he said it. Then the light left his eyes. Joe knew he was dead. He'd seen that same look in every whitetail he'd killed.

As Joe stared into the dead eyes, Little Fire shook his shoulder then said, "Joe, we have Jacob tied down in the sled, we should go."

Joe looked over his shoulder and said, "Yeah, we should go."

Joe and Fire Foot lifted the front of the sled and started for the village with Little Fire following behind.

CHAPTER 11

The Coyote

As soon as Mark met Aiyana, they hit it off. Right after Mark moved into the Iktumi household, he and Aiyana were spending a lot of time with each other in the evenings. It wasn't easy, he had a full schedule with Iktumi learning the healing Herbs during the day.

Mark was actually very proud of himself. He didn't get good grades in school. He didn't find anything interesting accept lunch. Maybe, lunch rated a little lower on the list. Going home rated number one on the list of good things about school.

When he and Iktumi started discussing the "Rites of Passage," he didn't like the idea of having a process of becoming a man. But after discussing it with Aiyana, he had a better understanding of why the village people celebrated the process. He thought it was nice the people of the village were involved in it.

Mark remembered back to when his Grandmother had talked to him about his drug use. She was concerned he wasn't going to make anything of himself. She was constantly reminding him that he was getting to an age where he needed to start thinking about his future. For Mark it was just easier to get high and not think about it.

He was a little worried himself, but he couldn't find anything interesting except drugs. Well, that wasn't true, he did find girls interesting. So interesting that he had a burning desire to be with one all the time. He and Aiyana hadn't wasted any time getting to that the first week.

Mark thought about Jacob, who was two months older than he. They had known each other, since Mark was born. Living next door to each other allowed them to be together all the time. He and Jacob were closer to each other, then they were to their own siblings. Mark couldn't understand why Jacob didn't show any interest in girls when they started their physical development.

As Mark and Aiyana spent more and more time together in the evenings, he didn't have any time to spend with Jacob. Mark knew it bothered Jacob that he couldn't be with him, but he couldn't control how he felt about Aiyana. He wanted to be with her all the time. Mark kept telling himself that Jacob had to understand, he really didn't seem to, though.

It wasn't Jacob who was completely free of his feelings of separation from the friendship. Mark could see Jacob and Joe were starting to become very close in their friendship. That bothered him, it crossed his mind more than a few times that Jacob was doing it on purpose just to piss him off.

Nobody had come between Mark and Jacob's friendship until Joe and Aiyana had entered their lives. Mark remembered when Grandma and Jacob's mother tried separating them as a punishment for sneaking drinks from the liquor cabinet. That didn't last, their spirits were crushed by the separation. Mark overheard his Grandmother talking to Mrs. Jericho on the phone one evening about how she just couldn't stand to punish them in that way. They both agreed that maybe they could find another punishment that wasn't so harsh.

Mark and Aiyana had started to take walks in the evenings, it was the only way they could be together. The walks also allowed Mark time to look for herbs. The herbs he looked for assisted Iktumi in healing patients. Aiyana enjoyed the walks for some of the same reasons. She would collect carrots and rhubarb along the path that would be saved for winter.

Mark asked, "Why do you collect food as we hike?"

"Me and my friends will be collecting food all through the autumn, because winter is coming."

Mark hadn't thought about winter. It was getting cold at night, but it hadn't occurred to him winter was coming. It wasn't something he ever thought about anyway, at home you just went to the grocery store to get food, so why worry about it.

Iktumi was teaching Mark how to trade for the roots and herbs that weren't native to the area. Iktumi also taught him the Flat-Landers' trade routes. Mark had to learn to barter for the supplies. The hardest part to learn was understanding the worth of the products being traded. He also had to know the value of the items he was receiving.

Iktumi told him there were rumors going around the village that Joe was trading animal skins with the Chinese couple who had the trading post at the mouth of the canyon.

"Really,". Mark said. He had no idea Joe was in the trading business. Mark said there was more to Joe than what people realized.

Early one evening Mark and Aiyana stood at the top of east hill overlooking the village as the sun set. They were talking about the Sleeping Demon that was in full view in front of them. Mark was trying to explain to Aiyana that the Sleeping Demon was in the world he came from. He pointed down to the area across the lake where he and Jacob's homes were going to be built. She asked if her village was still there because it would be right next to the lake.

Mark didn't have the heart to tell her about the future of her family. Hell, he wasn't sure now if any of it was true. He knew the Indians were at war with other tribes. They were also at war with the Europeans. The white man certainly wasn't innocent of atrocities against other peoples. It seemed like they were always at war with somebody. *It's so peaceful here*, he thought to himself. He couldn't imagine anybody would kill the whole population of the village just for land.

He remembered when he and Jacob were talking about having to register for the draft. They used to talk about what it would be like to be drafted. Jacob said in the conversation they should join before they were drafted, that way they wouldn't be separated. Mark said, he had no intention of joining the military. For that matter, if he was drafted, he would become a draft dodger. Mark remembered Jacob was angry with him when he said it. Jacob felt it was both their duties to go if drafted.

Jacob told him, "If I'm drafted then I'm going. It's my duty."

Mark asked Jacob if he would still go even if he didn't agree with the reasons for the war. Jacob told him there weren't any good reasons for war. It's human nature to be at war. Mark didn't agree with Jacob about going into the service, he did have admit, Jacob was right, it's human nature to be at war.

As the sun set, Mark was telling Aiyana where the high school was going to be built. He described the size of the building. He then turned and pointed behind them and said it was going to be built right on the top of the hill. He pointed to the north and said, "That's where the junior high school is going to be built." She was enjoying watching him as he pointed out all the things that were to come. She still didn't understand why her village wasn't there in his world.

Aiyana asked if he would explain what the difference was between the schools. He told her about the three levels of education. There was an elementary level for kids to learn the basics. She asked about the middle school.

Mark had to think about it for a moment. He said, "Middle school is where kids are institutionalized, because their in-between being a child and being a young adult." He wasn't serious about what he'd said but, then again.

Aiyana asked what was the high school. Mark explained that going into high school was the entry point to adulthood. This made sense to Aiyana, she said it's the same as their tradition on the "rites." Mark thought about it and said he wasn't sure that was the reason. In his world a person's "rites of passage" was celebrated within the family. In the village everybody in the community was involved in the tradition.

While they stood there talking, they both heard something running around in the weeds. When they first heard the sound, Aiyana became a little freighted. She moved closer to Mark. Mark liked it; it gave him an excuse to put his arm around her. As he wrapped his arm around her shoulders to comfort her, he said she shouldn't be worried he was there to protect her.

They could hear the footsteps running in a large circle around them as they listened. Mark said in the past, when he and Jacob took their dogs out on hikes, the dogs would do the same thing. The dogs would run around in large circles protecting them from predators. He said dogs and man had been friends for thousands of years, it was instinctive for the dog to protect humans.

"Why would a dog want to protect people?" Aiyana asked out of curiosity.

Mark said, "It's because people fed them. That's why they're so, loyal to humans."

Aiyana said, "That's strange, I thought the dog was food."

Mark did a double take at her. He'd never thought of a dog as food.

There was something running around in the field, though. When it stopped, Mark had a pretty good idea of where it was. He picked up a rock and threw it in the direction of where the sound of the footsteps stopped. When the rock came down and hit the ground a coyote jumped up in the air then disappeared back into the weeds.

Mark said, "I swear, I just saw a coyote jump out of the weeds."

Aiyana said, "I've occasionally seen a coyote running around the village."

Mark thought it was strange that a lone coyote would be running around the village.

He asked Aiyana if she was sure it was a coyote she had seen. Aiyana reassured him it was a coyote, after all she knew what a coyote looked like. It was starting to get dark, Mark said maybe, his eyes were playing tricks on him. He wanted to go down the hill to where he had thrown the rock. When they walked over to the area where he had seen the coyote jump, they saw paw prints.

"It's a canine paw print. I can't tell what kind of print, maybe it's just a dog."

They both agreed it was getting late and should return home. As they walked back to the village, Mark asked Aiyana if she would be interested in climbing the peak of the sleeping demon the following evening. Aiyana was a little surprised by the question. She wanted to know why, he was interested in hiking up the mountain.

"There's a healing root I'm looking for. I can only find it at a certain altitude."

"How long do you think it'll take to get to the top of the mountain?"

"I'm thinking around four hours round trip. I don't think it'll be necessary to hike to the top, because I'll probably find the root before we get that far."

"It would be fun to hike to the top to get a look around, though."

The following evening, they were preparing for the hike, Aiyana said she was concerned about returning in the dark. Mark assured her they'd be okay. Aiyana was uncomfortable with the idea of walking up a mountain in the first place, but at night. As she thought about it, she realized it would be a good opportunity for the two of them to spend more time alone.

They started the hike west toward the sleeping demon. Mark's plan was to hike up the canyon that separated the two mountains, which made up the image. The canyon in-between the two mountains looked to be the easiest access point to the larger mountain. He didn't want to hike the face of the mountain, because it looked to be a much more difficult hike.

The trail that led to the mountain became smaller and smaller as they approached the canyon. It then eventually faded away. Mark said it made sense the trail would end because nobody had any reason to hike up that far. There was no reason for the trail to continue. Aiyana thought it made since that nobody would hike there, because there was no reason to hike a mountain.

They crossed a small creek before starting up the mountain. They walked across the stream stepping on the rocks that stuck up out of the water. Mark was concerned about getting their feet wet, it was already cold outside. Aiyana wondered if it was the creek that fed the watering hole which sustained their way of life. Mark said he thought that was a very good observation. He said it probably was the creek, where else would the water flow.

They turned around at the mouth of the canyon to see a deer bouncing along the top of the weeds. It had a freighted look on its face as it ran across the field. It was dodging pine trees as it ran out of sight. Mark could swear there was something in the weeds chasing it. Whatever it was, wasn't visible, because it wasn't tall enough to show itself above the weeds. Aiyana said maybe it was the coyote again.

The two continued their accent up the canyon. Aiyana asked Mark if he was interested in having a family. Mark said he hadn't given any thought to it, he was too young to start his own family.

Aiyana asked, "What are you talking about?"

He said, "Where I came from people don't start families until they're in their twenties, thirties, or even older."

Aiyana was a little perplexed by what Mark said. She said, "I'll be a grandmother by the time I'm in my thirties."

Mark asked her, "Why would you want to be a grandmother in your thirties?"

"Because I'll probably be dead of old age by the time, I turn forty."

That whole concept was foreign to Mark's way of thinking.

Mark asked, "Why would you die of old age in your forties?"

Aiyana looked at him and told him to stop joking around.

"I'm not joking."

They stopped to rest; they both were having trouble breathing the thinner air.

While they rested Mark asked Aiyana if she was serious about having children.

"We've come of age, that's the reason certain parts of our bodies have started working, Mark. It's time to reproduce."

"I have to admit I've enjoyed the experience with you, since the first week I came here, but I'm not sure it's time to have children."

They started walking again, Aiyana heard the four-legged animal running off in the distance. As they listened, it was moving in a circle around them. Aiyana said she didn't think the animal was stocking them, because most animals don't stock humans. They joined hands as they continued the climb.

Mark said, "I think maybe, it's a bear."

"No, I don't think so, a bear wouldn't bother us unless we were between the mother and her cubs."

"It might be a mountain lion."

Aiyana said, "I don't think so, a mountain lion is afraid of humans. I've also never heard of a mountain lion stalking people, or a bear for that matter."

"Whatever it is, it's aware of us, but keeping its distance."

They continued to hike, until they reached the saddle. The view from the saddle was very impressive. The two looked out west over the mountains. Aiyana was very impressed with the view. Mark was pointing at the different peaks that stood out. Aiyana was just taking in the whole view. Mark pointed to the ridge of mountains that were off in the distance.

"That's the continental divide," he said with excitement in his voice.

Aiyana had no idea what the continental divide was. Mark explained to her the continental divide was the highest point on the continent. He said the water in the rivers flow to the east then on the other side of the divide, the rivers flowed to the west toward California.

He pointed to the highest peak to the north of them and said the mountain was called Longs Peak. Mark wanted to show Aiyana Pike's Peak, but couldn't, the mountain they were about to hike was blocking the view to the south. He said he'd show her Pike's Peak once they reached the top of Bear Peak.

They rested in the saddle for ten minutes, then started the climb up the mountain to the peak. Aiyana told Mark maybe they should turn around because it was getting dark. Mark said it didn't matter whether they turned around or not, in an hour it would be dark, so they'd still be returning with no light.

They were almost to the peak when they decided to take a break. They sat down facing east looking across the plains. They could see the watering hole from where they sat. It looked small from up on the mountain. They could barely see the village sitting next to the water.

Aiyana pointed out the large tribal community to the south. She said, "That's where the tribal leaders live."

Mark said, "I know that, because we're supposed to take Leroy and McCabe to them for trial."

Aiyana was a little surprised when Mark said it. "How do you know about the tribal council?"

Mark trying to backpedal said, "I've heard rumors about them."

Aiyana wasn't letting it go. "You just said we're supposed to bring Leroy and McCabe to the tribal council. Who's we?"

Mark looked into Aiyana's eyes and thought to himself, what am I going to say. Aiyana didn't say a word. She waited for Mark to explain.

Mark couldn't see any way out of the predicament he just put himself in. "Aiyana, try to understand that we weren't supposed to come to the village before it was attacked by Leroy Abrahamsen and George McCabe's army. We were supposed to show up after you and your people were massacred."

As soon as Mark told her that they could hear footsteps running down the mountain. The sound wasn't circling them anymore, it was running away from them.

"We weren't supposed to meet you, your family, or any of the people in the village. We were supposed to capture the two men that led the attack on the village. After capturing them, we'd take them to the tribal council. We knew where we'd find them, because they'd be building the new town in the area where the village had stood. I'm sorry I didn't tell you sooner, it's just I didn't know what to do, because I've fallen in love with you."

"I too have fallen in love with you, Mark. I'd fallen in love with you when we were talking to each other in my sleep. I knew we'd meet, because you were in my dreams. That means the guiding spirits are involved." She leaned over and kissed him on the cheek. "You shouldn't be sorry. What we need to do now is concentrate on preventing the killings from happening."

Mark looked down on the ground and said, "There it is."

"There's what?"

Mark pointed down to a little green florescent light glowing on the dirt. "It's a glow worm."

Aiyana looked very closely and said, "I've never seen a glow worm."

"The only time two people see a glow worm is when they're in love."

"Is that true?"

"Sure, it's true, you also only see it at seven thousand-foot elevations. The glow worm is related to the firefly."

"We don't have fireflies here, though. Fireflies live further east of here."

"I don't know, Mark; I've never seen or heard of a firefly. I'm quite fascinated with the glow worm, though."

Aiyana leaned over and kissed him on the lips. "There's something I need to tell you, since we're being honest with each other."

"What it was?"

Aiyana hesitated, then said, "I'm pregnant."

"Holy shit, I'm going to be a dad after all."

"Yes, Mark, yes, you are going to be a father."

He leaned over and started kissing her. She started to say no, then the feeling came over her.

The next morning, they awoke in each other's arms as the sun came up over the eastern horizon. Not only was it beautiful, it was warming them up. They were quite chilled from their overnight stay. Aiyana said they should go back to the village. Mark said they should at least climb up to the peak, before they returned home. Aiyana agreed to go to the peak, she wanted to see the view from the top of the mountain.

About five hundred yards below the peak they came to a rock formation that looked like a staircase made of stone. When they stopped to rest, Mark asked if she could make it to the top, she was having a hard time catching her breath.

"We've gone this far, there was no way I'm going to miss it."

They started the climb up the stone staircase to the peak.

When they arrived at the top, they stood in amazement at the scenery. Looking to the east they could see for miles across the eastern plains. There were small communities along the front range. They couldn't tell if they were native communities or white communities. They were so far away all they could see was the smoke from the fires that people were using for cooking.

To the west the view had a completely different ecosystem. The mountains jetted high into the sky. There were already snow-capped peaks.

Mark pointed to the highest peak to the south and said, "That's Pikes Peak."

Aiyana couldn't believe how beautiful the view was, as she took it all in.

Mark turned to Aiyana and asked, "Would you be my wife?"

"Of course, I will."

They stood there in each other's arms talking about how the last two days were the best days of their lives. They sat on the peak for a couple of more hours talking, before deciding to return home.

They started down the side of the mountain back to the saddle. It surprised both how much faster going down the mountain was then going up. Within twenty minutes they were resting in the saddle. Mark said it seemed to take forever to get to the top. Going down was much faster.

Aiyana said, "Maybe it's because, we slid halfway down the mountain on our butts." As they rested in the saddle Aiyana asked, "What plan do you, Mark, and Joe have? It sounds like nothing has gone according to your original plans."

"I don't know, because we haven't had time to talk about it. From the time we arrived in the village we've all been so busy; we haven't had a chance to talk with each other to make a plan."

"The three of you should sit down and come up with something."

"We need to, but we don't know when the massacre will take place, because we don't know what year this is."

They rested for a few more minutes then started down the canyon back to the trail. They walked back through the field of weeds until they found the trail leading back to the village.

As they walked into the village holding hands, Amitola ran up to them and said, "Jacob's been injured in a fight. Little Fire and Fire Foot went looking for Joe and Jacob this morning. When they didn't return from hunting last night."

White Lightning came out of the longhouse with Roaring Fire to greet Mark and Aiyana. White Lightning told Mark, "I had two additional scouts looking for them. They found them and reported back that Joe, Fire Foot, and Little Fire where going to be here with Jacob any minute."

Joe and Fire Foot came running into the village with the sled in tow. Mark could only say, "Oh my God," as he looked at Jacob. Jacob was ghost white, he had blood and dirt all over his body. His hair was completely blood soaked. Mark wasn't sure if he was alive. His shoulder and underarm looked like he'd fallen under a sewing machine that was running out of control. He also, had a cut running down his side, under his armpit that had been sewn up.

"What the fuck happened?" Mark asked as White Lightning and Roaring Fire untied Jacob.

They picked Jacob up and carried him into his teepee.

CHAPTER 12

The Long Sleep

*J*acob stood up and stepped off the sled. He was a little confused as he turned around to see Joe and Fire Foot running down the trail away from him. Little Fire was behind them bouncing from side to side off the sides of the trail as he followed the sled.

"Jacob."

He turned around to see Scott standing in front of him.

"What the hell are you doing here."

"I live here."

"You're dead, Scott, you can't be living here."

"I'm not dead, Jacob."

This must be a dream, Jacob thought to himself. It couldn't be Scott. He knew he died. He saw it with his own two eyes. But then again, I see him with my own two eyes standing in front of me. "I saw you drown."

"Are you sure you saw me drown?"

"No, I'm not sure."

He thought back to the morning Scott fell through the ice. Scott did have a point; he didn't see him drown. He just fell through the ice, when he bobbed back up out of the water, he was lifeless.

Jacob looked Scott over. He remembered they took him away in an ambulance. Then his family had a funeral for him.

"I remember the funeral."

"I'm not dead, Jacob."

"I remember falling through the ice, then bang I was here."

"What do you mean bang you were here>" He was trying to figure out if he had just arrived that minute.

"No, I told you I live here."

"I can't remember how long it's been, maybe a couple of years."

"A couple of years," Jacob said as he continued to look him over. "You don't look any older."

Scott said jokingly, "I come from a long line of good genes where nobody ages fast."

Jacob thought to himself he'd laugh, but he wasn't sure what he'd be laughing about.

Scott looked around the campsite then told Jacob he had made quite a mess.

Jacob looked around the campsite, where Ted and Sam's bodies lay and said, "Yeah, it is a mess."

"What'd happened?"

"I'm not sure. Joe was taking a piss off the side of the cliff over there."

"Who's Joe?"

"You know Joe," Jacob hesitated for a moment then said, "actually you don't know Joe."

Jacob was very confused when he asked Scott what it was, they were talking about. Scott said he was telling him about Joe pissing off the cliff.

Jacob said, "Oh, yeah, he was taking a piss ten feet in the air, when Ted came running up with a big-buck knife screaming, he was going to kill him for pissing on his head."

"Are you sure he was pissing ten feet in the air?"

"Yeah, Scott, I'm sure. I had this idea that I'd go after him with a rock to protect Joe."

"It looks like you did a good job of that."

"Well, that's actually Joe's work lying there. I ran toward Ted to bash his head, then I tripped and fell into the knife cutting my shoulder."

He looked down at his right shoulder and saw there was nothing there. No wound not even a tear in the shirt.

"Are you sure you were cut by the knife?"

"I can't see anything on your shoulder accept your shirt."

Jacob became more confused when he said, "No, I'm not sure."

"But you're sure Joe was pissing ten feet in the air."

"Would you forget about Joe's stream?" Jacob said, "Joe tore his shirt off and stuffed it into my wound. When he did, I screamed bloody murder."

Jacob asked Scott again, what he was doing there.. Scott said he already explained it to him. He lived there.

"I know you live here, but what are you doing in the campsite?"

"I was hunting whitetail dear to bring home to the family when I heard all the noise up here."

"What family?"

"I'm married to a Flat-Land woman. I have a baby boy. My wife's name is Kaya. My son's name is Little Pale Scott. Little Pale Scott is too young to go with me on the hunt."

"Give it ten more years, though, then I'll teach him to be a great hunter."

Jacob asked how it happened. Scott asked how did he think it happened.

Jacob said, "Well, I know how it happens." He looked more perplexed by the conversation.

Jacob reached out his hand to do the shake. Scott didn't remember the shake. Jacob taught him the shake. Jacob thought to himself he could have sworn it was Scott who taught him the shake, so why would he have forgotten it. Well, maybe the cold water effected his memory. As they shook hands Jacob congregated him.

"What's it like being a father?"

Scott said, "It's a great deal of responsibility. I'm always worried about having enough food for the baby and wife. It's different living here than it is in Table Mesa. Living in the hamlet, I'm a man with responsibilities."

"What's the hamlet?"

"It's the village where I live. In Table Mesa I was just a kid always being told what to do and when. Living here I'm a man; therefore I make my own decisions. You know, Jacob, I was very angry with you for a long time after I arrived here."

"Why?"

"You should have followed me out onto the ice."

"I looked through the ice and knew it was too thin to support our weight. I told you not to go out onto the ice."

Scott looked angry when he said, "We're friends, Jacob; friends stick together."

"Scott, the ice was too thin, I knew it was going to break."

"You should have stayed with me, Jacob."

Scott said, "You don't know what it's like to end up here alone."

"I suppose you arrived butt naked like Mark, Joe and I did?"

Scott looked at Jacob for a few seconds not sure what that meant. "What are you talking about, Jacob?"

"When we made the trip through the portal, it ripped the clothes right off us. When we arrived here, we had nothing on but our birthday suits."

"I have no idea what you're talking about, Jacob."

Jacob asked Scott how he met Kaya. Scott said it was a long story. He asked Jacob if he'd be interested in meeting Kaya and his son. Jacob said yes, he'd like to meet them both. Scott said both would be glad to meet one of his friends. He said he'd tell him how he met Kaya as they walked to the hamlet where he lived.

When they started walking Jacob asked how far it is. He was a concerned about being gone too long. Scott told him not to worry it was a couple of miles west. They set out on the hike west, not on a trail. Jacob asked why there wasn't a trail to the hamlet. Scott said it was a small hamlet and not a lot of people visited there.

Scott told Jacob his story as they walked through weeds. "When I first arrived, I was completely baffled as to what had happened. I vaguely remember why we were on the ice. It was strange when I fell through, I never got wet. I just appeared here."

Jacob asked, "Didn't you fly through space like a bat out of hell?"

"No, Jacob, let me finish my story. I wandered around for a few days trying to find something to eat. I recognized the landscape around me, but there weren't any buildings. There wasn't anything at all, but the lake and a bunch of weeds. I decided to go west through the valley in between those two mountains," Scott pointed. "I hiked through the valley, until it came out in an opening at the top. It was sundown and I was too tired to go any further, so I gave up."

"What did you do then?" Jacob asked with a worried look on his face.

"I fell asleep, Jacob. I was freezing my butt off. If you were here, we could have helped each other stay warm."

"Scott, I'm sorry I didn't make the trip with you. There was no way I was going to walk on the ice." Jacob had been trying to make eye contact with Scott, since they first met that day.

"I should kick the shit out of you, Jacob, for leaving me here alone." He sounded angry.

"We should be working together right now, Scott, instead of fighting." Jacob was thinking that it didn't sound like Scott at all.

"Luckily I still had my winter clothes on, or I would've frozen to death. In the morning when I awoke, I was being poked by a sharp object.

I could barely move, because of the cold. I managed to roll over onto my back to see what had poked me. As I opened my eyes and focused, I saw three men standing there looking at me. I was going to jump to my feet and fight, but it was no use; I was just too weak. One of them asked my name and what was I doing here. I told him my name. He said his name was Adahy, he then introduced his two friends standing by his side. 'This is Demothi,' as he pointed to his friend to his left. 'This is Elan,' as he pointed to his friend on his right. They both said hi at the same time.

"I was so hungry I asked them if they had any food. My pride wasn't getting in the way of begging. They gave me some of the meat they were carrying. It tasted like dried beef. It was dried beef, Adahy said. We trade buffalo skins for it. Sometimes we trade for dried pork. That's our favorite.

"Adahy asked me what I was doing out here without any tools to survive. I had to think about it for a moment, because I wasn't going to tell them the story of what had happened. If I did, they'd think I was an evil demon and kill me. I told them I fell and hit his head and couldn't remember where I was. I just woke up out here lost.

"Adahy told me their hamlet was a couple of miles up the trail in the direction of the sunset. If I wanted, I was welcome to stay there. I didn't think I had the strength to walk the distance to the hamlet. I wasn't going to stay where I was, because I wouldn't survive another night in the cold. 'Come, Scott, you can follow us to the hamlet.' Adahy reached out and clasp hands with me. He then pulled me up.

"It took weeks for me to get my strength back from when I first arrived in the hamlet. While I was recovering, I spent time getting to know Kaya. That's Adahy's sister. We hit it off. She didn't know English, but she did make her feelings known to me. I wasn't shy about my feelings for her."

Jacob said, "Well, Scott, you are consistent in one area."

"When I was strong enough to hike the trails again, Adahy took me with him on the hunt. He trained me in the bow and arrow. Then how to take down my own deer. He said it's important to be able to catch my own food. While out on the hunt Adahy, was always talking about women he had encounters with."

As Scott and Jacob walked into the hamlet, they were greeted by Kaya and her best friend Rada. Scott introduced Kaya as his wife. As Jacob observed Kaya, he thought she was almost too beautiful for her surroundings. She had long gold hair that hung down to her ass. She had very wide brown eyes. Her nose was long, not like a Flat-Lander's nose. She almost appeared to be an illusion. Scott started talking to the two women in a language that Jacob didn't recognize. Kaya went into one of the tepees and came out with a baby in her arms. Some of the other women in the village gathered around, they were curious about Jacob.

Scott picked up Little Pale Scott and told him, "This is your Uncle Jacob."

Jacob said, "Hi, Little Pale Scott."

The village women were starting to gather around Jacob. They were talking about how they loved his blue eyes.

"We've never met a man with blue eyes before." They continued to talk and giggle as they gave Jacob the complete lookover.

One of the women said, "I think his skin is to pale."

"Maybe he's a ghost."

Kaya and Scott decided they'd have a feast that evening to celebrate the two friends coming back together. The women of the village started cooking succotash for the feast. When they all sat down to eat, there was corn, smoked buffalo, bean soup, squash soup and succotash. Succotash had become, one of Jacob's favorites, since he had come to the village.

When the feast was over and the guest left, Scott and Jacob talked through the night. Scott was curious about Jacob's plans. He wanted to know how Jacob came to the area and why. Jacob had filled him in, on everything that had happened since Scott fell through the ice. Scott sounded a little jealous when he asked Jacob if Joe was his replacement.

Jacob told him it wasn't planned that way. Joe just kind of stepped into his place.

Scott asked how Mark was doing.

Jacob said, "Mark is happy living here. He's met a woman and fallen in love."

"Why do you sound angry, Jacob, when you mention Mark is in a relationship?"

"I never see Mark anymore."

"What's the problem?"

Jacob looked at the ground, then said, "I don't know."

Scott wouldn't let him off the hook that easily. "What's bugging you, Jacob?"

"There's a lot of things that bother me about Mark having a relationship."

"Jacob, I know you and Mark are best friends and were always together, but the two of you aren't married."

"It's weird, Scott, I like Aiyana and I'm glad Mark has found somebody. It's just... I don't know."

"Jacob, do you have sexual feelings for Mark?"

Jacob looked at Scott and thought it was a strange question to ask. He also thought it strange that Scott still wasn't making eye contact.

"Why did you ask the question?"

"Since I've known you, Jacob, you haven't shown much sexual interest in girls."

Jacob thought he should be offended by what Scott had said, he wasn't. "I haven't thought about Mark in that way."

"Do you like girls?"

"Yeah, I like girls. Yes, of course, I think about them and," he stopped again.

"And what, Jacob?"

"Come on, Scott, your questions are getting personal."

"I'm trying to help you understand yourself, Jacob."

Jacob asked Scott if he ever entertained those kinds of thoughts. Scott said, "Yes, I do."

"Even though you are married to Kaya, you still have those feelings?"

"Yes, I do, I have sexual feelings for both guys and women."

"Have you discussed it with Kaya?"

"Kaya and I have very deep conversations about human sexuality."

Jacob said, "I've always been curious about same-sex relationships. "Is she okay with it?"

"Yes, she is, in fact, Rada and Kaya are in a sexual relationship."

Jacob had a surprised look on his face. "Does the three-way relationship work for you?"

"Think, Jacob, of course it does. Rada is looking for a man to have a baby with her."

Jacob looked at Scott, he couldn't think of anything to say.

"She finds you attractive. She would like to have a baby boy with eyes like yours."

Jacob thought to himself he wouldn't know what to do with a woman.

Scott changed the subject when he asked Jacob again what he, Mark, and Joe's plans were.

"I don't know, because we didn't plan to arrive before the massacre took place. The Shet placed us on the edge of the village before the massacre. We hadn't planned on meeting any of the people in the village. Now, we've become a part of their community."

The three had become a part of the lives of the people in the village as much as they were apart of theirs. Jacob said he loved the Chief. He was like a father to him. Joe had become a part of his new family, also. Jacob could tell Joe loved his two new brothers Fire Foot and Little Fire. Jacob said Mark was in training to be a healer and he was good at it, too. Scott could tell Jacob was proud of Mark.

Jacob said, "Yeah, Mark was always in search of something. He's found it living here."

Jacob told Scott he didn't know what the plan was, because he and the other two hadn't had time to plan. One of the problems was they didn't know what Leroy or McCabe looked like. They were going to take the two to the tribal council south of the village for trial. Now, they didn't know when in time they were, so they didn't know when the massacre would take place, if it took place at all.

Scott asked, "Do you want to stay for a while in the hamlet?"

"Yes, I do want to stay. I shouldn't stay too long, though, because everyone in my village will be worried about me."

"Would you be interested in getting to know Rada better?"

"Yes, I would be interested in that."

Jacob and Rada had started to spend time together over the next couple of weeks. Rada knew a little English. Jacob couldn't recognize the language she spoke. Their conversations were mostly about same-sex relationships. He asked her a lot of questions.

Rada asked, "Why do you have a strong interest in same-sex relationships?"

"I'm looking for answers, because I hadn't been exposed to it, until moving to the village."

Rada and Jacob became very comfortable with each other as the weeks passed. Rada asked if he was interested in her one evening after dinner. Jacob said he didn't know; he hadn't had any experience in that area. She made it clear to him when he felt comfortable enough with her, she was ready. She said the two of them having a baby together would produce a strong child with good physical characteristics.

The following evening the four had been out on a walk after dinner. Scott and Kaya said they were going to bed leaving Rada and Jacob alone.

Rada asked, "Do you want to?"

"I don't know if I can do it with you, I have stronger sexual feelings for guys then I do for women."

Rada looked Jacob over and said, "There are other ways to conceive."

"How? I don't understand what you're saying."

Rada leaned over and whispered in his ear. "Do you know how to do that?"

"Oh, I get it."

She giggled and asked, "Well, Jacob?"

He said, "Now, that I know how to do."

"Well," she said, "you do that, then you give it to me. I'll take care of the rest."

"I'm not sure I want to be a father, yet."

"Jacob, I've seen fifteen summers, and it's time, my people don't live that long."

"Okay, that makes sense to me at least in this world."

Months later Jacob Jr. was born, the only problem was, she was Jacobina.

As Kaya came out of the birthing room, she said, "Congratulations, Jacob, it's a girl."

Jacob asked, "May I see her?"

"No, it's forbidden for men to be in the birthing room."

A few days later Rada brought the baby home. Jacob had been living with the threesome, since coming to the hamlet. Scott decided to have a coming home party for Rada and Jacobina.

During the party the Rada and Kaya got up and said, "Nature calls."

They left for the calling.

Scott and Jacob continued to have a conversation.

Jacob said, "I think it's great you and are fathers."

"Yeah, Jacob, it is great. Jacob, do you remembered when I told you, it was going to be very painful for you."

Jacob's expression changed from joy to confusion. "I'm not sure what you're saying."

"Come on, Jacob, think back to when Iktumi told Mark he didn't have to be afraid, because he was going to make it a painless death for him when he killed him. I told you it was going to be a painful death for you when I killed you."

Scott was looking into Jacob's eyes now. Jacob could see Dzoavits staring at him as he spoke.

Scott stood up, pulled a knife out, and slit Jacobina's throat.

Jacob screamed, "Oh my God, no."

Jacob lunged at Scott trying stop him. It was too late. He continued to charge Scott. Scott through the knife up in front of him in a defensive posture. Jacob continued the pursuit as Scott ducked then turned around as Jacob passed him. Scott wrestled him to the ground then sat on his chest and put the knife to his balls.

"What did you think, Jacob? Did you think I wasn't going to do anything about you Mark and Joe showing up here."

Jacob realized it wasn't Scott talking to him; it was Iktumi. "Iktumi, you're a fucking bastard.."

"Shut up, you little fuck. Haven't you figured out Jacob that I'm not Iktumi, I'm your friend Dzoavits."

Jacob coughed up some phlegm from the back of his throat and spit in his face. Dzoavits was so pissed with anger he raised the knife getting ready to plunge it into Jacob's head.

He stopped and said, "I'm not going to kill you yet, Jacob. I'm of my word, Jacob. Are you ready to be separated from your nuts? I'm going to stare into your eyes and watch the life drain out of you, while you bleed to death."

Jacob was trying to figure out how he was going to get out of it, when he saw Kaya sneaking up behind Dzoavits with a big stick. Jacob forced himself to look only at his face, so he wouldn't give her away. She raised the stick over his head and brought it down with a thud on his shoulder. Dzoavits screamed out, then rolled onto the ground moaning. Rada walked into the room and picked up the lifeless baby and walked out crying Kaya turned and followed Rada out.

As the two women walked out of the room a tall Native America Warrior walked past them as he entered the room. He had strong features in his face. It looked like his face was carved out of stone. He turned and looked at Jacob with green piercing eyes. His hair was long and grey, giving him a look of great wisdom. There were feathers coming out from behind his war bonnet that matched the color of the paint on his face. The only clothes he wore, were a pair of deer skin pants and moccasins. His upper body was bare chested with muscle tone that looked like a chiseled statue. Jacob had never met him but knew in his heart that the man standing before him was Shappa.

"This is between me and Jacob, Shappa. You need to stay out of this situation."

Shappa looked at Dzoavits, in a loud thundering voice bellowed, "Shut the hell up or I'll kill you right here on the spot."

Jacob realized Dzoavits respected Shappa, he immediately shut up. "Dzoavits, you will be judged for your evil and disgusting acts."

Shappa walked over to where Jacob was lying, knelt beside him and asked if he was hurt. Jacob was a little surprised by the gentleness in Shappa's voice when he spoke to him.

"I'm fine."

"Do you know what he did to me?" Jacob asked in a shamed voice.

"Yes, Jacob, I do know."

Jacob turned his attention to Dzoavits and said he was going to kill him. "Not if I'm able to kill and eat you first. That would've happened if Shappa hadn't interfered."

Shappa turned to Dzoavits and told him, "If you speak again, I'm going to shove this hunting spear down your throat."

When Shappa's attention turned back to Jacob, Dzoavits made his break and ran out the door.

Jacob yelled, "I'm going to kill you," as he ran out. Jacob thought it was strange, as he ran out the door he was transforming into a coyote.

"You didn't know he's a skin changer?"

"I didn't until now. Thanks for helping me, Shappa. Dzoavits would have killed me if you hadn't shown up."

"Jacob, you should have been paying attention to his lies."

"What do you mean?"

"He made a couple of mistakes in the conversations with you that you should have caught."

Jacob asked, "Like when Scott didn't remember the shake?"

"Yes, his story about how he ended up here."

"Yeah, he told me, he just appeared here with his winter clothes on after going through the portal."

"From your own experience, Jacob, you should have caught on after he told you that."

Jacob said, "I was frightened and confused when I first saw Scott. I wanted to believe he was somebody I could trust."

"You need to be aware of your enemy's deception. We've been trying to teach you that. You need to pay attention to the messages especially, when you're under stress. Wanting to trust someone, isn't a reason to have faith in what you're seeing. That mistake hurt you deeply, Jacob. You have a nemesis who wants to kill you. I want you to remember that. With that said, I want you to also remember there are people who love and care for you. There's one person who has exceptionally strong feelings for you. It even surprised me."

Jacob asked, "Who are you talking about?"

"I can't tell you that, Jacob. You'll find out for yourself. When the time comes, you need to be honest with him and yourself."

Jacob said, "Okay, I don't know what you're talking about, though."

"Just don't forget that there are people that love you, Jacob."

Jacob said he understood. Shappa gave him a look of doubt.

"No, I do. I think my mother loved me. I don't think my dad does."

"Why do you feel that way?"

"As far back as I can remember I wasn't able to please him. I think my dad wants me to be like him. I try, but it's not who I am."

"Can you give me an example?"

"A few years ago, dad told me it was time for the ritual to manhood. The ritual is a coming-of-age tradition in our family. When a member in the family starts puberty during their twelfth year. Their dad takes them out hunting for their first animal. After the kill, he teaches them to clean the animal. During the process they remove the heart and eat it, that marks the beginning of the trail to adulthood.

"Dad and I drove into the mountains to do the ritual. He taught me how to set up and patiently wait. As we waited, he told me about his ritual when he was twelve. He talked about how proud grandpa was of him. He also, talked about how proud he was of himself. He just raved about how it was the best day of his life. I didn't say it to him, but I wasn't interested in the ritual.

"When a whitetail came into view, I sighted it in. Dad was right behind me coaching. He asked if I had the dear in my sights. I said yes, I do. He asked if I was aiming at the boiler room."

Shappa asked, "What's the boiler room?"

"It's just a term we use."

"Why do you call it the boiler room?"

"The boiler room is what a hunter calls the area right behind the shoulder. If you shoot it in the boiler room, it usually kills the dear instantly. That way the hunter doesn't wound the animal, because it may run for miles suffering before it dies. I told him I had the boiler room sighted in for the shot. Dad asked if I had my finger on the trigger. I said yes, I do. He told me to slowly squeeze the trigger. I started to squeeze the trigger then hesitated."

"Why did you hesitate?"

"While I was looking through the scope, I was thinking when I fired the shot, I'd be taking a life. I didn't feel right about having that kind of power. I slowly lowered the barrel of the gun, then turned to look to dad for advice. He looked at me, then told me I was a total disappointment. He turned and started walking back to the jeep. He didn't say a word to me the whole way home."

Jacob looked at Shappa with a tear in his eye. He said, "I don't feel any connection to my dad, Shappa."

Shappa's eyes bore into Jacob's when he said, "Jacob, you and Mark are brothers."

Jacob said, "I know, Shappa, Mark and I are blood-brothers."

"No, Jacob, you and Mark are true-brothers. You both have the same father."

Jacob's eyes didn't leave the stare in Shappa's when he slowly asked, "You mean my dad fathered Mark, also?"

"No, Jacob, I mean Mark's father is also, your father."

Jacob slowly shook his head no as he said, "I don't believe that, Shappa; how can Mark's father be my father also?"

Shappa said, "Jacob, I can't explain to you what happened, but I can tell you with all honesty that you and Mark are the product of the same man."

"I feel like you're my father, Shappa."

"We are related, Jacob."

"Shappa, would have been disappointed in White Foot if he had done that?"

"No, Jacob, I wouldn't have been. White Foot isn't a warrior, but I do still love him."

"That's cool, Shappa. White Foot must love you also. Are you disappointed in me, Shappa?"

"No, Jacob, I'm never disappointed in you, I do worry about you, though. I'm always here for you, Jacob. I can't protect you from your life lessons, though."

"I'm sorry you had to learn the hard way with Dzoavits. I'm going to kill him."

"I know that, Jacob. Don't forget, Jacob, I'm always here for you. We can't stay in the spiritual realm any longer, Jacob."

Jacob became frightened when Shappa told him.

"Why can't I stay with you?" Jacob was almost pleading with him as he asked.

"I'll have to catch up with you later, Jacob. For now, I have to go."

Jacob pleaded with Shappa not to leave him.

Shappa said, "Jacob, you're back on your pathway."

As he walked out of the room Jacob said, "No, there's room on the path for both of us."

Jacob awoke from the long sleep.

CHAPTER 13

Who Cares for Jacob

Joe and Fire Foot had Jacob tied to the sled when they came running into the village. They were greeted by Mark, Roaring Fire, and White Lightning. White Lightning sent Fire Foot and Little Fire out looking for Jacob and Joe earlier in the morning. He knew the two had gone on Jacob's first hunt the day before. He became worried about them when they didn't return the previous evening.

The Chief and Roaring Fire untied Jacob and carried him into the small teepee. Jacob's teepee sat next to the longhouse. The floor space inside the tent was six feet by six feet. There was a small fire pit in the center of the room. Jacob's bed was a mattress of hay that laid on the ground opposite the fire pit. Buffalo skins laid on the bed he used for blankets.

As they carried him into his room, Mark and Joe followed behind. They laid him down on his back in bed. The Chief asked Joe what happened. Joe told him the story. The Chief turned to Roaring Fire and told him to gather some of his men, so they could go with him to investigate the campsite. As they left the teepee, Mark heard Roaring Fire ask the Chief what were they going to do at the campsite. As their voices faded away, Mark could barely hear the Chief say, they were going to clean up the mess.

Mark turned to Joe and said he was going to find Iktumi to see if he could help. When Mark returned with him, Iktumi looked Jacob over, then said there was nothing he could do for him. Mark told Iktumi Jacob needed his help. He asked him if he couldn't do anything for him or wouldn't do anything.

Iktumi said in an angry voice, "I've trained you in the healing herbs, why don't you treat Jacob?" He then left.

Mark looked at Joe and said, "If Iktumi wasn't my father-in-law."

Joe did a double take at Mark' he hadn't realized he and Aiyana were married.

The first night Mark and Joe spent the evening washing Jacob's body. Mark made it clear to Joe, it had to be done every night, because he didn't want any bacteria to get into the wound. They used soap-root to wash him. As they cleaned him, he'd scream out in pain. Jacob pleaded with them to stop hurting him. Mark asked him if it was his shoulder that hurt. Jacob didn't respond to Mark's question, he just continued to plead with them to stop.

Joe told Mark he was angry that Iktumi wouldn't help Jacob. "I think he knows who we are. I also, think he knows why we're here."

"I don't think Iktumi knows, because we arrived in the village before the massacre; therefore, he doesn't have any reason to kill us."

Joe could see that Mark was in denial about Iktumi. "I think Iktumi's physical body is possessed by a demon."

Mark became angry when Joe said it. "It's obvious Iktumi had nothing to do with Jacob being shredded like an old rag doll."

Joe understood by the way Mark said it, he was defending Iktumi.

"Iktumi's a Medicine Man, it doesn't seem right to me that he would turn his back on somebody who was injured."

"Tell me, Mark, is that something you would do when you become a healer?"

"Listen, Joe, Iktumi can make his own decisions."

Joe yelled at Mark, "It's your best friend lying there dying. So why are you defending the medicine man who's turned his back on him?"

Joe saw by the way Mark's facial expression changed he had gotten through to him.

Mark said, "Just for the record, I love Iktumi. He's taught me everything I know about medicinal herbs. He's also training me to be a healer. Iktumi is family. I'm not the same person I was before coming to the village."

Joe said, "None of us are the same person we were before we came here."

Mark asked, "What is it you're thinking?"

"While we played the Game of the Spirits, the demon made it clear to you and Jacob that he was going to kill both of you. We know Iktumi the man loves you because Aiyana is in love with you. I think the demon was planning to kill both of you, until you and Aiyana fell in love. The reason I think this, is because I believe the demon is communicating with Iktumi the man."

"What you're saying doesn't make any sense. Why would Iktumi spend the time guiding me through the 'rites to pathway' if he was planning to kill me?"

"White Lightning didn't give him a choice when he told him he'd be your guide," Mark said. "Iktumi trained me in the healing arts. He didn't get in the way of Aiyana and I falling in love. He's made me a part of his family. I just don't agree with what you're saying, Joe."

Joe said, "I think the demon hasn't taken complete control over Iktumi yet. Iktumi's fighting that."

"I don't think you are right, Joe."

Joe thought to himself that Mark can't see through the deception.

Mark thought about it for a minute then said, "I don't think Iktumi has any idea who we are, because we showed up before his family was massacred."

"You've already said that, Mark, your feelings for Iktumi are getting in the way of your clear thinking."

Joe did raise some doubts in Mark's mind.

Mark said, "Remember the first day we were in the village standing in front of the council. Iktumi read all three of our auras. He told me that during one of the herb training sessions. He later without thinking told me he couldn't read Jacob's aura. I'm thinking maybe that isn't true."

"Why do you think he read Jacob's soul?"

"I asked him if he read minds. He said no, he didn't read minds. He read souls, then he said he could read anyone's soul. I asked him what information did he receive, when reading a person's soul. He was reading the persons, wants, needs, passions, and fears."

Joe asked, "Do you think Iktumi read Jacob's soul?"

"Yes, I do think so."

It was late October, Mark and Joe were sitting next to Jacob talking as he laid on his bed. This had become a nightly ritual since Jacob had been injured. Mark would stay by Jacob's side during the day taking care of him. Joe would show up in the evenings after warrior training and take care of him through the night.

Mark asked, "Are you staying all night with Jacob?"

Joe said, "Yes, I started sleeping next to him every night, because I can't leave him by himself."

It was Joe and Mark who took care of him. White Lightning was the only person in the village who would come to visit. Jacob had a high fever that wouldn't go away. The village people were very superstitious about the sickness the settlers had brought from Europe. Half their population had been decimated by the illness the pioneers carried. They believed the never-ending fever Jacob had, was one of those illnesses.

To feed Jacob, Joe had come up with an interesting idea. He formed a funnel out of dried buffalo hide. He and Mark would put the tapered end into Jacob's mouth then pour water and liquid food into the funnel. Aiyana would bring food to the door and leave it for Mark and Joe to feed him. The food she left was mashed down to soup. In the evenings they'd sit Jacob up and pour the food down him. Sometimes, they were able to wake him up long enough to get him to swallow on his own. Jacob would usually fall back a sleep, before they were finished feeding him.

Mark started treating Jacob with medicinal herbs, since Iktumi refused to. When Mark first started treating his wound, Joe had questions about what the herbs were. Mark didn't think anything of the questions. As time went by, he began to realize Joe was becoming protective of Jacob.

"What's that, Mark?" Joe asked.

Mark said, "It's echinacea."

Joe asked what it was used for.

"Echinacea is very good at helping wounds heal," Mark said, "it also helps boost Jacob's immunity from disease."

"What the hell is that one? It's a strange-looking root."

That Mark said with a little pride, "This is Devil's Claw Root. Devil's Claw Root will help take the inflammation out of the wound."

Joe was impressed with Mark's knowledge of the herbs and roots. Mark pulled another one out and was studying it. Joe enjoyed the idea of using herbs for healing. Mark combined the roots and herbs into a bowl. He had one more herb to throw into the pot.

"What's that one?"

"Melaleuca Alternifolia," Mark said as he took delight in his new-found knowledge.

"What's that good for?"

"It's also, a good anti-inflammatory."

"How do you find all of these Herbs?"

"I trade for 'em. I can trade for anything."

"I know that, I've been to the trading post."

Mark said, "I don't trade at the Chongs' Trading Post."

"Where do you trade?"

"The Flat-Landers have trade routes all over the country."

"They do?"

"Yeah, the tea tree oil comes from as far away as the Pacific Coast."

"Really." Joe said, "I'm impressed with the idea of trade routes."

"I know you are; I've heard you've been trading a lot of furs at the Chongs'."

"What are you trading furs for?"

Joe said, "Whiskey and guns."

Mark pulled out some little red berries and asked Joe if he knew what they were.

"Yep, they're cranberries."

"That's right, Joe."

Joe said, "I've drank a lot of cranberries juice in my day. Cranberry juice is good for bladder infections."

"I don't know, Mark; I don't think Jacob has bladder infection."

"It's good for warding off other infections," Mark said.

When it was time for Joe to remove the stitches in Jacob's shoulder, Mark prepared a treatment. Joe watched as Mark put all the ingredients into a mixing bowl. He mashed them down with the wooden-masher-gadget.

"Do you have name for the wooden-masher-gadget?"

"I can't think of one."

Mark mixed the ingredients. He asked Joe if he'd get the hot water that was heating on the fire and bring it to him. Joe went over to the fire, grabbed the pot of water then brought it back.

Mark told him it was time to pull the stitches out of the wound. Joe went to work cutting the stitches then pulling them out of Jacob's shoulder.

"How many stitches did you sew into the shoulder?"

"I counted eighty-one."

When he finished pulling the stitches out of the shoulder, Mark had him come around to where he was sitting to help with the treatment.

Mark told Joe to slowly pour the water into the bowel as he mixed everything together.

When he finished mixing the ingredients, he said, "Oh, I almost forgot the sage."

"I know what sage is; how's that going to help Jacob?"

"It'll help reduce the fever."

When Mark was finished mixing the poultice, he started to apply it to the wound. When he did, Jacob cried out.

Joe yelled, "STOP, you're hurting him!"

"I'm not hurting him."

Mark looked at Joe. When he looked into Joe's eyes, he felt threatened. He thought to himself that Joe had become overly protective of Jacob.

"The treatment won't hurt him. You can help me apply it if you want to, Joe."

"I promise Jacob won't feel anything."

"Okay, but, if he cries out again, we'll have to stop."

Mark applied the poultice to his shoulder. When he finished with that part of the wound, he had Joe raise Jacob's right hand over his head, so he could treat the gash in his armpit.

As Mark looked at the scar under Jacob's arm he said, "It's lucky the knife didn't cut his face, because that is one ugly scar."

When Mark finished the treatment, he laid a cactus pad over the treated area.

Joe and Mark sat back then had a conversation.

Mark told Joe, "Jacob is very lucky the knife didn't hit the artery in his arm. Where did you learned to stitch wounds?"

"My dad used to stitch the dogs when they had a run-in with an animal. Sometimes the dog would get into a fight with another dog. Dad told me it was too expensive to take the hound to the vet. When I was ten, he taught me how to sew stiches."

As the weeks passed into December, Mark and Joe sat next to Jacob talking about why he wasn't waking up.

Mark was baffled about it. "He's still sleeping. He couldn't be in a coma because if he was, he wouldn't be talking. He has to be dreaming though, because he's talking and crying in his sleep."

Joe said, "Jacob talks in his sleep all night."

"I know that."

"I can understand everything he's saying while talking in his sleep. Do you listen to what he's talking about while he sleeps, Mark?"

"Yes, I do."

"What's your opinion about what Jacob is saying?"

"Jacob and I have been friends our entire lives and I love him, no matter what." Mark paused then said, "I don't care either way."

Joe looked into Mark's eyes and said, "I love Jacob also, but not in the same way you do."

Mark started to ask Joe what he meant. He didn't have to ask though, he realized what Joe had just told him. As they sat there looking at each other, Mark was thinking nobody in their wildest dreams would ever suspect that of Joe.

"Please, Mark, don't tell Jacob what I just told you."

"I can't make a promise like that."

"Why?"

"If I were to keep a secret from Jacob, he'd know I was hiding something from him. I know Jacob, in his mind it would cast doubt on my loyalty to him. I'd also, feel I was deceiving him."

"You need to be honest with Jacob and tell him how you feel about him."

"I'm afraid to tell him."

"What are you afraid of, Joe?"

"If Jacob knows how I feel, he'll end our friendship."

"Jacob won't end your friendship if you tell him you're in love with him. He will, though, if you're not honest with him."

Jacob continued to talk in his sleep as they sat by his side.

Mark said, "I don't understand why he's hallucinating."

"I don't think he's hallucinating."

"What do you think's going on with him then?"

"I don't think his soul's in his body. I think it's somewhere else."

The thought frightened Mark. He asked, "Why do you think something like that?"

"I know, because I sleep next to him every night. I listen to the conversations he has until I fall asleep. He's alive, but his essence isn't in his body. It's interacting with someone or something."

Joe changed the subject, when he said they'd been in the village for six months. They still hadn't made plans to capture Leroy Abrahamson or McCabe and bring them to the tribal elders for trial. He was right. The problem was, they were supposed to have shown up after the massacre took place, not before. It would have been much easier to show up, after the massacre, because they knew Abrahamson and McCabe would be building the town of Table Mesa right there.

Mark had been thinking about it for months. He remembered when he wrote the prayer down on paper. He'd written: "It is necessary for us to go to the area and time of the massacre after it took place, east of the Sleeping Demon by the lake."

When he mentioned it to Joe, Joe said they weren't chanting that. Mark had written the prayer down. Joe was the one who memorized it. Mark and Jacob hadn't had time to memorize it, they just followed what Joe was chanting. Mark asked Joe to repeat the prayer.

Joe chanted, "It is necessary for us to go to the area and the time before, the massacre took place, east of the Sleeping Demon by the lake."

After hearing it, Mark realized the Shet had placed them where they ask it to. The Shet place them by the lake, next to the village, before the massacre, not after.

Joe said, "Yeah, by the lake next to the village, butt naked."

Mark said they didn't know when the massacre was going to happen, because they didn't know when in time they'd been placed. Shit, they didn't know if the massacre would happen the next day or in twenty years.

Joe said they should be working on a plan as Mark was getting ready to leave for the evening. Mark agreed they should. He wanted to wait, until they had Jacob back on his feet. Mark left and said as he was walking out of the teepee, they'd have time to plan. Joe didn't agree with him but didn't have a chance to argue because Mark left.

The following evening after training Joe showed up at the teepee.

Mark said, "Jacob has a very high fever tonight. It's higher than it usually is."

Joe could see from the amount of sweat on Jacob's body, he was burning up. Joe said maybe, Jacob wasn't going to make it. Mark told him to shut up and have faith. Mark told him they had to bring his fever down.

Joe looked at Mark, shook his head, then asked, "What can we do?"

Mark said, "I remember watching a movie where one of the characters had a fever. The doctors put him in an ice bath."

"That's great for a movie, but are we going to find ice around here."

"We have ice, the lake's frozen over. We'll break a hole in the it next to the shore. Then we'll lay Jacob in the water, long enough to bring the fever down."

Jacob was talking as the two pick him up and carried him out of the tent to the lake.

Mark said, "When we lay Jacob in the bath, we need to keep his shoulder out of the water. You know when we go into the water, we're going to freeze our nuts off."

Joe said, "I'm not using mine anyway, that's part of the worrier training."

"What is?"

"When a warrior is in training for the hunt or for battle, it is strictly forbidden to be sexually active."

They carried Jacob into waste deep water then gave him his bath. They both bitched about how cold they were. They kept his body submerged in the water for as long as they could tolerate. When they tried to carry him out of the water, they were both having problems with the muscles in their legs working. They carried him back to his teepee. They wrapped him in the buffalo hide to warm him up.

Jacob began to speak clearly as Mark and Joe wrapped him. He wasn't talking to either one of them. Jacob said, "I don't feel any connection to my dad." He wasn't conscious, so he wasn't speaking to Mark or Joe.

Mark asked, "What did he mean by that?"

Jacob's eyes were still closed when he said, "I know Shappa, Mark and I are blood-brothers."

"You mean my dad fathered Mark also?"

Jacob slowly shook his head no, "As he said I don't believe that, Shappa. How can Mark's father be my father also?"

Joe began to cry as he sat by Jacob's side listening. As Mark observed Joe crying, he thought to himself that Joe must have a heart in there after all.

Mark looked into Joe's tear-filled eyes and said, "Jacob's hallucinating, because of the fever."

Joe looked at Mark and said, "No, he's not."

"I know you live with your grandmother. What happened to your parents?"

"My mother died when she gave birth to me."

Joe stared into Mark's eyes then asked, "So what happened to your dad?"

"He died a few months before I was born."

"How did he die?"

"I don't know, my grandmother refuses to talk about it. Why are you asking?"

"If what Jacob is saying is true, don't you think that's a little suspicious?"

"Joe, Jacob's hallucinating," Mark was becoming angry as he said it.

Jacob rolled his head in the direction of Joe and slowly opened his eyes. It took him a while to focus on who was sitting there. "Oh, it's Joe."

"Why are you crying?"

Joe leaned over and hugged him, "I thought you were dying."

"It'll take more than trying to cut my arm off at the shoulder for you to get rid of me."

When Joe was finished slobbering all over Jacob, Mark leaned over and gave him a hug.

Mark said, "Welcome back," then he started crying.

"What are you two crying about, it's only been a couple of days,"

Joe asked, "What's the last thing you remember?"

"I remember falling into the knife then, you stuck a big ass needle in me. I must have passed out, because I can't remember anything after that."

"Who was the guy who chased you with the knife?"

Joe explained who they were and how they had arrived there. "I remember the story of Ted and Sam. When Scott drowned in the lake, Sheriff Justice mentioned two guys, who had gone missing in 1950. All that was found of them were their clothes by the shore and one of their dad's cars."

Mark said, "Now we know what happened to our clothes when the we went through the portal."

Joe said, "Yeah, our clothes are lying next to the lake."

Joe told Jacob he was lucky he'd passed out, because he poked him with the needle eighty-one times.

Jacob said, "I didn't have a choice when I passed out."

"You should have stayed awake for the whole sewing job. It only took an hour to sew you back together."

"The least you could have done, was give me a bottle of whiskey to chug before you went to torturing me."

"Why would I waste a good bottle on that?"

Jacob said, "I feel like I've been sleeping for a couple of days."

Joe told him it'd been nine weeks.

"Nine weeks, what have you been doing?"

Mark shook his head then said, "What have we been doing? We've been wiping your fucking ass, that's what we've been doing."

Jacob smiled at Mark, "It's better to wipe somebody's ass than it is to kiss it."

Joe said, "Yeah, we've been kissing your ass too." Joe told Jacob, "Thanks for saving my life."

"I didn't save your life. I tripped and fell into the knife when I threw the rock."

"It gave me time to load the arrow; otherwise, Sam would have killed me."

"You can't blame him, after all you were pissing on him."

Jacob told Joe, "Thanks for saving my life. I'm sorry I hit you in the eye."

"I probably had it coming since I was sticking needles in you."

"I didn't feel anything after you stuck me the second time. I thought I was going to die before I passed out, though."

Mark excitedly said, "I have some good news."

Joe and Jacob both said "What?" at the same time.

"Aiyana and I are married." He looked at Jacob who was staring down. "Shit, Jacob, I'm sorry we don't hang out anymore. Are you angry with me?"

"I'm not angry, I miss being with you all the time. I'm happy for you and Aiyana. You two are perfect for each other."

Mark leaned over and hugged Jacob. He said, "Shit, Jacob, you need to start eating, because when I hug you, it feels like I'm hugging a skeleton." Mark said, "I'm going to be a father."

Jacob said, "What the fuck."

"That's right, Uncle Jacob."

Joe asked if Iktumi knew.

"Not yet, we haven't figured out how to tell him."

"You better not wait too long, because it'll start to show eventually."

"I know things are different between us, Jacob, but you have Joe looking out for you. He's pretty good at it too."

Jacob said, "Yeah, Joe and I are getting close. We were sleeping together under the stars the night before I was injured."

Joe said, "We've been sleeping together every night for the last nine weeks."

"I hope you've been a perfect gentleman the whole time."

"Of course, I'd never take advantage of an injured person." Jacob thought for a moment then said, "All we do is sleep, though."

"No, all you do is lay there."

"Well, Joe, if you made a move on me, maybe I wouldn't just lay there."

"I don't know how to make a on a woman, so how would I know what to do with a guy?"

Jacob said, "I know somebody that does."

They both looked at Mark. Joe asked Mark to explain it to him.

Mark looked up in the air and said, "I don't kiss and tell."

Joe turned to Jacob and said, "Well, we'll get it out of him one way or the other."

Mark looked at Jacob also, then said, "I'll take that as a threat, we all know what happens to people who cross Joe."

Mark stood up and said Aiyana was waiting for him to come home. He told Jacob he still loved him like a brother. He said to Joe as he was walking out the door, he should bring the whiskey stash with him the next time the three of them were together.

As Mark left, Joe turned to Jacob and said there was something he wanted to talk to him about.

"Jacob, were you joking about us sleeping together?"

Jacob was about to start throwing the jokes out again, when he realized by the way Joe was looking at him, the question he'd asked came from the heart. There was a moment of silence as the two looked into each other's eyes.

Jacob thought to himself, Joe knew him well enough to know if he lied, he'd know. He thought if he told him the truth, he'd still know. So, either way, Joe knows.

"Your question comes from the heart."

Joe didn't say anything, he just looked at Jacob.

"Joe, the way the people in the village view human sexuality is completely different from what we've been taught. There's men with women

relationships. Men with men relationships and women with women relationships. Some of people have sexual relationships with the opposite
sex and with the same sex. This culture is so casual about sex, I feel a
person can be themselves.

"I'm always talking about girls, but what I think and what I say isn't
always how he feel inside. I was confused about my sexuality, until we
came to the village, now I'm no longer confused."

Jacob became very flush in the face when he said, "Joe, if you are
asking me if I have sexual feelings for guys, the answer is yes. I just told
you something I thought I'd never tell another person. Did you ask me
because you wanted to know or are you making the move on me?"

When Joe started his answer, his voice was shaking. "Before we
came to the village, I was confused about my feelings also. I try to think
about girls in that way, but I want to be with a guy." He corrected himself when he said, "I don't want to be with a guy, I want to be with you,
Jacob." Joe's face turned completely red when he said it. "I feel the same
way about the village people. It's strange how living here has changed
me. It's also changed the way I viewed same-sex relationships." Jacob
thought about it for a moment then said, "Living here didn't change
you, it just allows you to be yourself. There's something else about the
people in the village I want to talk about. As humans these people phys-
ically have two sexes. The more I interact with the culture, I think the
people don't have two sexes, they have three."

Jacob didn't follow what he was saying.

"I think they have an in-between sex."

Jacob asked, "Do you mean a third gender?"

"Yes, during one of the village ceremonies Fire Foot was dressed
in a woman's costume. He was also playing the role of the women.
The next day when I saw him at training, I asked him why was he
wearing a women's costume and playing the role of a women in the
previous evening's ceremony. Fire Foot told me it was because, he
is a woman."

"He's not a woman, Jacob. The next day during training when we were changing clothes, I could see he had a dick. When I saw that, I said to him, you're not a woman, you have a penis. He said, 'Joe, you don't understand, my body is male, my soul is female.'"

Jacob thought about it then said, "Yeah, that makes sense."

"There's more I want to talk to you about, Jacob. John and I are from Colorado Springs. Last year I met a guy, who had moved from Trinidad. He was telling me about a clinic there that did sex change operations."

"What's a sex change operation?"

"If a person has a male body, but they believe they're a woman, they can go to the clinic to have their gender changed, or vice versa."

"Can I ask you a personal question, Joe?"

"Sure."

"Do you think you're a woman in a man's body?"

"No, I feel I'm male on the inside even though I'm attracted to guys. Are you a woman on the inside, Jacob?"

They both were very curious about each other's answers.

Jacob said, "I also feel I'm male on the inside. I do understand it, though, if a male felt they were female on the inside, or vice versa."

Joe said, "I'm glad you feel you're a man inside, because I wouldn't want them to cut your dick off."

Jacob paused for a moment thinking about a couple of different ways he could take that. "Well," he said, "I wouldn't want them to cut your dick off either."

Jacob said, "I'm not trying to change the subject, but I must go to the shit-pit."

"Do you think you're ready to go on your own?"

Jacob started to stand up, felt woozy, then sat down.

"Let me help you up, Jacob."

Joe slid his shoulder underneath Jacob's left underarm, then lifted him to his feet. As Joe lifted him up, Jacob investigated Joe's face and could see by his expression, he genuinely cared about him.

When they returned to the teepee, Joe helped him lay back down on his bed. "I should probably give you some room, Jacob. Do you want me to leave?"

Jacob asked, "Where would you go, you've been sleeping with me for the last two months."

"I'm still welcome to sleep with Fire Foot and Little Fire."

Jacob looked deep into Joe's eyes then asked, "Would you please, sleep with me tonight, like you've been doing for the last two months, but tonight would you hold me in your arms?"

Joe thought to himself, when he did, it was going to end his warrior's career. Joe paused then said, "Yes, Jacob, yes, I will."

CHAPTER 14

Retreat

As Mark packed his only bag for the pilgrimage to the Shet, he was thinking he must be crazy to think about attempting the trek in the middle of January. He knew the temperatures at night were dropping below zero. He had experience with below zero temperatures when he was younger growing up in Table Mesa. He always knew when it was zero or lower, because the snot in his nose froze when it was that cold.

Mark remembered back to when he and Jacob took the bus to the ski area one day. They spent the entire day skiing until the resort closed around four. Jacob told him jokes the whole way up the hill on the ski lift. They were laughing so hard, they didn't think about the cold.

One morning they had come to the top of the mountain on the lift. There had been a cross wind that was so cold, they both swore they were going to freeze to death before they reached the top of the mountain. When they did finally arrive at the end of the ride. The outside thermometer read twenty-five below zero. As they slid off the chair at the top of the mountain, they could barely move they were so cold.

When they skied down the mountain, Mark had to stop, he kept getting brain freeze headaches as they accelerated down the hill. Jacob was pushing Mark to keep going. They'd warm up as they skied down the mountain. Every time they started to accelerate Mark had to stop, because it was too painful to continue. When Jacob asked what was the problem, Mark complained that every time he hit a certain speed, he just couldn't handle the pain in his head.

Mark told Jacob he was going to the lodge after one run. Jacob said he was going to keep skiing. There was no way he was wasting the sixteen dollars he spent for the lift ticket. They split up at the bottom of the mountain. Mark said if it warmed up later in the morning, he'd catch up with him as he walked toward the ski lodge.

Mark walked into the lodge and immediately walk over to the café to spend a quarter on a soda pop. He half chugged the soda before he looked for a place to sit down. He wasn't alone in giving up to the morning cold. There were people in the lodge hanging out drinking beer.

Mark walked over to the fireplace and sat down on the couch next to a couple of guys in their twenties. They already had a buzz from drinking. Mark knew they were buzzed by the way they were talking. When he sat down, one of them turned and said hello. Mark said hi back. He asked Mark if he was a local. Mark said that yes, he was local. The other guy asked Mark how the hell he could stand the cold there. Mark explained them that it wasn't always that cold.

They told Mark they were ski bums. Mark thought, that would be something that he'd like to do someday. He then introduced himself. They introduced themselves as Chuck and Bob. Bob stood up and said he was going to get another beer. He asked Chuck if he was ready for another one. Chuck chugged his beer and said sure, why not. Bob asked Mark if he wanted another soda. Mark said no, he'd have a beer. Bob said okay and walked off.

He returned from the bar with three cans of beer. He sat down next to Mark and told him to give him the soda can. Mark handed the soda

can to Bob, who filled it up with one of the beers. He handed it back to Mark. Mark was kind of surprised but took a chug anyway. Bob told Mark the next round was on him. Mark said he only had a couple of dollars, if he got a beer out the deal, he'd buy.

Three beers later the three were laughing at all the jokes Mark had learned from Jacob. Bob and Chuck had all kinds of stories from their travels around the country. They were telling Mark about all the women they had encounters with during their stays in different ski towns. They told him if he wanted to get laid by a different woman every night, then he must be a ski bum.

Around noon Mark saw Jacob walk into the lounge looking for him. He yelled at Jacob to come over and join them. Jacob came over and sat down next to Mark. Mark introduced Chuck and Bob to him. Jacob reached out and did the shake with the two guys. He could see all three were drunk already. Jacob said he was thirsty, then asked Mark if he could have some. Jacob chugged the entire can before Mark could stop him. He then burped and said he must catch up to all of them.

Bob and Chuck started laughing then asked if Jacob had been skiing that morning. He said yeah, he had been, but it's was just getting colder as the day went on, so he'd giving up. Mark told Jacob he was buying the next round. Jacob said he only had five dollars; he'd buy if five dollars would cover the cost of the beers. Chuck stood up and told Jacob he could get the next round. This one was on him.

The four spent the rest of the afternoon talking and drinking. When four o'clock rolled around Mark and Jacob were having so much fun they missed the bus going home. Bob told them not to worry, he'd give them a ride back to town.

It was a tight fit as the four packed into the bug. As they started down the mountain on the snowpack road, they were fish tailing. Mark and Jacob got a kick out of the ride. Chuck took them all the way to their houses and dropped them off. As the two drove off Chuck was yelling out the window goodbye and maybe they'd see them again.

As Mark continued to pack for the week-long pilgrimage, he thought to himself he and Jacob had the best day of their lives that day on the mountain not skiing. Then he thought it was the best day of his life, until he came to the village. He didn't think Jacob would agree with him about the village. He was having a hard time living there.

He thought about how living in the village had changed him. He'd found the women of his dreams. He found his place in life as a healer. All he had to do was finish the week-long retreat, then the whole village was planning a celebration of accomplishment for him.

Fire Foot would be finishing his rites, also. There was going to be the "rites" celebration, where everybody in the village would participate. The celebration would have a feast of food, dancing, then White Lightning would give them new names. After Mark and Fire Foot received their new names, they'd became, totally new adult members of society.

Joe would have been finishing his "rites," but he blew it when he and Jacob started their relationship. Joe had told Mark he didn't care if he wasn't allowed to finish. Mark thought it probably bothered Joe a little, he was very competitive. Joe had what he wanted, though' his prize was Jacob. Even Jacob knew Joe was in love with him and cared very deeply for him.

Mark thought, he should have known Jacob had those kinds of feelings. He and Jacob had cut each other's index fingers and sworn on their blood-brother-ship that neither one of them would speak to another human about their sexual experimentation phase. Jacob seemed to enjoy the whole thing while, for Mark it was just a curiosity thing.

And Joe, Mark thought, he'd never in his wildest dreams thought that about him. The thing about Joe was, if he wanted something, he went after it. He wanted Jacob, he got him. Mark thought back to the evening Jacob awoke from the long sleep. Joe asked him how he felt about what Jacob had been talking about in his sleep. The more he thought about it, the more he realized, Joe wanted to find out his feelings about same-sex relationships, before he told him how he felt about Jacob.

Iktumi had spent the last seven months preparing Mark for the week-long retreat. Mark wasn't as confident about the week as Iktumi was about Mark's newly learned skills. Mark was going to have to spend two days hiking to the Shet. He'd have to spend four days praying for direction. Then he'd have to spend a day hiking back to the village.

He'd already planned the route. He'd take the same route to the top of the mountain he and Aiyana had taken earlier in the fall. Once he reached the top of the mountain, he'd follow the ridge south, which would take him to the Shet. The problem was the snow on the mountain would slow him down significantly. The other problem was the cold. If he was lucky, he may have a couple of days where the Chinook winds would blow. That would bring the temperature to something tolerable.

Mark had his pack full of dried pork when he started the hike. The pork was a gift from Joe and Jacob. Joe had become a regular customer at the Chong Trading Post. There was talk in the village about what Joe was receiving for his trades. Fire Foot and Little Fire knew what Joe was up to, but they wouldn't say a word, even when cornered. Joe was their brother, and they were loyal to him.

He had enough food to survive the seven days. He had the peyote for the prayers. He had clothes and a coat made of buffalo hide. The coat fell all the way to his feet. When he arrived at the Shet, he'd need to figure out shelter. He had a very small tent made from buffalo hide, that would only be good for sleeping.

Mark set out before sun rise. He wanted to get as far up the mountain as he could before night fall. It was bitter cold as he started up the trail in the direction of the Sleeping Demon. As he walked along the trail, he heard the snow crunching under his feet. He thought to himself all the ski gear he had at home would come in handy. Even a good pair of hiking boots. The boots Aiyana made for him were keeping his feet warm, but they weren't as sturdy as his hiking boots.

There were light snowflakes swirling around his head as he walked the trail. About half an inch had accumulated on the ground as he walked closer to the mountain. The snot in his nose was frozen. As the snowflakes fluttered to the ground, it made the trail icy which made it slippery. Mark was getting pissed as he slid along the trail. The four-letter words started to come out of his mouth at his own surprise, He hadn't cussed as much as he did before they came to the village. Jacob told him the reason he didn't throw out the four-letter words as much, was because he was in a relationship.

When Mark arrived at the flatiron that laid at the base of the mountain, he turned right and followed the trail for mile before starting up the trail that led him to the base of the canyon. The trail faded away as he approached the small canyon that led up to the saddle. It was going to get difficult from here, he thought to himself as he started the climb.

As he made the accent up the canyon, he was having a difficult time keeping his footing. The trail had frozen over. There was a light coating of snow on top of the ice. He was able to step on the rocks to keep his footing. The problem was there were places in-between rocks that were icy, so he'd have to take his time trying to move up the trail on the ice.

He was giving himself a ration of shit for making the stupid decision to go in January. He couldn't have made the retreat any earlier, because he'd been taking care of Jacob. Now that Jacob had awoke and started his recovery, he could do the retreat. He didn't want to make the trek later in the spring, because he was going to be in the ceremony with Fire Foot and the other graduates, who were finishing their "rites." The baby was also due in March or April, so waiting was out of the question.

It was around one in the afternoon when Mark took a break. He wanted to sit down. He didn't dare, he didn't want to get wet. As he stood there, he thought he was probably halfway to the saddle. The hike was taking longer than he expected. It was twice as hard trying to climb up the trail on ice and snow.

He thought by the time he arrived at the saddle, it would probably be dark. He had to make it to the saddle, though. There wouldn't be anywhere in the canyon to camp. It was just too steep to set up the tent.

He remembered back to when he and Aiyana had hiked to the saddle, they had found flat ground with boulders surrounding the area. He thought that would be a good place to set up camp.

When he arrived at the saddle, it was after dark. The wind was blowing from the north. It was bitter cold. Mark set up camp behind a boulder. There was no point in trying to build a fire. The pine needles he needed to start a fire were damp.

He broke some tree limbs off a pine tree and used the branches to pitch his tent. It was so cold that he just said, the hell with it. He crawled into the tent and fell asleep. To his surprise he slept all the through the night. It was getting light outside when he awoke. The wind was blowing hard from the west. Mark realized, as he was climbing out of the tent that the temperatures were warmer than the previous evening.

He climbed out of the tent and looked around to see that it was a beautiful morning. The sun had just risen over the east. When he turned around and look at the continental divide, it was a spectacular view. The sky was a dark crystal blue with snow-covered mountains peaks complementing the sky. Mark was thinking to himself that he'd spent his whole life in Table Mesa, he had never appreciated the view to the west until now.

When he camped that evening, he wanted to be at the foot of the Shet. He was thinking he'd have to hike over the peak to get there. There was no other way, if he took the front of the mountain, he'd get stuck in a boulder field. He couldn't take the back side of the mountain either, it was to snow packed.

The wind continued to blow as he hiked to the peak. When he arrived, he went around to the east side. The east side of the mountain gave him protection from the wind. While he sheltered from the wind, he made his plan for the hike to the shet.

As he looked at the Shet from where he was sitting, he thought it would take maybe an hour and half to make his way over to it. He had to keep in mind though that there was no trail. It was mid-afternoon, so it would be dark when he arrived.

As he approached the Shet it was getting dark. He had to climb a small rock canyon to get to the foot of it. There was just enough light for him to do the climb. He climbed up the rock formation for about thirty feet. When he reached the top, there was flat ground that had dead underbrush on the top of it. He smiled as he knew that it would make the perfect campsite. It took about half an hour to set up camp. As he climbed into the tent for the second night, he was thinking the next morning he'd take the peyote and start his vision quest.

When he awoke the following morning, he was looking forward to his day. He was looking forward to three days of tripping on peyote. He had taken peyote in the past for recreational reasons, this was going to be better, because this time he'd be given some direction in life.

He took the peyote then prayed. When the drug started to take effect, he became overwhelmed with emotions. At first, he was very frightened then depressed. Then he started to laugh at nothing. The laughing turned to sorrow, then fear as he realized, he had never felt that way before after taking the drug.

The spirits began to swirl around Mark's head telling a story. As this story unfolded, Mark realized they were showing him something about Iktumi. Iktumi was running down the mountain that made up the Sleeping Demon. It was the morning Jacob had been injured. Mark thought it strange how Iktumi's body appeared to move as he ran. His body movement appeared to look quadrupedal, instead of bipedal.

Iktumi had run down the mountain, crossed over the saddle, down the steep canyon. He'd just reached the base of the mountain when he heard a couple of boys from the village calling Jacob and Joe's names. Iktumi wasn't interested in why the two boys were looking for them. Even though he was going to kill Jacob, now that he knew why he was there.

He was going to save his revenge on Jacob for another day, because he was planning his revenge on Ted Beasley. Ted's grandfather had been involved in the killing of his family. It took Iktumi years to set Ted up for the kill. He and Sam had just arrived the previous evening by way of the portal. Poor Sam's family didn't have anything to do with the massacre of the village, he just happened to be with Ted when the time came to bring him through the portal. Iktumi wanted to kill Sam just for fun, but because his family was innocent of any atrocities against his family, he couldn't touch him.

Iktumi's plan was to be there waiting for Ted to come through the portal the previous evening. When he appeared from 1950, Iktumi was going to run up to him and tear his balls off with his teeth. He'd then watch him bleed to death. The plan changed though, he had been following Mark and Aiyana up the mountain the previous evening.

Iktumi wondered around the area for a while, looking for Ted. He smelled meat cooking, so he went to investigate. He followed the smell with his nose to Joe and Jacob's camp. When he peered through the trees, he could see Ted lying on the ground with an arrow through his head. Sam was lying in a pool of blood about five feet away with an arrow in his side. Iktumi could see that Sam didn't have much time left before he died.

Fire Foot and Little Fire were tying Jacob to a sled. As Iktumi peered through the trees he could see that Jacob had been injured, he had one hell of a gash on his shoulder. He thought to himself, it was too bad he didn't get to be the one to cut Jacob. He then became angry with Joe; it was obvious he was the one who got the kill on Ted. I told that little fucker to stay out of this, he thought to himself. Joe just needed to give him one more reason, then he'd tear his balls off too.

As Iktumi viewed the seen, he was thinking to himself, all he'd have to do was run over there and tear Jacob's throat out with his teeth. Joe was over next to Sam talking to him about something. He was thinking it would be the prime time to kill Jacob. The problem was he had promised Jacob it was going to be painful for him. If he just ripped his throat out, it'd be over. He wanted Jacob to suffer before he killed him.

Iktumi was thinking of a plan when he came up with the idea. It looked like Jacob was going to die anyway from loss of blood. When Joe and Fire Foot picked up the sled and started to run back to the village, Iktumi would just follow behind as they ran. The movement would probably kill Jacob anyway. Iktumi was a little surprise at how fast he had his chance. As soon as they started running off with Jacob's body tied to the sled, Jacob's soul left his body. As his soul stood there confused about what had happened, Iktumi changed form from a coyote to Scott.

Mark could feel the peyote wearing off by the way he felt. He could tell he was getting ready to heave his guts. Mark rolled over onto his stomach, then got up on his hands and knees to throw up. As he threw up all the dried pork he'd eaten earlier in the morning, he wondered why the spirit guides were showing him that story.

He rolled over onto his back and laid there looking up at the Shet. He could see by the location of the sun, it was already late afternoon. Probably around four, he thought there was only one hour of light left, so he didn't want to take more peyote. As he laid there trying to figure out the message of the vision. He realized he wasn't thinking clearly from the peyote, he decided he'd wait until the next morning to try to analyze it.

Mark woke up early the next morning. The winds were still blowing. If the wind stopped, it would become very cold again. He ate breakfast then, laid down under the Shet to take the peyote. He still didn't understand why the spirit guides had told him about Iktumi.

As Mark laid there waiting for the drug to kick in, he thought about the previous days trip. He had heard of shapeshifters in folklore. The werewolf was a perfect example of a shapeshifter. When he and Jacob had been playing the Wizards Game with some friends, there was a were-bear in one of the maps.

His grandmother had told him stories of skin changers. She'd made it clear to him that talking about the subject was taboo. If the subject was discussed at all, it would only be discussed in families, which meant it wasn't to be talked about with outsiders. After she told him that, she never talked about it again.

The spirit guides must want me to know that Iktumi is a skin changer. As he laid there thinking about it. He didn't appreciate Iktumi following him and Aiyana up the mountain. The more he thought about it, the more it bothered him that Iktumi had been following them around. That evening on the mountain wasn't the first time he'd heard the coyote running around them. He'd heard it a couple of other times. Aiyana had mentioned, she had seen the coyote running around the area of the village.

Mark suddenly came to the realization that Iktumi knew the reason that he, Jacob, and Joe were there. Since, they arrived in the village, he didn't think Iktumi knew who they were. Joe was right after all. Iktumi had to of known though, he'd been planning to kill Ted Beasley when he came through the portal.

The peyote started to kick in as Mark was trying to think the whole thing through. As he drifted off into the spiritual realm, he was thinking Iktumi had made it clear to he and Jacob while they were playing the game of spirits that he was going to kill them both. The only difference between the killings was Iktumi was going to make it a painful death for Jacob.

As the spirit guides appeared in front of Mark, he understood they wanted him to follow them. He sat up from where he was laying and started to follow, he realized he didn't have to walk. They floated down the face of the mountain back to the trail that led to the hunting grounds. Mark knew where the hunting grounds were, Joe was always telling him stories about his hunting trips. Mark remembered Joe wouldn't shut the hell up about him taking Jacob through his "rites ritual."

They continued to float down the mountain to the campsite where Jacob had been injured. As they approached the sight, Joe and Fire Foot ran by them with the sled in tow. Little Fire was following from behind, crying. As Mark looked at Jacob in the sled, he could see Jacob was dead. It confused him as he thought about it, when Joe and Fire Foot arrived in the village with Jacob the morning he was injured, Jacob was alive.

The guides never talked to Mark when he was in the realm. He just understood the message. He didn't understand this message, Jacob was alive and recovering. When Mark and the guides arrived in the campsite, the guides dissipated. As they left, Mark understood he was to stay with Jacob and not leave his side.

In the campsite standing before him was Jacob and the demon Dzoavits. Mark remembered the poster on Jacob's ceiling. He understood by the conversation they were having that Jacob thought the demon was Scott. It was obvious Jacob was very confused about the conversation. Mark could sense Jacob was very frightened also, he was doing a good job of hiding it.

As he stood there observing the conversation between the two, he could sense the rage in the demon. The rage was irrational as Mark picked up on the energy from him. He could see his anger wasn't about anything at all. It was just pure evil.

Jacob and Dzoavits started walking away. Mark knowing Jacob was in a great deal of danger, yelled at him to stop. Jacob not hearing him continued to walk. Mark followed them listening to the conversation. The conversation between them frightened him as the three walked. Dzoavits was telling Jacob a bunch of bullshit about how he had a hard time surviving when he first arrived there.

They were a few minutes into the hike when the demon told Jacob about how he had arrived there. Jacob asked him about the trip through the portal. His answer should have made it clear to Jacob that he'd never been through the portal. He told Jacob he fell through the ice and ended up there with all his winter clothes on.

Mark remembered when Joe told him about his conversation with Sam. He told him, he and Ted arrived through the portal butt naked. Jacob knew the three of them arrived through the portal naked, so why wasn't Jacob following up on the lie about coming through the portal with clothes on him?

As the trail led them through the valley west, it became foggy and there were ferns growing on either side of the trail. Mark became claustrophobic as the plants and trees grew closer and closer to the trail. He had never seen a weeping willow tree, they didn't grow in the climate where they lived, he knew from seeing pictures of them, the trees lining the path were those trees.

They hiked up a canyon, at the top, they came to a flat clearing. On the other side of the clearing was a small hamlet with a longhouse that didn't look like anything Mark had ever seen. It looked like a village that belonged in England during the dark plague. As they approached the small hamlet, Mark had a feeling of gloom. The same feeling, he had when walking near the lake across the street from his house.

When they entered the settlement, two old witches came out and greeted Jacob and the demon. Mark couldn't believe his eyes, the two looked to be at least a hundred years old. Dzoavits spoke to the two women in tongues. As Mark listened, he realized he could understand every word they were saying.

It was obvious the two women knew him. He told them he needed their help in making Jacob believe he was Scott. The two laughed and said they could see right through him on it. Dzoavits said they owed him, and he was there for payment. They wanted to know what he was up too. He explained that Jacob had been involved in the death of his family members, therefore he was seeking revenge.

They asked the demon what was it he wanted them to do. He told them one of them needed to play the role of his wife. He wanted to carry it further and say the two women were also in a sexual relationship on the side. The two laughed, that wasn't far from the truth. He told them he'd led Jacob to believe he was the father of a baby boy.

The two giggled and asked him how he'd gotten away with having a baby with one of them when they didn't remember him sleeping with

either one. Dzoavits told them to shut up and go along with it. Rada
said she had the body of a baby boy that died a few years back. She
could cast a spell on Jacob leading him to believe the baby was alive.
She said they could also lead him to believe the baby was a pale face.

Rada walked behind Jacob and cast her spell. Kaya went into the
longhouse and came out with the dead baby boy in her arms. The
demon introduced the two women to Jacob. He introduced the boy as
Little Pale Scott. It appeared there were more people starting to gather
around, Mark could see they were just ghosts. He understood, Jacob
thought they were real, he was interacting with them.

The peyote was wearing off as Mark saw the image of Dzoavits and
the two witches assaulting Jacob. He screamed no, he didn't want to
leave Jacob there alone. He had the feeling of nausea again. As he
flashed back to his camp site at the foot of the shet. Mark threw up his
guts. When he was done throwing up, he became angry.

Mark sat there thinking about the evening Jacob awoke from the
long sleep. He hadn't said anything to he or Joe about his experience
in the realm. He'd been talking and screaming in his sleep for nine
weeks while they took care of him. Mark remembered back to the evening after Joe and Fire Foot brought Jacob back to the village. He and
Joe washed his body. He was covered in blood, dirt, and barf.

While they washed him, he was screaming in pain. He kept pleading with them to stop. Mark yelled at Jacob; he was trying to get him
to understand they had to wash him. When he screamed out that it
hurt, Mark asked if it was his shoulder that hurt. Jacob just screamed
no and pleaded for them to stop.

Mark felt depressed, it broke his heart to think of what Jacob must
have endured. He was talking out loud asking himself why Jacob didn't
say anything to him. He knew from the visions Jacob had full memory
of everything that had happened to him.

Something happened though, Jacob's body was in the teepee with
he and Joe, twenty-four hours a day for nine weeks. His soul wasn't.

Mark had no idea what to do. He thought if he took the peyote the following day, he couldn't stomach watching Jacob being assaulted by the demon and the witches again.

He thought, what would he do when he returned to the village? He thought, and what about Jacob? Would he act like he knew nothing, or would he confront him? He didn't want to think about it anymore that evening. It was dark and he wasn't thinking straight anyway. He decided he'd go to bed and decide in the morning.

When Mark awoke, he was thinking clearly. The winds had stopped. It was cold outside. As he climbed out of the tent, he said, "The hell with the retreat." He decided to start down the mountain. He thought to himself, *The Shet is just as evil as the demon.* The faster he left this place, the better off he'd be for it. He packed up and started his decent down the mountain.

CHAPTER 15

Jacob's Recovery

Jacob, Joe, and Little Fire were sitting around Joe and Jacob's teepee sharpening the arrow heads they were going to use to hunt meat for the Rite's celebration. Little Fire was proud when Jacob asked if he'd join them on the hunt. Little Fire danced around the village in excitement for half an hour bragging to anybody who would listen.

Little Fire was chipping away at the arrowhead flint rock while Joe packed the food for the day. As he sat on the ground, Jacob was trying to figure out how to attach the arrowhead to the top of the arrow shaft. He asked Joe for a third time how to do it. Joe dropped what he was doing and said he'd have to show him the technique. He sat down next to Jacob and showed him how it attached.

"The first thing you must do is cut a slit on the end of the shaft. Then push the arrowhead into the slit at the top of the shaft and tie the sinew around the arrowhead to keep it secure."

When Jacob finally had the knack for inserting the arrowheads into the shaft, he had to figure out how to attach the feathers to the tail of the arrow. Joe explained to him he needed to use hide glue to attach the feathers. Jacob thought the sinew would work better. Joe told him, he could do it either way both ways worked. Jacob wasn't convinced so, he decided to do both methods.

As they were getting ready to leave Joe asked Jacob, "Are you sure you're ready for the hunt?"

"Of course, I'm ready." Jacob's recovery was taking much longer than they had anticipated. When Jacob had awoken from the long sleep, he was nothing but, skin and bone. Mark and Joe had done everything they could to keep food in him during his sleep, it wasn't enough. It took weeks to get him up on his feet and walking on his own.

Jacob couldn't walk across the teepee without falling back on Joe, who was helping him through rehab. It was quite impressive that Joe never complained during Jacob's long sleep or helping him in his recovery. Joe cleaned up after him for the nine weeks Jacob slept. Every night he would give him a sponge bath. Mark had made it clear to him, it had to be done. He told him they couldn't take a chance bacterium would get into the wound, infecting it. If that were to happen, Jacob would die. So, Joe was willing to do anything to keep Jacob from dying, therefore he did everything Mark told him to do.

There was a foot of wet snow on the ground as the three started in the direction of the Sleeping Demon. Jacob commented about the dampness of the snow, "It feels like March, the snow is so deep and wet."

Joe said, "I don't agree, I think it's April, the days are getting longer."

Little Fire asked, "Can you explain to me what a month is?"

Joe was in the lead making the trail as they hiked. Jacob and Little Fire found it easier to follow Joe's footsteps than trying to make their own trail. Little Fire was following behind Jacob as the sweep, while they moved through the snow. The foothill leading up to the Sleeping Demon wasn't very steep, Jacob was having a hard time breathing.

Joe turned and asked, "Are you okay, Jacob?"

"I need to get back into shape."

"You're making a comeback after nearly starving to death. I'm amazed you're doing as well as you are."

Little Fire told Jacob, "I'll help you get into shape, Jacob."

Jacob turned around and said to Little Fire, "That's a nice thing to say."

"I'll do anything to help Joe too, because he's my brother. You're my brother also, Jacob, because you're married to Joe."

That made Jacob feel good when Little Fire said that to him.

Joe turned and said to Jacob, "Both Fire Foot and little Fire are loyal to us."

Little Fire said to Jacob, "Joe told me I was going to be the one to teach you to use the bow again."

Joe not looking back, told Little Fire, "You weren't supposed to tell Jacob that."

Jacob said to Little Fire, "I appreciate having a good teacher, who will help me learn the bow again." Jacob said to Joe, "You've done a good job teaching Little Fire how to speak English," in between heavy breaths.

Little Fire told Jacob, "Fire Foot and I taught Joe all of the swear words in the Flat-Land language. That was after he taught us all the swear words in English."

Joe said, "Yeah, Jacob, both Fire Foot and Little Fire swear right in front of Roaring Fire in English. He has no idea what they're saying."

Little Fire said, "Doing that is fun, even though dad knows we're cussing."

Jacob asked, "What are we hunting?"

Joe said, "We're going to take a buffalo down."

Jacob stopped, then said, "Maybe, we should talk about this."

"Not to worry, Jacob; I have it all worked out."

"Ahh, how are we going to carry a buffalo back to the village?"

"We're not. We're going to slaughter it where we drop it."

"Okay, so what do we do once that's done?"

"There's five warriors, who are going to meet us later to help carry the meat back to the village."

"Is Fire Foot one of the warriors joining us?"

"No, he and Mark are in rehearsal for the 'rites' celebration."

Jacob said, "The way I'm feeling, I may not be able to carry much of the meat back to the village."

Little Fire told Jacob, "You don't have to worry, because you're not going back to the village after the kill."

"What do you mean?"

"We're going to gut the animal, then skin it for the hide. The warriors will pack the meat back to the village."

Joe interrupted Little Fire before he could finish spilling the beans. "That's enough talk, Little Fire."

Jacob asked Joe, "What is it we're going to do?"

"We're going to take the hide to Chongs' Trading Post."

Before Jacob could ask what it was, they were going to receive for the hide. Little Fire said, "We're going to get a musket."

"Are you talking about a black powder musket?"

"Yep, an 1841 Mississippi rifle."

Joe turned to Jacob and said, "That baby will blow the heart out of a man from fifty yards away. It's a beauty, not like the piece of shit, my dad has."

Jacob said, "It looks like we're graduating from bows and arrows to rifles."

Little Fire said, "Joe has a collection of guns for the coming war." He said, "Joe's going to train Fire Foot, me and you in the use of firearms."

Jacob said, "Apparently there's some things that I've missed over the last two months. Maybe, I should be filled in on the reason you have guns."

Joe said, "I've started a collection of firearms to prepare for the attack on the village."

Jacob asked, "I take it, you've told Fire Foot and Little Fire what was going to happen to the village?"

Joe could tell by the Jacob's tone he was pissed. Joe turned to Jacob and said, "I'm sorry I went over your head and made a command decision, you need to understand while you were incapacitated, I had to keep moving the plan forward."

Jacob wandered aloud sarcastically, "That's a good idea to tell Fire Foot and Little Fire what's going to happen."

Joe became angry when he turned to Jacob and said, "I have no intention of standing by, while people I love are slaughtered." Joe said, "Last January I was at the Chongs' Trading Post, trading for the Dragoon."

"What's a dragoon?"

"I almost forgot to tell you, Jacob. I traded some furs to get a gun for you. I bought the Dragoon for you, because you aren't able to fire a rifle with you wounded shoulder." Joe said, "I have a pretty good idea of when the massacre is going to take place."

"How do you know?"

"You told me when it was going to happen."

"What are you talking about?"

"It's in your wagon train story. You know, the one about Josh and his family moving to the front range. The wagon train left Independence, Missouri, in April 1852. When I was at the trading post in January, the Chongs wished me a happy new year. I asked them what year is it. Mrs. Chong said it was 1852."

Jacob thought for a second, "Of course that makes sense."

Mark had explained to him they fucked up the prayer when they were reciting it.

Joe said, "You meant to say I fucked it up."

"No, Joe, we fucked up the prayer. The Shet couldn't have place us any closer to the time of the massacre, because we requested being placed before the attack on the village. The attack took place a few weeks before the first day of summer, 1852. The portal can only be accessed on the first day of summer, therefore for the Shet to place us before the attack, it had to place us on the first day summer 1851."

197

As the three hunters approached the ridge overlooking the buffalo herd Jacob stopped to ask Joe, "How are we going to bring a buffalo down with arrows?"

"I came up with the idea from you."

Jacob not being amused by the word games told Joe, "You don't need to play on words anymore."

"Let me explain, Jacob. The morning they brought you back to the village with the injury to your shoulder, Mark and I spent the afternoon into the evening washing your body. You were covered in blood, dirt, and vomit. You kept going into convulsions as we washed you. You also, had the dry heaves. We'd roll you over onto your left side, so you could throw up, nothing came out of your stomach. You'd just cough up blood.

"While this was happening, I was confused as to why you were throwing up blood. Mark said you weren't throwing up blood. Most likely your right lung sack was punctured from the knife wound. That puncture was letting blood leak into that lung."

"It sounds like I was dying."

"You were dying, but you didn't."

"I'd be dead if it weren't for Mark, Joe, Fire Foot, and of course you, Little Fire."

Little Fire proudly looked at Jacob and said, "I helped to clean you also. I was running back and forth from the lake to the teepee with fresh water all afternoon into the evening."

Joe said, "I think it's your will to live, and some help from a higher power, that you didn't die."

"So, what does that have to do with bringing a buffalo down with arrows?"

"The next day, I was talking to Roaring Fire about you. I was concerned you would die from a punctured lung. Roaring Fire assured me, that if you did die, it wouldn't be from a punctured lung. I asked him how he knew that. He said humans have two lung sacks, not like a buffalo, who only has one lung sack. That's how a hunter brings a buffalo down with a spear or arrow. You puncture the lung, in turn it collapses, and dies."

Jacob turned to Little Fire and asked, "Is that true?"

Little Fire just shrugged his shoulders.

Jacob said, "Before we go over the ridge for the kill, I should use a tree for target practice."

Joe said, "That's a good idea."

"I'm not sure I can even pull the arrow back."

Jacob set up and took his stance. As he tried to drawl the arrow back with his right hand, it was obvious he was in a great deal of pain. His arm shook uncontrollably from fatigue as he continued to draw.

When he let go, the arrow went about five feet and dropped to the ground. After the arrow hit the ground, Little Fire looked at Jacob and said, "It looks like we have some work to do."

Jacob looked back at Little Fire and said, "It looks like we do."

Jacob turned to Joe and said, "Maybe, I should start training with the Dragoon."

"We'll be training soon, Jacob. We're also going to start training in hand-to-hand combat."

Jacob didn't need Joe or Little Fire to tell him he wasn't going to participate in the kill. It was obvious he couldn't get an arrow to go far enough or powerful enough to hit a buffalo, much less bring it down. Jacob volunteered to gut the animal after Joe and Little Fire killed it. Joe said the three of them would have to work on processing the animal once, it was brought down. It was just too big for one person to work on with the amount of time they had.

Joe told Little Fire to come over next to him, so he could explain the plan. "We're going to sneak up on the buffalo. We're going to set up for the kill side by side about twenty yards on the left side of the animal. Little Fire, tell me your plan of escape, in case the bison turns on us."

Little Fire said, "If the animal turns on us, I'm going to run like hell."

"I already know that. What direction are you going to run. I need to know what you're going to do, so I can drawl the animal's attention away from you."

Joe told Little Fire, "I want you to aim at the boiler room. You're going to have to concentrate on aiming at the ribs, because you need to sink the arrow in between two ribs."

Little Fire said, "I know where the boiler room is on a deer. Where's the boiler room was on a buffalo?"

"You have to aim about a third of the way up the chest, between the shoulder blade and the leg bone. An honorable and disciplined hunter will kill the animal with one shot."

The three hunters walked over the ridge and started down the hill. As they move into the trees, Joe pointed to the animal that he wanted to take down. He leaned over and whispered to Jacob and Little Fire to follow him on their stomachs.

There was nothing between the trees and the target except a field of snow. The three laid on their stomachs and worked their way over to the target buffalo. As they approached the animal, he became suspicious and moved away. They scooted closer. The buffalo moved again.

Joe told Little Fire, "We're going to have to set up at a right angle to the animal. You need to move fifteen feet forward, then fifteen feet to the right. That's where you're going to set up. I want you to signal me when you're ready."

Jacob asked, "What's the plan?"

"You and I are going to be the bait, Jacob. I'm going to do a deer roar, to see if I can trick the bison into turning around and coming back to investigate the noise. I'm going to aim for the eye, hoping to get a brain shot through the eye socket."

"Do you know the odds of getting a bull's eye?"

Joe smiled and said, "Yeah, I know the odds, but this isn't a bull's eye, this is a buffalo's eye."

Jacob pulled his buck knife out of the sheath hanging on his hip. "I may as well have a weapon in case the buffalo charges."

Joe almost said, "Be careful, we know what happened the last time." He decided it would be better not to say anything.

"Jacob, stand in sight of both me and Little Fire, because you're going to give the one, two, three with a hand signal."

Jacob moved into sight of both hunters.

Joe told Little Fire, "Jacob will count to three with his fingers. On three we'll take our shots at the same time." Joe looked sincerely at Little Fire and said, "Concentrate, Little Fire."

Joe gave off his deer roar.

Jacob said, "That didn't sound like a deer roar."

Joe not looking over at Jacob said, "It doesn't matter, the bison is walking toward us."

Jacob turned to see that indeed, the buffalo was walking over to investigate the sound. He walked within twenty feet of them. He stopped. Little Fire looked like a statue. His stance was in perfect form as he aimed at the side of the animal.

Joe told Jacob to start the count. When Jacob's third finger went up, Joe launched his arrow. The arrow swished through the air hitting the buffalo to the right of the eye bouncing off. A half second later, little fires arrow sunk into the side of the animal. Joe and Jacob waited to see if it would drop. Instead they saw fire in its eyes. Joe yelled "fuck" as he took off to the south at full run. Jacob said the same thing and took off running to the north. Of course, the buffalo took off chasing Jacob. Little Fire got off another round hitting the animal in the ass, which only pissed it off more.

Jacob was running as fast as he could as he heard the heavy breathing coming from behind him. He thought about turning and taking a stance with the knife. He was so frightened, he dropped it as he ran. He didn't have to look back to know he was just about to get trampled. He heard a big thud and slush sound hit the ground behind him. He wasn't about to stop and look, so he just looked back as he ran. The buffalo was lying in the snow on its side trying to breath. Jacob could see Little Fire hit him in the lung with the arrow, because of the way the animal was trying to breath. It stopped breathing and just laid still.

Jacob turned and started to dance as he screamed, "That's the best shot I've ever seen."

Joe ran over and gave Little Fire big hug. Joe yelled at Little Fire, "You're going to have the best reputation as a hunter in the village."

Jacob walked over to where Little Fire and Joe were dancing. He said, "Little Fire, the great buffalo hunter, who took a buffalo down with one shot of an arrow. Not a gun, but an arrow."

Little Fire looked at the both and asked, "Did you doubt me?"

"Well, we'll never doubt the great buffalo hunter again."

Little Fire had a proud look on his face as Jacob said it.

The three rolled the animal over onto its back and started to work. When they finished pulling the guts out, they skinned the carcass. When they finished removing the hide, they quartered the carcass. As they were finishing up their work, the five warriors showed up to help carry the meat back to the village.

Joe told them as they walked up to them, "This is Little Fire's first buffalo kill."

The three hiked to the trading post. When they arrived, the Chongs were very impressed with the hide they had brought them to trade for the musket. Jacob bragged about how Little Fire was the one who brought down the buffalo. Mrs. Chong told Little Fire nice shot as she handed him some dried pork.

While Joe and Little Fire were doing business with the Chongs, Jacob was looking around the trading post for some clothes. Mr. Chong asked him what was he looking for.

Jacob said, "I need to find some western style clothes and boots that will fit Joe and me."

Mr. Chong said, "Oh, you and Joe are tired of playing Indians, ha, ha, ha," as he laughed.

Jacob said, "Yeah, something like that," as he continued to look.

Mrs. Chong came over to where the two were talking and said she had some clothes that would work. She would have to measure them first, then tailor the clothes.

"It'll take a couple of weeks, though," she said.

Joe walked over to see what Jacob was up to.

Jacob asked Mr. Chong, "How much does a horse cost?"

Mr. Chong looked at Joe then said, "You have an interesting friend, White Indian Joe."

Mr. Chong turned back to Jacob and said, "A pack horse will cost twenty-five bucks. A good riding horse will run about seventy-five bucks."

Jacob asked, "How much is a buffalo hide worth in dollars?"

Mr. Chong said, "I'd probably give you three dollars a hide. I'll give you that price, because you are good friends with Joe, otherwise I'd only give two bucks, fifty for a hide."

Mrs. Chong said, "If you bring the bison tongue, we'll give you twenty cents for that. We can make five cents on that deal."

Joe asked Jacob why he wanted a horse. Jacob said they were going to ride out to the Denver Camp and visit family. Joe knew what Jacob was thinking. "Are you sure that's a good idea?"

"I'm not sure of anything," Mr. Chong said. "I can find you a ride out to the Denver Camp and back for much less than what it would cost to buy a horse."

"How can you do that>"

"There's supply wagons coming and going between the Denver Camp and the Boulder mining supply camp. For a small fee, the wagon leads are willing to take a couple of passengers."

When Mrs. Chong was finished measuring Joe, she walked over to Jacob and started measuring him.

Mr. Chong said, "There's a small surcharge for getting the rides lined up to and from the camps."

When Mrs. Chong finished with the measurements, she said the clothes would be ready in two weeks. She walked over to the counter and pulled out a bottle of whiskey and handed it to Joe. She said the bottle was for being their best customer.

Jacob said, "That will come in handy at the 'rites' ceremony."

Joe said, "I'll add it to the collection."

The Chongs thanked the guys as they left the trading post. When they arrived at the village it was getting dark. Little Fire ran off toward home to tell Roaring Fire and Fire Foot about his kill. Jacob and Joe went to their teepee to call it a night.

When they entered their teepee, Joe threw some wood into the fire pit and started a fire. Jacob laid down in bed.

Joe asked, "Do you want anything to eat?"

"No thanks, I ate a ton of dried pork."

As Joe walked over to Jacob he said, "I'm full also." He laid down next to Jacob and asked him to raise his right hand over his head.

"Are you checking my scar?"

"No." He rested his head on Jacob's underarm. "Does that hurt?"

"No, it tickles, though. Why do you always liked to snuggle on my right side?"

"I'm more comfortable lying on your right side then I am on your left side."

"I think you like to lay your head on your handiwork."

"Ahh, no, that's not the reason."

"I know the reason."

"What do you think?"

"The sweat gland under my right armpit was destroyed by the knife cut, so it doesn't smell as bad as the left armpit."

"Your body odor doesn't bother me, Jacob."

"So, I have B.O.?"

"Well, sometimes."

"My right armpit reminds me of a nerd."

"What do you mean by that?"

"When I look at the hair under my arm, the scar runs right down the center of my armpit. It looks like a dorky kid with his hair parted right down the middle of his head."

Joe turned his head and said, "Let me have a look." As he was studying Jacob's underarm, he said, "You're right, the part in the middle of your armpit is exactly center. You have the same amount of hair on both sides of the scar. So, stop complaining."

Joe laid his head back under Jacob's arm. "I can't do anything about your right armpit. If you want, I can do some work on the left armpit, so you have a matching set."

Jacob thought about it for a moment. "If I give the go ahead, then you may want to consider, you will probably have to wipe my butt and wash my balls for eight or nine weeks, while I recover."

"I'll have to reconsider my offer, I didn't like wiping your butt, but I did enjoy giving you a sponge bath every night."

"Oh, really, and what parts of my body were you washing that gave you enjoyment?"

"I'm not telling; besides it was Doctor Mark's orders that you receive a bath every night."

"Did you bother to argue about the orders?"

"Of course not."

"Are you finished guessing why I don't like laying on your left side?"

"I've run out of all the good reasons."

"I always lay on my back before I fall asleep. When I'm about to fall asleep, I roll over on my left side. When I roll to my left, I put my head on your chest and fall asleep, while listening to your breathing. If I lay on your left side, I'll roll away from you."

Why does it matter if you roll away from me if you're falling asleep?

Joe snapped at Jacob and said, "It just matters, Jacob. If you'd stop falling asleep first, you might understand what I want."

"Jeez, sorry I asked."

They laid there for a few minutes before Jacob asked, "Are you still pissed at me?"

"What are you talking about, Jacob? I'm never pissed at you."

"You sounded pretty upset with me."

"I'm not upset with you, Jacob. I'm upset about the situation."

"I'm sorry, Joe, I love you and I want to, it's just I can't stay awake."

"I understand, after all you are still recovering, I wouldn't want to hurt you."

"You don't have to worry about that."

"Are you talking about what you can handle or are you talking about my size?"

"I can handle it, Joe."

"Jacob, I must ask you this question."

Jacob was looking up at the shadow of the fire dancing on the tee-pee walls. He knew what Joe was going to ask him. Jacob said in a whisper, "Go ahead and ask."

"Jacob, when Mark asked you if you remembered what happened to you while you were in the spiritual realm, you told him you didn't remember anything about it."

Jacob laid there thinking, *He's now going to tell me he knows I was lying.*

"Jacob, I was with you every night for nine weeks, your body was in the teepee with me, your soul wasn't there."

Jacob stared at the walls and didn't say anything.

"Jacob, what happened?"

Jacob hesitated before he spoke. "Dzoavits and two witches repeatedly raped me and molested me while they had me trapped in the realm." Jacob just looked at the shadows dancing on the teepee walls as he continued. "They took my semen and impregnated one of the witches." He paused then said, "A couple of days after Rada and my baby girl was born, Dzoavits slit the baby's throat from ear to ear." He said it with no emotion in his voice.

"After the demon slit Jacobina's throat, he tackled me, he sat on top of me with a knife to my balls. He was going to cut my nuts off and stare into my eyes while I bled to death. He wanted to watch the life drain out of me."

Joe had turned and was looking into Jacob's eyes as he talked. Jacob had never seen that kind of anger in Joe's eyes, it scared him. Joe said in an angry voice, "I'm going to fucking kill Dzoavits."

Jacob told him, "No, you're not going to be the one who kills him, we both are going to do it."

"Is Dzoavits the demon in the poster?"

"Yes, the problem we have, Joe, is Iktumi is processed by Dzoavits. We're going to have to kill Iktumi to get to the demon."

Joe looked concerned when he said, "Mark's not going to like this."

"No, he's not."

"Jacob, how could everything that happened in the spiritual realm take place in nine weeks? It takes nine months from conception to when a baby is born."

"Time's not linear in the spiritual realm. Everything feels like it's happening at the same time. It was confusing when I was in there, it's like everything is scrambled. I still experienced everything that happened to me, though.

"When we were playing the spirit board game with Scott, he kept egging the demon on. He was so pissed off, he suggested a challenged. He knew Scott would except, because he had a big ego. When Scott did accept the challenge, he invited the demon to possess him. When Dzoavits gained possession of him, he antagonized him until he committed suicide. Dzoavits can't possess a person without their invitation. "Dzoavits had almost kept his promise to kill me, except Shappa interfered."

"Was that the conversation you were having right before you woke up from the long sleep?"

"Yes. When Shappa appeared, Dzoavits yelled at him to not become involved. Shappa told him to shut up or he'd kill him. Dzoavits instantly yielded to Shappa's demands."

Joe said, "That tells me Shappa has power over the demon."

"That's what I think also."

"Why didn't you say anything to Mark or me when you awoke from the long sleep?"

"I don't want Mark to know. Dzoavits is getting information either from Mark or Aiyana or both. What they know, the demon knows. If I read Mark correctly, he has told Aiyana everything."

"Do you know how Iktumi is getting information out of Mark?"

"Mark told me about a coyote that follows he and Aiyana, when they go out for walks."

"Mark mentioned that to me a couple of times, also."

"It's not unusual for a coyote to hunt alone, but it's unusual for it to hang around humans."

"It appears to me that you've thought a lot of this through, Jacob."

"I had a lot of time to think while Dzoavits and the two witches had their fun at my expense."

"What's the plan, Jacob?"

"Do you think anybody would miss a lone coyote, who became ensnared in a trap, then disappeared?"

Joe smiled as he looked at Jacob.

"Jacob, with all the shape shifting and deception that goes on around you, how do you know it's me laying here next to you?"

"When I look into Dzoavits' eyes I see the hate and rage of a demon. When I look into your eyes, I see kindness. When we're together, you've always been gentle with me and you've never hurt me. Believe me, I'd know if it wasn't you, Joe."

"There's something else bothering me, Jacob."

Jacob said, "We may as well get everything out in the open."

"I've been thinking about the portal. It can only be accessed on the first day of summer. If we decided to go home, most likely Mark won't go with us. I know Mark, there's no way he'll leave Aiyana. He's fallen in love with her. Mark's a soon-to-be father. In the near future he'll be a healer."

"You're right, Joe, Mark won't go back. He's found his place in life."

"Do you think you could go home without him?"

Jacob began to cry when he said, "I don't know."

"Jacob, if I decided to stay, you wouldn't leave me, would you?"

Jacob began to cry uncontrollably. Joe waited until Jacob stopped crying to get his answer.

When he stopped crying, he said, "When I awoke from the long sleep, you asked me for my feelings, when I gave them to you, I gave myself to you. If you want to live in the village, then I'll stay here with you. I can't stand the thought of not having you in my life."

Jacob reached over and took hold of Joe's hand. He asked, "Would you be interested in having kids with me?"

"How can we do that?"

"Do you know that Pabria and Padma are in a relationship>"

"I do know that."

"They asked if you and I would be interested in fathering children with them. I thought if you might be interested in the two of us donating, we could start a family with them. That's if you're interested."

Joe said, "Yes, Jacob, I am interested. I'd also, be interested in spending the rest of my life with you."

The two laid there for a while, not saying anything. Jacob was trying to stay awake; he was drifting off.

"Jacob," Joe whispered.

Jacob very quietly said, "Yeah." He could hear Joe talking, he couldn't stay awake.

Joe's voice became more and more distant as Jacob fell into a deep sleep. Joe laid there listening to Jacob's breathing. He thought to himself how peaceful and regular Jacob's breathing was.

He thought back to the first two weeks after Jacob was injured. His breathing was like a fish gulps air when it's out of water. He'd seen that with his grandmother days before she died. He remembered how relieved he was when Jacob started to breath normally. He knew Jacob was going to survive when he started to breath without gulping for air. Joe began to cry, as he thought about Jacob screaming in pain night after night pleading for them to stop hurting him. He laid there for a few minutes crying then rolled to his left, put his head on Jacob's chest, and drifted off to sleep.

CHAPTER 16

Judgment Day

*J*acob and Joe hiked up the hill to the east of the village. "Why do you want to use a snare trap to catch the coyote, Jacob?"

"I want the coyote to suffer before it dies."

"The leg-hold trap is much more efficient."

"The problem with the leg-hold trap is Iktumi is intelligent. If his leg is trapped, he'll transform into a human, then he'll just use his hands to get himself out of the trap. If we use the snare trap, it'll tighten around the coyote's neck. That makes it easier to tie him up once we catch him."

"The problem with the snare trap is it could kill him before we get him tied up."

"Either way, Joe, his fate is sealed." Mark and Aiyana make it a ritual almost every evening to stand at the top of the hill and watch the sun go down behind the Sleeping Demon."

Joe said, "If Iktumi is following Mark and Aiyana almost every time they're up here, then there should be fresh canine tracks."

The two walked around the area, until they came across some tracks.

"What do you think, Joe?"

"Those are canine paw prints."

They followed the tracks, which circled around the top of the hill.

Joe said, "Iktumi must be up here almost every night by the looks of all the prints."

As they walked the circle of tracks, Joe was looking for a place to set the trap. He stopped at an area along the trail and was studying it.

Jacob asked, "Do you think this is a good place to set the trap?"

"No, this isn't the right place."

They continued to follow the circle of tracks.

"What are you looking for, Joe?"

"If we're going to use a snare trap, we have to set it to catch the coyote without bait. Iktumi's not going to fall for food, he won't have any interest in it. He'll also know it's a trap. We need a place along the trail that has high weeds on both sides." Joe stopped. "This is it, Jacob." As he pointed, "I think I can make it work in this spot here." Joe studied the area for a while, "Yeah, I can make it work."

"How are you going to build the trap?"

"On either side of the trail are high weeds that will hide the three stakes we'll use for the base of the trap. You see that sapling tree there, Jacob?"

"Yeah."

"We'll use that sapling to tie the snare."

Joe hesitated for a few moments while he thought about it.

"Joe, what's taking you so long to figure this out?"

"We'll place two stakes parallel to each other about two feet apart along the trail behind the weeds. Then we'll tie a stick across the two stakes about three inches below the top. We'll hammer a stake perpendicular and center of the first two on the other side of the tail. That'll set the base of the trap."

"After the base is set, you'll tie a rope around the top of the tree sapling. I'll pull it down and tie it to the top of the trigger. At the bottom of the trigger we'll tie the rope snare. The snare will lay on the trail. When Iktumi runs under it, he'll hit it, releasing the rope holding the bent limb of the tree. When the tree is released it'll pull the snare tight."

Jacob looked a little skeptical, "Do you think this is going to work, Joe?"

"I don't know, I've never set a trap without bait. If Iktumi is running around like a dog, then he'll have his nose down sniffing the trail. If he's doing that, he may not see the stick that's hanging across the trail. That stick will be the only thing visible. All he has to do is hit it knocking it loose. That will release the tree, which will pull the snare tight. If all goes well, we'll have our coyote."

They hiked back to the village to get the tools they needed to chop the wood to assemble the trap. As they walked down the hill Joe asked, "Jacob, I've been teaching the hand-to-hand combat class for months now. Where are you learning the moves you're using? I don't know the majority of battle techniques you're using."

"White Lightning's been training me in militant conflict. He's also, training me in the use of the tomahawk."

"I didn't know White Lightning's been training you."

"We decided after I was injured that maybe, it'd be a good idea to train me how to fight."

"Will you teach me some of the moves?"

"Yes, I will, Joe."

As they walked into the village, Jacob said, "Thanks for the Dragoon."

"No problem, Jacob, you weren't lying when you said you knew how to handle guns. You have a good aim."

"Next time we're at the trading post I want to buy a holster for it. Where are you keeping the other guns stashed?"

"They're in a cave just at the foot of the Sleeping Demon. I discovered it while hunting. I can take you up to the cave if you're interested in seeing it."

"I would like to see it."

"We have to go in that direction anyway, the trees are bigger as we approached the mountain. We need the bigger trees trunks for the first three stakes of the trap. It has to be thick wooden stakes that hold a coyote, who might end up turning into a man."

They hiked up the trail leading to the mountain. When the trail turned to the right, Joe led Jacob off the trail to the left through a fern garden.

As they traveled through the garden, Jacob said, "I feel like I'm floating, I can't see my feet. I can only see the tops of the plants."

Joe said, "The fern patch is a good place to hide if you ever need it."

"I hope there isn't a snake down there, we wouldn't know It, until one of us is bitten."

Joe said, "Yeah, until one of us is bitten."

They dipped down under a rock, then came up in a crevasse that was behind one of the flatirons which laid up against the mountain. They climb the crevasse for about thirty feet. It flattened out as they reached the top. Jacob said, "Holy shit," as he looked at the mouth of the cave. He looked around the area of the mouth. The cave was completely hidden from view, except for the one place they were standing.

When they entered the cave, it looked like a small cavern with nothing in it. Joe told Jacob to follow him. They walked into the cavern about fifteen feet and looked around.

Jacob asked, "Where are the guns?"

"That's the best part about this hiding place, you can't see it, even if you stumbled into the cave."

They walked to the back wall. Joe climbed up the wall about ten feet. At the top of the wall was a shelve that dropped behind a rock ledge.

Jacob climbed up to have a look. He was surprised at what Joe had stored up there. There was seven guns, four bottles of whiskey, and a box of cigars.

"When did you start smoking?"

"I don't smoke unless I'm going to be an uncle."

"I hadn't thought about that. What do you think we're going to be called, Uncle Joe and Uncle Jacob or Uncle Joe and Aunt Jacob?"

Joe laughed. "Five warrior friends of Fire Foot's joined."

"I know we already have Fire Foot and Little Fire recruited. Are they in addition to the five making it seven?"

"Yes, there's seven recruits total."

Jacob said, "The odds are getting better, we still need more fighters, time's running out." Jacob asked, "How's Little Fire's training going."

"He's almost fully trained. He's a fast learner. He picked up the moves fast."

"Does Little Fire understand the rules put in place?"

"Yes, he does."

"Can we trust him completely?"

"We've earned his loyalty, Jacob."

"He'll make a good assassin then?"

"Yes."

As they were getting ready to leave Jacob suggested they bring one of the bottles.

"I'll grab the box of cigars also. Do you want me to grab a couple of guns?"

"It's not a bad idea, maybe you should grab all of them."

"Are you going to a have your gun when we catch Iktumi?"

"I'll probably be carrying my gun for now on."

The two walked back through the fern garden down the hill to the pine forest. That's where they went to work assembling the wood they'd need for the trap. They downed a tree with an eight-inch diameter trunk. Joe sharpened the ends of the three stakes that would be driven into the ground for the base of the trap. Jacob was cutting the other pieces that would be used for the trigger.

Joe said, "Shit, I almost forgot to tell you, the Chongs are going to rent us their mule for a couple of days. We can pick up three gallons of lamp oil, when we're there to get the mule. We can use the mule to carry the gallon jugs back to the village."

Jacob said, "We need to pick up more black powder also."

The following evening, they sat about fifty yards downwind from the trap. They were high enough on the hill that they could see Mark and Aiyana on their evening walk. As they waited, they heard something running in a big circle around the two as they walked. When Mark and Aiyana stopped at the top of the hill, they turned and looked at the sunset.

Aiyana was startled when she heard a coyote yapping. She turned and looked down the hill to see if she could see anything. When the yapping stopped, Mark turned her around to look at the sunset over the Sleeping Demon. Aiyana asked if they should go investigate. Mark told her no; most likely the coyote was chasing a rabbit.

Jacob ran up to the coyote, who was caught by its hind leg in the trap. He couldn't hit the animal until Aiyana and Mark turned around. As soon as they did, he hit the coyote in the head, knocking it unconscious.

Right before Iktumi lost conciseness, he felt something reach into his midsection. He lurched forward, then took off like a bat out of hell. Iktumi was flying through space at an incredible velocity. Then just as fast as that happened, Bang, he was standing in front of a panel of two men and a woman.

Iktumi recognized all three. There was, Hania, Shappa, and Alo. Shappa spoke first, he told Iktumi he was there to be tried for crimes he commented in the spiritual realm.

"I haven't committed any crimes in the spiritual realm."

Shappa told him he was charged with murder, rape, molestation and torture.

Iktumi asked, "Who, did I supposedly commit these crimes against?"

Alo told him, "You committed the crimes against White Lightning's son, Jacob. The murder charge is for killing Jacob's daughter, Jacobina."

Iktumi screamed, "Fuck Jacob, there was no crimes committed against his physical body!"

Hania told Iktumi, "You will show respect for the court and not use foul language."

Shappa said, "Iktumi, you're lying, you and the two witches committed the physical attacks on Jacob, while Dzoavits committed the attacks on his soul."

Iktumi looked at Hania; he could see the age in her face.

She said, "A spiritual attack is just as damaging to a person's soul as a physical attack."

"Why am I accused of committing crimes, when it's Jacob who committed crimes?"

Hania stood up and pointed her finger at Iktumi. Iktumi observed her; she had her blue trial skins on with a blue turquoise necklace that had a mystical glow. She didn't have the look of a Flat-Lander. Iktumi thought to himself that she must be at least eighty years old with that big nose and even bigger ears.

Hania sat down, then gently said, "Iktumi, Jacob committed no crimes against your family."

Alo asked, "Iktumi, do you recalled the morning Jacob was injured?"

"Yes, I do remember that morning."

"Did you appear in front of Jacob in the form of his friend Scott after Jacob's soul left his body?"

In a defiant tone, Iktumi said, "Jacob and Scott aren't friends."

Shappa said, "They were friends until you and Dzoavits killed Scott."

"Don't play word games with the court," Alo said.

Iktumi almost asked Alo if he was a man. He was thinking Alo was very feminine with that silk smooth grey hair that was very long. And those facial features were very feminine. Alo was wearing a white rob, Iktumi asked himself where did he find that.

Alo asked Iktumi, "Did you appear in front of Jacob in the form of somebody that Jacob trusted?"

Iktumi stood there thinking for a moment. Hania demanded that he answer the question. Iktumi said, "Yes, I did."

Shappa said, "You, stood in front of Jacob and had a conversation with him leading him to believe, that you were somebody he trusted. Shape shifting for deceptive purposes is strictly forbidden."

Alo said, "You then invited him to the hamlet. When he agreed to go with you to meet your nonexistent wife, you spent the entire hike to the hamlet telling him lie after lie, grooming him for the attack."

Iktumi thought to himself that he better not asks Alo if he's a man or a woman.

Alo asked Iktumi, "Do you realized the seriousness of the atrocities you committed against Jacob?"

Iktumi asked Alo, "Do you realize the seriousness of the crimes Jacob is guilty of against my family?"

Hania said, "The only things Jacob is guilty of is being frightened and vulnerable which, you took advantage of."

Shappa continued with his statements, "When you and Jacob arrived in the hamlet, Rada and Kaya were also in a deceptive form leading Jacob to believe, they were much younger than they were. That's strictly forbidden."

Iktumi said, "I can't speak for the two ladies."

Shappa said, "When Jacob wasn't paying attention, Rada cast a spell on him, leading him to believe that a dead baby was Scott's living son."

"That's bullshit."

"Rada admitted to that at their trial." Iktumi's eyes widened as he realized, the two witches had been put on trial.

Alo said, "When the three of you gained his trust, you repeatedly rape, molested, and tortured him, while he was trapped in the spiritual realm."

"Jacob consented to having sex with us."

You could see fire in Shappa's green eyes when Iktumi said it. "Jacob didn't consent to any of the abuse you inflicted on him. He bonded with his captors like any human does in captivity. Nobody in this room, believes he would have consented to having sex with the three of you, if he hadn't been led to believe you were somebody else."

Iktumi yelled, "You can't prove any of this," as he began to realize his fate.

Shappa said, "You're not the only one who can read souls, Iktumi. I didn't have to ask Jacob what had happened to him. I could feel the pain and suffering emulating from his soul, because you abused him. I could read that from his soul just in the ten minutes I spent with him in the realm."

Hania asked, "Whose idea was it to take Jacob's semen and impregnate one of the witches?"

"I don't know what you're talking about." Hania was looking down reading. "Rada stated in her testimony to the court at her trial (it was Iktumi's idea to impregnate her with Jacob's semen). Rada also stated she didn't want anything to do with that kind of behavior, but Iktumi had dirt on her from a crime she committed years earlier. She conceded to your demands after you threatened to expose her."

Hania continued reading Rada's statement from the court proceedings. "Rada further stated, she knew Iktumi was going to harm the baby after she was born. She pleaded with you not to harm the child. He gave his word, he had no intention of hurting the baby. Shappa said Rada stated, 'A few days after the child was born you slit the baby's throat in front of Jacob.'"

The three judges asked the guards to escort Iktumi out of the court, so they could discuss a verdict. When Iktumi was brought back in, he stood in front of the council.

Shappa said, "Iktumi, you've been found guilty on all charges. You're sentenced to death."

Iktumi screamed when the verdict was read. He yelled, "It's Jacob who committed crimes against my family. He's the blue-eyed devil."

Shappa, not taking pity on Iktumi told him, "The person you hurt the deepest is the person who will carry out the sentence."

Iktumi started screaming in hysterics when he realized, it was Jacob who would put him to death. He was dragged out of the court room yelling he was innocent.

CHAPTER 17

Little Fire's Assignment

Little Fire was proud when Jacob selected him for the first assigned hunt. His brother Fire Foot was selected to go on the hunt with him. Fire Foot was a fully trained warrior, he'd be graduating at the following evenings "rites" ceremony. Little Fire was proud of Fire Foot, he was the fiercest of the newly trained class.

As the two walked to the campsite where Jacob had been injured, Little Fire was talking about how much he looked up to Jacob and Joe. Little Fire iodized Joe.

Fire Foot asked, "Why do you look up to Joe?"

Little Fire just bragged about how smart Joe was. "Joe's a great hunter, trapper, and fighter. He has the fierceness in his eyes of a warrior god."

"What do you think, Jacob?"

"Jacob is our leader. Even Joe knows that."

"Why do you think Jacob's the leader and not Joe?"

"Joe always looks to Jacob for direction. They're both smart, but Jacob makes the decisions."

Little Fire said, "Joe has great power, but when he's with Jacob, he's a purring kitten."

Fire Foot thought Little Fire was right, Joe would have graduated at the "rites" ceremony the following evening, except he gave up his warrior's career to be in a relationship with Jacob.

Little Fire said, "If not for Jacob, Joe would be a killer without a conscience. Joe's love for Jacob is a counter-weight to his evil side, which balances the two sides of him."

Fire Foot told Little Fire he had good intuition about people.

When the two reached the campsite, they turned and looked west. They stood there looking at the canyon they were going to hike.

Fire Foot looked at Little Fire, he had no fear in his eyes. He asked him, "Are you sure you want to go through with it?"

"It doesn't matter what I want. I was selected for the hunt; therefore, I'll carry it out."

Fire Foot thought to himself, *I hope Little Fire's loyalty to Jacob doesn't get him killed.*

The two started through the weeds to the west in the direction of the canyon. As they hiked, Fire Foot told Little Fire, "I'm proud of the way you handle yourself in the hand-to-hand combat training."

"I wanted to pursue a career in the warrior's path like you, Fire Foot, but I changed my mind."

"Why, are you still taking the combat classes if you changed your mind?"

"I still want to fight, after talking to Joe about guerrilla warfare, I decided to pursue that."

"I've never heard of guerrilla warfare. What is it?"

"It's a whole new approach to war. Because of the disadvantage we have in the upcoming war, we need a different approach to warrior battle training we receive."

"I know Joe's been training you on the side after classes."

"Under orders, I'm only to talk about my training with you, Joe or Jacob."

"Under guerrilla warfare tactics what is it you're training for?"

"Assassin."

Fire Foot said, "We're going to have to talk to father eventually, because we don't have enough warriors to fight the battle."

"That's up to Jacob to talk to White Lightning. If White Lightning believes Jacob's story about the massacre, he'll order Roaring Fire to provide more fighters."

"What if he doesn't?"

Little Fire looked at Fire Foot and said, "If he doesn't, then it's up to us. Until then, we keep our mouths shut."

The two reached the top of the canyon, then stopped to look around the area. They hid in the tall weeds as they searched for their prey. As they looked around, they could see the area at the top of the canyon was flat with weeds and weeping willows trees. They looked across the clearing through the trees and saw an old longhouse.

They observed the house for a while, then decided to move closer to get a better observation.

Fire Foot said, "It looks like nobody is living in it."

Little Fire said, "We should be careful around the long house while looking for prey."

They decided to avoid the house as they moved around the area just in case somebody lived there.

As Kaya and Rada were peeking out of a crack in the wall, they were having a conversation about the two hunters that were sneaking around outside.

Kaya said, "They're probably two huntsmen, who are out hunting and have wandered too far from home."

Rada said, "I don't see two hunters out there; I see two lamb chops for dinner. That sounds good to me, we haven't eaten meat in quite a while."

The two women decided to shape shift to their beautiful twenty something selves for the introduction to their dinner for the evening.

Rada complained about the amount of energy it took to transform and keep the form.

Kaya said, "It's because we're hungry. We'll be just fine after we have the boy stew."

Fire Foot and Little Fire were in the bushes about forty feet from the house, when the two ladies walked out to start a fire in the pit that was in front of the house. As the two women stirred the fire, one of them called to them asking if they were lost. They kept their mouths shut and waited to see what would happen next. She turned and looked right in the direction of where they were hiding. Fire Foot was startled when he realized she knew exactly where they were.

Rada in a sweet voice said, "You need not be frightened. We know you're probably lost and afraid."

Kaya said, "There's nothing to be afraid of, we're just two old women." She hesitated, then said, "Two young women here." Kaya said, "There's nobody else around."

Fire Foot whispered in Little Fire's ear, "When we come out of hiding, we'll tell them were lost. Maybe, we can get a free dinner."

Fire Foot and Little Fire slowly stepped out from behind the bushes. Kaya looked at Rada as the two emerged from the bush and said, "They look so innocent." She turned back to them and said, "You're welcome, to join us for dinner this evening."

Rada laughed under her breath.

They walked within twenty feet of women then stopped. Kaya asked them if they were lost.

Little Fire said, "No, we're not lost."

Rada said, "You look lost. Are you two out hunting today?"

Fire Foot said, "Yes, we're hunting."

"It's obvious you haven't had any luck today, because you don't have any meat."

"We haven't caught our prey yet."

"What are you hunting?"

"We're hunting two witches."

Right as Little Fire said it, they raised their bows and fired the arrows. As soon as the arrows flew, they immediately reloaded and waited. Fire Foot's arrow entered Rada's leg. She fell to the ground as soon as it hit her. When she fell, she dropped her wand. Kaya was able to get her wand out. She was ready to cast an attack when Little Fire's arrow passed through her hand causing her to drop the wand. The two witches then transformed back to their old selves.

Fire Foot told Little Fire to cover him while he went to retrieve the wands. Little Fire told him not to touch the wands. He said just break them in half with a rock. Fire Foot walked over to the where the women lay. He took a rock and busted both wands in half.

Rada asked, "Why would you attacked two helpless women who just wanted to help you?"

Little Fire said, "It's because we're under orders."

"By who?" Kaya asked.

"By Jacob," Fire Foot said.

As soon as Fire Foot said it, Rada knew their sentence was commencing.

Rada said, "Shit, I thought maybe, the court had forgotten about us."

Kaya said, "I told you the court doesn't forget. It just takes its time to carry out the sentence. Most likely, Iktumi will be joining us soon."

Fire Foot bound the women's hands with rope. He walked them into the longhouse where he tied them to the main support beam of the building.

Kaya asked, "Do you know why Jacob gave the order to incapacitate us?"

Little Fire said, "I don't ask, because I don't question Jacob's orders."

Fire Foot and Little Fire walked out to the woodpile to haul firewood back into the building. As they brought the firewood into the house, they were piling it up around the two bound women. It took a couple of hours to get enough wood piled up around them. After they were finished piling the wood, they went outside and waited.

They waited until they saw Jacob and Joe come over the top of the canyon. They had a body of a man laying a crossed the back of the mule. He had a hood over his head so they couldn't see who he was.

As they walked the mule up to them, Little Fire asked, "What took you so long to get here?"

Joe erupted into an angry tantrum, "The fucking stubborn mule stopped five times on our way up the canyon. I finally got the fucker to move when I dumped some black powder on his ass and lit it."

Jacob said, "I still don't know how we're going to explain it to the Chongs."

Joe said, "At least we won't have to explain why we killed it."

Jacob told Little Fire and Fire Foot they needed to go home.

Fire Foot said, "I want to stay."

Joe said, "You both need to go home."

Jacob told the two, "You don't need to see what's going to happen."

Little Fire said, "I want to stay, I earned the right to watch the fire."

Joe told Little Fire, "Not this time. Now both of you go home."

Both turned and walked away without any more arguing.

Jacob dropped Iktumi down onto the ground and dragged him into the house. He propped him up, then tied him to the main support with the witches.

Rada asked, "Jacob, please find it in your heart to forgive me."

Jacob ignored her. "She was my baby as much as she was yours. Killing our baby, hurt me as much as it hurt you." He removed the hood tied over Iktumi's head.

Jacob went outside to where the mule was tied and grabbed two gallons of lamp oil. He went back into the house and started pouring it over the three bound captives. While he was pouring the oil over the three, Joe grabbed the vile of black powder. He came back into the house and laid a trail from the support post to the door.

Iktumi was screaming at the three judges about how unfair it was that Jacob would be the one to carry out his execution as he was dragged from the court. He then felt the force reach into him and grab him in the midsection. There was a powerful lurch forward as he flew through space again then stopped. He was back in his body. He realized his hands and feet were bound. He looked around to see he was in Rada and Kaya's house, tied to the main support beam.

Jacob finished pouring the oil. He stepped back and looked at Iktumi as he screamed at him about how he was going to kill him. He kept screaming he was going to kill him the next chance he had.

Rada said, "I know you're going to light the fire; I just want you to forgive me for what we did."

Jacob didn't say anything as he walked over to the door. He knelt then lit the black powder.

Iktumi watched as the flame jetted down the trail of powder. When it hit the lamp oil, they all went up in flames. Jacob and Joe back off about thirty feet from the building as it went up in flames. They stood there listening to the agonizing screams and the howling fire until everything went silent. They waited, then there was a loud howling scream that came from the embers.

A black mist rose above the flames then jetted in Jacob's direction. It swirled to within a couple of feet of him and stopped.

Jacob told Dzoavits, "Don't bother because you're not invited."

Joe said, "You shouldn't bother with me either, you're not invited here either."

There was a loud howl as the mist shaped demon turned and took off south.

Joe asked, "Where do you think Dzoavits will go?"

"He's going to the only place that will have him. The Shet, the devil's home."

CHAPTER 18

Celebrations

The people of the village gathered in the Long house council room for the "rites" celebration. The evening agenda would be assembling the people until everyone was in the festivity room. White Lightning would introduce the three who completed their transitions. After the introductions there would be a feast for dinner. After dinner a celebration dance performed by the graduates. Then every member of the village would join in dance.

It took a while to assemble everyone into the council chambers. When they were settled, White Lightning started his introduction speech. "Thank you all for joining us tonight. We the clan of the village, who belong to the larger family the Flat-Landers whose ancestry belongs to the Plains People, assemble once a year for the 'rites' celebration. The celebration is the final stage of the three phases of the 'rites to pathway.' Tonight, we society, welcome back our new adult members, who have shed their childhood skin.

"The first graduate to be introduce tonight is at the top of his class. Fire Foot set three very difficult goals. One was to graduate at the top of his class in warrior training which he achieved. The second and more difficult goal was to be recognized as a third gender member of society. The third goal was to be recognized as the warrior with a male and female spirit."

White Lightning signaled Fire Foot to approach the council table, where he would receive his new name. Fire Foot walked up to the table and stood before the council.

White Lightning said, "The people of the village are proud of your accomplishments. Roaring Fire and I had a difficult time trying to think of a name for you. We decided to go with the name your brother Joe recommended."

White Lightning said, "All the people in the room are witness. From this point in time forward, Fire Foot's full name will be Phoenix Fire. Phoenix Fire will be recognized as the warrior of the third gender. He will also be recognized as the warrior with male and female spirit. Phoenix Fire's childhood journey has ended. I and all the people in this room welcomed you as a new adult member of society."

White Lightning addressed the crowd, "The next graduate hasn't lived with us for very long. Last summer when I placed Mark in Iktumi's care, I had no idea he would excel as fast as he did. Mark is completely and unconditionally accepted by the people of this village. That gives him more support to further achieve his goals.

"Mark picked up the Flat-Land language almost immediately. Like it was his first spoken language. When he was schooled in the healing power of herbs, he excelled rapidly to the understanding on the level of Healer. When Jacob was injured Mark spent every day caring for him, until he had recovered enough to take care of himself. What Mark's achieved in keeping Jacob alive, shows he has exceptional qualities and integrity.

"With all of Mark's achievements, he's still found time to commit to a lifelong relationship with Aiyana. Mark and Aiyana are going to be parents soon. That will bring a new member into our society and village."

Everyone in the room cheered.

White Lightning signaled Mark to approach the council to receive his new name. Mark stood before the council thinking the last time, he stood in front of them, he thought he'd be put to death. He wondered to himself, why Iktumi isn't here for the celebration. Iktumi had been talking all week about how he was looking forward to the "rites" celebration. Mark couldn't stop thinking about it, he knew Iktumi was proud of him.

White Lightning said, "I have to be honest with you, Mark. I couldn't think of a name for you either. I wanted to give you a name that showed respect for your previous culture and our culture. I did get advice from one of your friends."

Mark asked, "Can I guess who it is?"

White Lightning gave him a nod.

Mark said, "It's Jacob."

White Lightning smiled and said, "Yes, it's Jacob." White Lightning said, "All the people in this room are witness. From this point in time forward Mark's full name will be Marcus Aesculapius the healer. Mark will be recognized as a Healer. Son of Iktumi, spouse of Aiyana. Marcus Aesculapius's childhood journey has ended. I and all the people in this room welcome you back as a new member of society.

"The next to be introduced is Padma. Padma set some high goals for herself. Padma set a goal of being the first women to take the warrior training and graduate. I and everyone in the village are proud that Padma set difficult goals and achieved them.

"Padma, will you please approach the council. I'd like to give a shout out on other achievements in your life that aren't recognized. Padma can build a teepee faster than anybody in the village. She works the land, farming the vegetables that we eat. When Padma isn't in training, she sews, weaves, and cooks. She's the fastest teepee builder in the village. In my opinion Padma's the ultimate survivalist.

"All the people in this room are witness. From this point in time forward, Padma's full name will be Doba. The studious, clever, and practical one. Doba's childhood journey has ended. I and everyone in this room welcome you back as a new member of society."

The feast was huge, there were tables set up throughout the chamber. Set on one of the tables was pots full of succotash, three sisters' soup, single bean soup, single squash soup, and corn on the cob. The next table over, had roasted buffalo, roasted dear, and roasted rabbit. There were pots of popcorn scattered around the room. There was sassafras tea, black tea with cranberries, and water for drinking.

When the feast was over, and everyone was stuffed full, White Lightning announced the ceremonial dance would begin. He said, "The dance for this evening will be performed by the three graduates. The three graduates who perform the pantomime dance will represent three spirits. Doba will represent the female spirit. Mark will represent the male spirit. Phoenix Fire will represent the third gender spirit. When they're finished with their program, the entire village will join in dance."

As the evening wind down, people started to go home. Jacob and Joe invited Mark, Aiyana, and Phoenix Fire over to their teepee for a drink, a real drink. White Lightning and Roaring Fire were still at the council table talking as the last five left the longhouse to continue to party.

White Lightning said, "I was contacted by the spirits in my dreams. They asked me to clean up a mess in the hamlet."

"Is it Jacob and Joe, again?"

"Yes, your other two sons Little Fire and Fire Foot are also involved."

"I should've known they were involved, because of their loyalty to Joe and Jacob."

"What'd the four do?"

"I don't know. They're up to something, but I don't know what. They're the next generation to come of age."

Roaring Fire asked, "Does that mean our time is coming to an end?"

"I don't know that either, Roaring Fire. The spirit guides told me more, but I can't share the information with you at this time."

The five were sitting in Jacob and Joe's teepee talking through the evening. Joe told Phoenix Fire about the hospital close to where he used to live that did sex change operations. Phoenix Fire was intrigued by the idea that a person could have their physical body changed to their real gender.

Joe said, "When I first heard about the clinic, I was uncomfortable with the idea of somebody who is transgender. But, since I met you, Phoenix Fire, it doesn't bother me anymore. I love you, Phoenix Fire, because you're my brother."

The two stood up and hugged each other.

Mark asked Joe, "Where's the other bottle of whiskey? I heard from Jacob you pulled two bottles from the stash earlier this evening."

Joe said, "I'd almost forgot."

He went over to the bed and pulled it out from under the buffalo skinned blankets. He sat back down and opened it. He took a chug then, passed it to Mark.

Mark put the bottle up in the air and said, "Here's to you, Joe." He then took a big swig.

Mark asked Aiyana if she wanted a sip. She said the baby was too young to drink, so maybe another day. Mark handed the bottle to Phoenix Fire who took and chug, then spit it out as soon as he tasted it. He asked, "What the hell is that crap?"

Jacob told Phoenix Fire, "Since you don't like whiskey there's be more for me."

Phoenix Fire handed the bottle to Jacob.

Jacob took a swig, then said, "AHHHH, it's been a while since I tasted that."

Phoenix Fire said, "I don't understand how you can stand that shit."

Jacob said, "You just need to develop a taste for a good bottle of aged whiskey."

He handed it back to Phoenix Fire who said, "It's not for me."

They were chattering away, when Doba stuck her head in the opening of the tent to say hello. Jacob told her to come in and join the fun. Doba said she and Pabria had come over to discuss a couple of things with he and Joe.

She said, "Maybe, it would be better if we came back tomorrow."

Joe said, "It's not a problem, come in and join the fun."

The bottle of whiskey was passed to Pabria as she and Doba sat down.

Pabria took a chug and said, "That's good. What is it?"

Jacob told her, "It's a drink that will put hair on your chest."

"Doba may not like hair on my chest. It wouldn't bother me, though. Where can I get a bottle for myself."

Joe told her, "You can find some at the Chongs' Trading Post. It costs a buffalo hide for a bottle."

Pabria said, "I can probably handle that."

Aiyana said she was going to go home. She told Mark, he could hang out with his friends for a while if he wanted. Mark said he'd walk her home, then come back for a while longer to visit, since he hadn't been able to spend much time with Jacob lately.

Phoenix Fire said, "I'll walk you home. I need to go anyway; I have somebody I'm going to meet later."

Aiyana and Phoenix Fire said goodbye and left.

Mark hung out for about an hour, then said, "I'm going to take a piss. I'll head home after that." He asked Jacob if he'd come outside with him, he had something he wanted to talk to him about.

Jacob said, "I need to take a piss also." He got up to join Mark.

Jacob and Mark were standing side by side taking a leak. Jacob asked Mark, "What's on your mind?"

"I need to talk to you about Iktumi."

Jacob thought to himself, what the fuck was he going to tell Mark, if he asked him if he had anything to do with Iktumi's disappearance? They both tucked back in.

Mark said, "When I was on my retreat, I took peyote for vision quest. When the spirit guides contacted me, they took me to the campsite where I witnessed the conversation between you and Iktumi. The spirit guides made it clear to me, I wasn't to leave your side."

Jacob could see that Mark was about to start crying.

As Mark started to cry, he said, "I followed you both all the way to the hamlet. It broke my heart to see what the demon and the two witches did to you." Mark burst in tears.

Jacob pulled Mark against him in a tight bear hug and held him, until he stopped crying.

When Mark stopped crying, he said, "I have to go home to Aiyana." As he walked off, he told Jacob, "If you killed Iktumi, I understand why. If you did, Jacob, please don't tell me."

When Jacob returned to the teepee. Joe and Pabria had obviously hit it off. They both were drunk.

Joe was telling Pabria, "If I was straight, I'd go for you. I like your chubby cheeks."

She had the face of a Flat-Lander; she was a little overweight, though.

Pabria and Joe were laughing and giggling when Pabria said, "Well, I'm strong, so we can have plenty of kids, maybe twenty."

Joe looked shocked when she said it, he thought to himself maybe, it was a good thing they both were gay, he may not be able to keep up her.

Doba looked at Jacob when he walked in and asked if he was okay.

Jacob said, "Yeah, everything's fine."

She told Jacob that Joe and Pabria were quite drunk. Joe had already agreed that he and Pabria were going to have children together.

Jacob said, "We discussed it, since you had mentioned it a couple of times in passing."

Doba said, "That leaves you and me to have our own children."

Jacob looked at her; she was quite attractive. She had the face of a Flat-Lander which Jacob found very attractive. Her hair was jet-black, not like most Flat-Landers who had brown hair. She had a band around her head with one peacock feather coming out from behind it. She was still wearing her ceremonial dress made of deer skin.

Jacob said, "We should have this conversation after everyone has sobered up."

Doba agreed, "That may be a good idea."

Jacob asked Doba how she thought the kids should be raised.

She said, "We want both you and Joe in the children's lives. Under our tradition, the girls will live with the us, until their grown. The boys will live with us, until they're seven, then they'll live with you and Joe."

Jacob said, "That sounds good to me." He looked over at Joe and Pabria and asked, "Is that okay?"

They both were in such a good mood they both said it didn't matter to them.

Doba said, "There's something else Pabria and I want to discuss with you. There are rumors that you're recruiting for an army. We'd be interested in joining Jacob's army. We heard it was a new asymmetrical style of warfare training."

Jacob said, "I'll discuss it with Joe as soon as he sobers up."

She reached out and shook Jacob's hand, then said, "Okay, partner."

As soon as Jacob and Doba shook hands, Mark ran in screaming, "Aiyana's in labor!"

Doba said, "Shit, I have to go to the birthing room, I'm one of the nurses." Doba said to Pabria, "We both have to go to the birthing room, Aiyana's going into labor."

Pabria yelled, "Bye, Joe," in a real loud voice. As she passed Jacob she said, "OH, hi, Jacob, when did you get here?"

Jacob and Joe walked over to the birthing room. When they walked in, Mark, Phoenix Fire, and Little Fire were already in the room. Jacob asked Mark why he wasn't in the birthing room with Aiyana. Mark said there were no men allowed in the birthing room when a woman's giving birth.

Mark shrugged his shoulders and said, "Tradition I guess."

As they stood waiting, Phoenix Fire told the group about the time his aunt was giving birth to his cousin. He'd been waiting in that very room when the baby came out. His aunt screamed she was going to kill her husband for doing it to her, right as the baby came out.

Mark asked, "Why would she scream that?"

Phoenix Fire said, "I don't know."

The nurses were telling Aiyana to push, push, push, then they said to breath. She was pushing hard when she screamed something out. Mark said she sounded like the devil, but he didn't hear what she said.

Jacob said, "I think she said, she was going to kill you for doing it to her."

Phoenix Fire said, "That's what I heard, also."

Mark looked at everyone and asked, "What did I do?"

Little Fire told Mark, "It's one of those things you need to figure out on you own."

Jacob said, "I have no idea why she'd be so pissed off that she'd sound like the devil himself."

Phoenix Fire said, "Maybe, it was something you did and forgot about."

Mark said, "I can't remember anything."

They were still pondering why Aiyana would be so upset with Mark, when they heard a baby's cry coming from the birthing room. They all started slapping Mark on the back and telling him good job. Joe handed out the cigars he'd been saving for the occasion.

They were smoking their stogies when Pabria came out of the birthing room and congratulated Mark for being the father of a baby girl.

Phoenix Fire said, "I was sure the baby was going to be a boy."

Little Fire said, "It's fine with me. I wanted a sister."

Mark stood there with a proud look on his face.

Jacob said, "You're an old man now."

It was three in the morning when everyone decided to call it a night. As Joe and Jacob walked back to their teepee, Jacob was telling Joe they only had about three hours to get some sleep, before they'd have to get up, then walk to the Chongs to catch their ride to the Denver Camp. Joe told Jacob he was unsure about going to the Denver Camp and talking to Josh. Jacob said if he had any better ideas he'd be open to them.

They woke up at six in the morning and set out for the Chongs' Trading Post.

Jacob asked, "Did you remember to let Phoenix Fire know to tell White Lightning and Roaring Fire, we'd be out hunting for a few days?"

"I did tell him."

"Did you let Mark know?"

Jacob said, "Yes, I've told Mark everything we're doing."

"What did Mark say when you told him?"

"He said he's worried about us."

When they arrived at the Chongs', Mrs. Chong told them their clothes were ready. She asked them to try them on, so she could see if it was a proper fit. Mr. Chong said he was going to charge them an additional surcharge for returning his ass with a burn spot on his ass. He started laughing.

Mrs. Chong was very impressed with how they looked in their western clothes. Mr. Chong said, "Wow," as he looked them over. He said they looked like regular cowboys. Mr. Chong walked over and grabbed two cowboy hats off the shelf and handed it to them. He said, "You can pay us the next time you visit."

As they were standing there talking, an old bushwhacker walked into the room and introduced himself. "Hello, I'm Benjamin Johnson from the Denver Camp. I work for the Platte River Colony, running supplies to the Boulder mining supply town here at the mouth of the canyon. I'll be leaving in the next twenty minutes for the Denver Camp. If you're going to ride with me, you should meet me out front."

Jacob thanked him as he left the trading post to load the wagon.

Joe turned to Jacob and said, "I haven't heard that accent, since we came to the village."

Jacob agreed, "It's strange to hear somebody speak English."

It was late in the evening when they arrived in the Denver Camp. Old Ben told them where they could find Josh Jericho and his family as he pointed in the direction of their burned-out wagon. They thank him as they walked in the direction of the Josh's wagon.

Ben said as they walked away, "I'll be leaving the day after tomorrow around six in the morning. If you're going to ride back to the trading post with me, you should be there at five-thirty."

They walked over to the wagon and looked around the campsite. Jacob was in awe, as he stood looking at the burned-out wagon. He'd heard and told Josh's story of the wagon train numerous times. The story was well over a hundred and twenty years old. He couldn't believe, he was standing there looking at the actual wagon right in front of him.

He heard a voice from behind him ask, "Do you need something?"

Jacob's eyes widened, when he turned around and thought, he saw his dad standing there. Jacob asked, "Are you Josh Jericho?"

"I am. Who are you?"

"My name is Jacob; this is my friend Joe."

Josh said, "I'd introduce you to the wife and kids, but they're all down by the river washing clothes. If you're here to steal something, you shouldn't bother, everything of value was lost in the fire."

"We're not here to steal anything. We just want to talk to you."

"If you're looking for work, don't bother asking, there's no money either."

"We're here to talk to you about your agreement with Leroy Abrahamson."

Joe looked over at Jacob with a surprised look on his face. He was thinking Jacob should've shown better diplomatic skills than launching right into the conversation.

Josh looked Jacob over, then asked, "Have we met before?"

"No, we haven't met."

Josh became angry, when he asked Jacob, "What is it you think you overheard?"

"I've heard you and Leroy discussing plans to move people out of their village."

Josh asked, "Are you a little fucking weasel who hides under wagons listening to other people's conversations?"

As soon as he said it, Joe told Josh he was a fucking dumb-ass and there was no reason to call Jacob names.

Josh looked at Joe and said, "You look like Captain Dumb Fuck Joe. Daddy just left, high tailing it south, running away from you, his idiot son. He's ashamed to be seen with you."

Jacob told Josh, "We're not looking for a fight. We just want to talk to you."

Josh said, "Maybe, Leroy would kill all three of us, if he heard from some weasel hiding under a wagon that we had a conversation."

Jacob said, "We're just asking you to reconsider your decision."

Josh said, "Listen, you stupid fucking idiot, you don't know what my decision is, therefore you are wasting your time asking me."

That was the last straw for Joe. He told Josh, "I'm going to stick a knife in your forehead if you insult Jacob again."

Jacob told Joe to back off.

Josh said, "Yeah, little Joe, you should back off and listen to your man. By the way are you the bitch?"

Joe had the look in his eye when he said, "The only reason I'm not going to kill you is because Jacob won't let me."

Josh said, "I see, Jacob's the boss. Do you make love to Jacob when he tells you to?"

Joe said, "What you just asked me is one more reason I'm going to kill you the first chance I get."

Jacob told both, "Insulting each other isn't going to get anybody anywhere."

Josh asked, "What's your problem anyway, Little Joe?"

Joe was yelling at Josh when he said, "The problem with you is you're a stupid fucking prick. When you made the decision to leave Missouri on the wagon train, you knew there would be risks involved traveling with a young family across the plains. You decided to take the trek across the country anyway. Then when the wagon train was attacked, and your son took an arrow through the heart killing him instantly. You didn't take responsibility for your piss-poor decisions."

Joe was almost shaking he was so furious. He continued to rip Josh. "Then you arrive here and make an agreement with Leroy to massacre an entire village of innocent people, because you want revenge for your son's death. I'm sure you have second thoughts about what is going to take place, but you justify it by telling yourself, it's in the name of revenge for my son, Toby."

Josh wasn't saying anything as Joe continue. Joe asked, "What kind of man are you? Everything we've heard about you, doesn't sound like the man who's planning to kill every man, women, and child, who lives in our village. Jacob is right, we're not here looking for a fight with you. We're just asking you, if you were thinking of making another stupid decision, that maybe, you'd reconsider it. That's if you're the kind of man, we've been told you are."

Joe wasn't finished yet, when he heard a man from behind him ask what was going on. Joe turned to see who he thought was Mark standing there with a gun pointed at him. Josh told White Foot to put the gun away. They were just having a friendly conversation. White Foot said it didn't sound like a friendly conversation. Josh told White Foot to just put the gun away. White Foot put the gun back into the holster.

White Foot asked again, "What's going on?"

"Jacob is talking to me about Leroy. He thinks Leroy is planning to massacre the people in the village."

"I've been up there two times with Leroy negotiating with White Lightning. Leroy is adamant about them moving. I don't think he's planning to kill anybody."

Jacob asked with a surprised look on his face, "Did you just say you've been to the village twice already?"

Josh stood there for a moment in thought, he looked at Jacob then said, "Leroy is planning to kill everyone in the village."

White Foot said, "I had no idea. I can't take part in the murder of innocent people."

Joe said, "We know that."

Josh said to Joe, "You and Jacob seemed to know a lot of things." Josh told Jacob, "Jackline and I had already discussed it. I already told Leroy I wasn't going to take part in the attack. Jackline isn't as persuasive as your man Joe, but she did get through to me."

White Foot asked Josh, "Why didn't you say anything to me?"

"I didn't make my final decision until yesterday."

White Foot said, "Shit, McCabe and his men pulled out earlier this afternoon to go out on patrol. I was wondering why Leroy was riding with them."

Jacob turned to Joe and said, "We have to return to the village."

"How are we going to do that? We don't have a ride back to the trading post until the day after tomorrow."

Josh asked White Foot if he'd hitch the horses to the wagon. Josh said, "While you're hitching the wagon, I'll go down to the river and let Jackline know we'll be gone for a few days." When Josh returned, the four set out for the village.

CHAPTER 19

Battle Cry

When Josh returned from talking with Jackline, he climbed onto the wagon and took control of the reins. He asked White Foot if he'd be interested in riding shotgun out to the village. White Foot accepted, but made it clear it wasn't his fight therefore he wasn't going to get involved. Jacob and Joe climbed into the back of the charred wagon bed.

Josh told Jacob they'd go as far as they could with the day light they had. They wouldn't be able to go any further after dark. Jacob asked White Foot when Leroy and his men left.

White Foot said, "They left three hours ago, they'd have to stop after night fall also, because they wouldn't risk having the horses walking the trail at night."

They pulled off the trail and set up camp as it became dark. Jacob had a worried look on his face when he asked Josh, "Are you sure Leroy and McCabe will stop for the evening?"

White Foot said, "They have a mitrailleuse they're towing with them. There's no way they'd drag that thing at night."

Jacob asked, "What's a mitrailleuse?"

Joe said, "I think it's a Gatling Gun."

Josh asked, "What's a Gatling Gun?"

Joe realizing the Gatling Gun hadn't been invented yet said, "It's a rapid-fire gun that's used on the battlefield in Europe."

White Foot said, "That's probably why we haven't heard of it."

Jacob asked, "Is the mitrailleuse a rapid-fire gun?"

White Foot said, "Yes, it can unload multiple rounds very quickly."

Jacob turned and said to Joe in a whisper, "The Gatling Gun was built here in the United States."

"I know, Jacob, it was used by the Union during the Civil War."

"Why did you tell them it was in use in Europe?"

"It wasn't invented until the 1860s."

"Oh, I see, it hasn't been invented yet."

Josh walked over to the wagon and grabbed a bottle of whiskey. When he returned, he said, "I had this on my list before me and the wife and kids left Missouri."

Jacob said, "I know, I've seen the list."

Josh didn't catch what Jacob said, because he was working on opening the bottle. Josh sat down after opening the bottle. He took a swig, then passed it to White Foot.

As the four were getting tipsy from the whiskey they became friendlier. White Foot asked, "Jacob, what happened to your shoulder? I can see you've been injured, because of the lack of mobility in it."

"I was injured in a fight."

"It must have been one hell of a fight."

"Yeah, the other guy got the best of me."

"Did you lose bad?"

"Let's just say I didn't win that battle."

"What happened to your shoulder, White Foot?" Jacob had told the wagon train story multiple times in his life. He already knew the answer but thought it would be interesting to hear the story from the horse's mouth.

"Captain Joe, who incidentally looks like your Joe, cauterized it after he pulled an arrow out it. The arrow almost passed through me. It wouldn't have been as painful if the arrow passed all the way through my body."

Joe said, "If the arrow had passed all the way through your body, it could have killed you."

"I got to tell you, Joe, having somebody shove a red-hot poker into my shoulder made me feel like I was going to die."

Jacob said, "I thought I was going to die when I was stitched up without anything to kill the pain."

White Foot said, "Luckily I passed out before he had a chance to burn the other side."

Jacob said, "Me too."

White Foot took his shirt off to show off his battle wound.

Jacob said, "Shit, that's one ugly scar."

Joe handed the bottle to Jacob and said, "That's what Mark said about your shoulder."

Jacob said, "White Foot, I'll bet you ten dollars I can beat that scar." Jacob took his shirt off to show his battle wound.

Josh said, "Holy fuck, dude, did you get run over by a horse and buggy team?"

"No, I really did get attacked by a knife-wielding maniac."

Josh asked, "What'd you do to piss him off?"

"I didn't do anything, Joe pissed on him."

Josh and White Foot laughed.

White Foot said, "It looks like a good doctor stitched it for you."

"No doctor, it was Joe who stitched me up."

White Foot said, "So, Joe pisses on the guy. You almost get killed. Then Joe sews you back together."

"That's pretty much the story."

Josh asked Joe, "Did you learn how to stich soldiers' injuries on the battlefield?"

Joe said, "No, my dad taught me how to stitch the dogs when they were in fights with other dogs. Once, one of the dogs tore into a porcupine. We had to pull all of the needles out of his throat."

"Your dog probably learned a lesson about porcupines after that."

"No, every time he saw one, he'd still go after it."

The bottle was back to Joe. He took a swig.

Joe asked White Foot, "Why do you kept referring to me as Jacob's, Joe? I know by the way you look at him, you're in love with him."

White Foot said, "I had a white mother and a Flat-Land father."

Jacob said, "We know that."

Josh said, "You two seem to know a lot about us. Do you care to tell us where you get all of your information?"

Joe said, "Let's just say news travels fast in these parts."

White Foot said, "The Flat-Land culture is much more excepting of same-sex relationships than the white man's culture. It still goes on in white man's culture, it's just taboos to talk about it."

Josh asked Jacob, "Are you comfortable talking about it?"

Jacob said, "Before, I and Joe moved to the village I was uncomfortable, but I'm not anymore." He asked if White Foot and Josh would keep it between themselves. He said, "Our lifestyle is accepted in the village. I'm worried about the culture outside the village."

White Foot, "You know, Jacob, you and Joe are ahead of your time."

Jacob said, "I'm not so sure of that."

The bottle passed to Josh. He took a swig, "When I was a kid there were multiple farmhands who worked on my parents' farm. Two of them were two guys in a relationship. I accidentally walked in on them one afternoon when they were kissing. They begged me not to say anything, because they'd be hanged if they were discovered. I promised them I wouldn't say a thing. As time passed, I grew to love them as friends. After a while, I didn't feel their relationship was any different than my parents' relationship. Don't worry, Jacob, we won't say anything."

Josh turned to Joe and said, "I'm sorry for being a smart ass earlier today."

"It's all right, I don't hold grudges."

Jacob told Josh, "You have to admit, you're a little defensive."

"I wasn't sure if Leroy put you guys up to it. I just told him yesterday that I wasn't going to go along with the planned attack on the village."

Jacob told Josh he and Joe loved the people in the village. Josh said, "I know you do, because you wouldn't have confronted me if you didn't. Don't worry, Jacob, White Foot and I will get you guys to the village."

The bottle came back to Jacob. He took a swig.

Josh asked Jacob, "Are you sure we haven't met before, because I feel a connection to you."

Jacob said, "No, we haven't met before." He wanted to tell Josh, but he knew he wouldn't believe him. He thought, if what Shappa said about his father was true, then they weren't even related.

They called it a night after the bottle was empty. Josh said it would be light around five-thirty in the morning.

White Foot said they should try to be on the trail as soon as it was light. He said, "Maybe we can put a little less time between ourselves and Leroy."

It was late in the morning when Josh's wagon rolled within a couple of miles of the village.

"Jacob."

As soon as Jacob heard the voice, he knew it was Little Fire.

"Little Fire, what are you doing out here?" He was standing on a rock overlooking the road.

"Roaring Fire told me to come out this way and look for you."

"How'd Roaring Fire know we'd be on the trail?"

"Mark told him where'd you'd gone."

"Why did Roaring Fire send you out looking for us?"

"Some of our scouts saw some men scoping out the village from the surrounding hills. They counted maybe, four or five men on the east hill.

There's a larger group of soldiers on the other side of the south hill. Roaring Fire thought they're going to attack the village."

Joe told Little Fire to climb into the wagon. Little Fire jump in the wagon and sat facing Joe. Joe rubbed his fingers in the charcoal that lined the inside of the wagon bed. With the residue from the charcoal on his fingers he drew lines on Little Fire's face.

Joe asked, "Are you ready for battle?"

"Yes, Joe."

Joe pulled his knife out and made an incision on his index finger. He drew lines of red on Little Fire's face in-between the black lines. Joe then painted his own face.

Jacob asked Josh to stop the wagon just below the top of the east hill. Jacob, Joe, and Little Fire walked up to the top of the hill to get a look. As they peered down the hill through the weeds, they could see four men working on the mitrailleuse. It was set up and ready to fire. It looked as though they were waiting for a signal.

Jacob asked, "Little Fire, does Roaring Fire have the warriors in a defensive position?"

"Yes, Jacob, he does."

"How many men did the scouts count on the other side of the south hill?"

"I'm pretty sure there's twenty-five men."

Jacob looked at Joe and said, "It looks like there's twenty-nine men total." Jacob asked Joe, "What kind of weapons do you think the group on the south hill are carrying?"

"They probably have a musket with bayonets. They're probably carrying handguns also."

Jacob said, "The soldiers will start their charge as they came down the south hill. They're not going to have time to reload, which means they'll be planning to fire once, then go into hand-to-hand combat."

"Little Fire, what's Phoenix Fire's location?"

"Roaring Fire stationed him and ten warriors on the west side of the south hill. That will allow them to catch the soldiers in a crossfire when they charge."

"Where's Roaring Fire's location for battle?"

"Roaring Fire and White Lightning and the rest of the warriors are placed between the south hill and the village."

Jacob turned to Joe and said, "White Lightning must not be aware of the rapid-fire gun."

Joe said, "They have four men on that gun."

"Do you think you and Little Fire can take out the four on the gun?"

"Yes, I do. What're my orders?"

"You and Little Fire are going to kill the gun crew. After killing them, you're going to disable the gun."

"What weapons do you and Little Fire have?"

"I moved the muskets to our teepee. The only weapon I have on me is my knife."

Jacob turned to Little Fire, he could see he was pumped up. "Do you understand your orders, Little Fire?"

"Yes, Jacob."

"What weapons do you have?" He could see Little Fire didn't have his hunting bow.

"I have a knife also, Jacob."

Jacob said, "I'm going try and retrieve the guns in the teepee. When I do, I'll take them to Phoenix Fire's warriors, maybe that'll help their odds."

They looked over to the top of the south hill and saw a man on horseback with a red flag. The rider paused then raised it. As soon as the flag went up in the air, the mitrailleuse fired. It sounded like fifty guns fired in succession. Lead balls poured down on the village. After the gun fired all of its ammo, the men operating the gun went to work reloading.

Jacob turned to Joe and said, "I'll get the goddamn guns to Phoenix Fire." He yelled an order to Joe, "Take that fucking mitrailleuse out of commission."

Joe turned to Little Fire and said, "Here's the plan, Little Fire," as they both dropped into the weeds."

Jacob took off to the north. He was going to circle around back to the village.

Joe and Little Fire made their way down the hill using the weeds as cover. As they approached the gun team, Joe viewed the operation of the gun. He could see there were four men total, one was a guard, the other three were operating the gun.

One of operators spun the crank, until all the rounds had been fired from the chamber. Once the rounds were spent, they removed the plate to be reloaded. After removing the plate, it would be exchanged for a fully reloaded one.

The third person would load the used spent plate with lead balls. He'd get it ready for the next round to be fired. The first two men would assemble the fully reloaded block of lead balls into the gun assemble, then start the process over, spinning the crank, firing multiple rounds into the village.

The fourth man was standing guard. He faced the rear, scanning the area with his eyes to be sure they weren't flanked from behind. He thought he'd seen something move across the top of the weeds out of the corner of his eye. When he turned to look, he couldn't see anything moving but the weeds swaying in the breeze. He decided to not worry about it, he didn't think anybody would try to sneak up on them.

Joe and Little Fire were about ten feet apart in the weeds. Joe signaled him to come a little closer to him, so he could give him his instructions. Little Fire crept up next to Joe.

Joe whispered, "The guard has to be taken out first or we'll never get our chance to take the gun out of operation. I think the guard may have caught a glimpse of us, he's not following up. We both need to keep that in mind as we move through our plan.

"Little Fire, you're going to kill the guard and the person reloading the block. Both men are on the left side of the gun. I'm going to kill the two on the right side of it. You have to circle around south, then work your way back to where you can approach the guard from the side. You're not to strike, until the gun starts firing again. We'll be using the sound of the gunfire to cover our movement.

"Little Fire, you have to make the first move taking out the guard. When I make my move, I'm going to take out both of my men within seconds of each other. After you make your first strike, you are to move to the second without paying attention to anything that's going on around you. You have to concentrate on your two strikes, nothing else. You're not to make your move, until signaled."

Before the two separated, Joe said, "Little Fire, use the killing method I taught you."

As the two split up, Joe could see Little Fire was full of adrenaline. He thought to himself, Little Fire better not blow this. Joe made his way north then circled around to the side. He then started the approach to his kill. Little Fire made his circle, then approached the men from the other side.

When Joe and Little Fire were set, their prey was between them completely unaware of them. Joe signaled Little Fire to wait until the gun started firing. He pointed to the guard. After pointing to him, he gave Little Fire the slit his throat signal by crossing his index finger over his own throat. The gun began to fire.

Little Fire charged the guard so fast that he never saw what hit him. Little Fire lunged toward him landing on his back. As he latched on to the guard, he brought the knife around and slit his throat from ear to ear. As the guard was falling to the ground, Little Fire stuck the knife in his gut and cut to the right. When they hit the ground, Little Fire rolled over once then flew back up onto his feet and charged the soldier spinning the crank. He never saw Little Fire coming as he repeated the same move on him.

Joe made the first kill on his attack. When he made his move to the next, the soldier had pulled his gun and was pointing it at him. He made the mistake of hesitating long enough for Little Fire to make his third strike. As Little Fire took him down, his gun discharged, the lead ball barely missed Joe. The two ducked back under the weeds. Joe thanked Little Fire, then told him good job.

It sounded like thunder as the horses came up over the south hill. McCabe was leading the charge as they descended on the village. Phoenix Fire and his warriors fired their arrows into the passing men. Half the soldiers turned to take aim at the Flat-Land fighters to their left. When they turned White Lightning and his men stood up out of the weeds and fired on the group.

Leroy had fallen back from the formation and rode around the lake toward the village. When he was close enough to the village to walk, he left the horse tied to some dead wood by the lake. He snuck into the village. He was thinking to himself, he'd finally get some of that Flat-Land pussy he'd always been craving. He sneaked into the longhouse and peeked into one of the rooms.

It looked like the village medicine man was in there with a woman. She was trying to get her baby to stop crying. Leroy thought for a moment about checking another room, then said fuck it, she'd do.

Mark turned to see who was entering the room when Leroy punched him in the nose so hard it shattered the cartilage. Mark dropped to the ground. He tried to stand back up. As he tried to get up, he fell back down from the dizziness. On the third attempt to get up, Leroy punched him in the side of the head knocking him unconscious.

Aiyana screamed at the top of her lungs.

Leroy said, "Hi, I'm Leroy the lion."

She screamed again. He walked over and slapped her. He then told her to shut the fuck up. She continued to scream as he spread her legs. She kicked him in the nuts.

He slapped her over and over again, yelling, "You should me more careful of the big dick that's going to make your day."

Jacob was moving through the village as the mitrailleuse was being reloaded. He only had about thirty seconds to move while the rapid-fire gun was quiet. He'd almost been caught out in the open when the last round of lead balls rained down on the village. Jacob looked for a rock to hide behind, he knew the lead balls would start to pour down any second.

As he waited, it took longer for the gun to start firing. The pause continued for a longer period than the previous three times. Jacob thought Joe and Little Fire must have been successful in removing it from service. He started to make his way to the teepee to retrieve the guns.

When Jacob moved passed the longhouse, he could hear a woman screaming. He thought to himself, *I should go to the teepee first and retrieve the guns.* He changed his mind when he heard another scream. He walked toward the longhouse to investigate.

He entered the house and followed the sound of the screams to the Iktumi household. When he peeked into the room, he could see Mark laying on his back on the floor. Mark wasn't conscious. His nose was flat. There was blood all around his head that had leaked from his nose. Jacob was relieved to see Mark was still breathing.

As he moved around to see more of what was in the room, he could see Aiyana laying on her back on the bed. She was using Leroy's name as she pleaded for him to stop. Leroy was standing with his back to the door. He had Aiyana's legs spread wide. He was just about to go in for the rape. He told her to shut her fucking mouth or he'd make it especially fun for her.

Jacob stepped into the room with his gun pointed at Leroy. He said, "Leroy, this has gone far enough."

Leroy turned and threw his knife at Jacob hitting him in the right hand. He then charged him. Jacob realize he didn't have enough time to pick up the gun. Leroy was swinging wildly as he approached him. Jacob raised his hands to block the punches. Leroy swung going for body punches, which Jacob blocked with his arms.

Leroy wasn't making any progress with body blows. He started swinging his fists at Jacob's face. Jacob was reacting without thinking as he blocked the punches and threw his own punches into Leroy's face. Jacob didn't have time to think about the combat training White Lightning had been teaching him. White Lightning had told him, when he was in battle the moves would just become instinctive. They were as Jacob started to get the upper hand.

Jacob swept Leroy's feet, then spun around and body slammed him onto the floor. When they came down, he pulled Leroy into a scissors lock with his legs. They had fallen next to the knife. Jacob immediately grabbed the knife. Jacob squeezed tighter around Leroy's throat. He'd almost put him to sleep when Leroy bit into his thigh and tore a chunk out of it. Jacob yelled "fuck" then, he stabbed Leroy in the right eye. Leroy screamed, while starting to bite again.

Jacob yelled, "Fuck you, Leroy," he stuck the knife in his other eye. Leroy was flopping around when Jacob stuck the knife in his gut then cut to the right. Jacob held him down, until he stopped moving.

Jacob stood up and yelled, "The fucker bit a chunk out of my thigh." He yelled, "Goddamn it, that fucking hurts."

Mark woke up complaining about his nose hurting.

Jacob said, "Fuck your nose, that freak took a bite out of me."

The battle outside the village was now hand-to-hand combat. McCabe's men had used up their ammunition. The warriors had used all their arrows. They charged into battle with tomahawks. McCabe's army was fighting with the bayonets and swords. They were starting to lose; they'd taken to many casualties at the beginning of the battle from arrows.

McCabe left the battle. He turned, then rode around the lake toward the village. He'd seen Leroy go into the village. He decided that he'd go kill the chickenshit for running out on him before the battle. He was going to ride into the village, kill Leroy, then ride north. He'd have to build a new army so he could fight another day.

McCabe walked into the Longhouse looking for Leroy. He'd known him for years; he knew what he was up to. As McCabe entered the longhouse, he heard someone yelling from one of the rooms. He peered into the room and saw Leroy laying on his back dead. He stepped into the room and pointed his gun at Jacob. Aiyana yelled at Jacob to duck. Jacob moved to the side. McCabe told Jacob he was going to kill him for killing his friend. He raised the gun and pointing it at his face.

Josh came through the door with a stick in his hand. He hit McCabe in the arm so hard it shattered the bone in his forearm. McCabe dropped the gun when Josh hit him. Josh took another swing hitting McCabe in the back. McCabe fell to the ground when Josh hit him the second time. Josh told McCabe if he moved, he'd crush his skull with the stick. McCabe stayed down. White Foot entered the room with rope in his hand. He tied McCabe's feet and Hands.

The battle outside the village had ended. The warriors were hacking up the remaining men who were wounded. Phoenix Fire and the warriors were starting to build a pile of wood they'd use to cremate the bodies of the dead. There was another group of warriors, who were collecting their dead to be taken to the burial ground.

Josh, White Foot, Joe, and Jacob dragged McCabe out of the longhouse. They picked him up and threw him over the back of a horse. Then they tied his hands and feet together under the horse's belly.

McCabe asked, "Why aren't you going to kill me?"

Jacob said, "We're taking you to the Tribal Council where you'll be tried for murder."

McCabe was yelling, "I'll get revenge on you for this."

Jacob said, "I've heard that before."

Jacob thanked Josh for saving his life.

Josh said, "I couldn't stand by any longer. White Foot and I watched Joe and Little Fire kill the four men firing the mitrailleuse.

That Little Fire is one hell of a fighter. I figured we couldn't just stand by and do nothing any longer."

They walked the horse McCabe was tied to up the hill to the wagon. They through him in the back.

Jacob said to Joe, "After we returned from the council, we'll collect all the horses and corral them. There must be at least thirty of them," as he looked over the battlefield.

Joe said, "We can start training the warriors to ride and fight."

Jacob said, "Yes, that'll give us an advantage in the coming war."

Josh turned the wagon around and started heading south in the direction of the Tribal Community. White Foot was riding shot gun. Joe, Jacob and McCabe were riding in the back of the wagon. McCabe wouldn't shut up. He kept threatening to kill Jacob for killing Leroy. Jacob took a buffalo hide strap and tied a gag over McCabe's mouth.

Jacob asked Josh, "Have you made any decisions?"

"Jackline and I are talking about farming. We lost everything in the fire, so moving to California is out of the question."

Jacob said, "There's plenty of farmland on the top of the east hill. It has one hell of a view of the Sleeping Demon." He was thinking to himself it would be nice to have the family close.

Joe told White Foot, "There's plenty of single-woman in the village. Would you consider staying, also?"

White Foot said, "I don't know if I'm ready to settle down."

Jacob and Joe looked at each other. They both knew what White Foot said wasn't true.

Jacob told White Foot, "You'd make a good father; you should think about raising a family here."

They dropped McCabe off at the tribal council then, headed back to the village. The whole way back Jacob was showing Josh the different areas where he could farm. He'd point in one direction and say, "You could build your house there."

Josh smiled and said, "Okay, Jacob, I'll consider it. I have to talk to Jackline about our future."

White Foot smiled at Josh then turned to Jacob and said, "I'll take it under consideration also, Jacob."

During the battle White Lightning had been hit in the gut by a lead ball. When the battle was over Roaring Fire and Phoenix Fire carried him to his teepee. As he laid in bed, he told Phoenix Fire he had to find Jacob as soon as possible. He needed to talk with him, before he passed. Phoenix Fire left looking for Jacob.

White Lightning told Roaring Fire they needed to talk; he didn't have much time. He said, "Roaring Fire, you're my best friend. We've been friends since, childhood. We've also fought many battles together and won all of them. Roaring Fire, you were there by my side when my wife and son died from the illness."

White Lightning asked Roaring Fire, "Do you remember the conversation we had after the 'rites' ceremony?"

"Yes, I do."

"The other thing the spirits had told me, was Jacob was supposed to have died, the morning he was injured in the campsite."

"What kept him from dying that morning?"

"Dzoavits lured Jacob's soul into the spiritual realm after his soul left his body. He was hell bent on making Jacob suffer before he passed. Because, he held Jacob in the spiritual realm for too long, Shappa got involved. When Shappa became involved, he sent Jacob's-soul back to his body in the teepee with Mark and Joe."

White Lightning said, "That changed the time continuum."

"Did it change Jacob's future?"

"It changed his future and past. In turn, everybody's past and future has been changed."

"Do you know what took place between Jacob and Dzoavits in the spiritual realm?"

"I don't know."

"Jacob and Joe didn't help matters, when they killed him." When he and Roaring Fire had cleaned up the mess in the hamlet, they'd found Iktumi's medicine man necklace in the ashes.

Roaring Fire said, "If Jacob hadn't told us about the planned attack on the village, we'd of lost the battle."

White Lightning said, "You're right, we wouldn't have won, we'd been caught completely off guard."

White Lightning said he had been thinking about the day the three had appeared out of thin air. He said, "I entrusted Joe's wellbeing to you, in turn you adopted him, making him one of your sons."

Roaring Fire said, "Iktumi adopted Mark, in turn Mark became Iktumi's son."

White Lightning said, "I adopted Jacob, he became my son."

Roaring Fire said, "Oh, fuck."

White Lightning said, "Because, Dzoavits changed the timeline by not allowing Jacob to die, he changed the future. Originally, I thought the three would spend a year with us going through their 'rites,' then they'd be sent back home the following summer. I don't think that's going to happen anymore."

White Lightning looked into Roaring fires eyes and said, "When you became my best warrior, you pledged your loyalty to me."

Roaring Fire knew what White Lightning was going to ask.

"Jacob already has Phoenix Fire's and Little Fire's loyalty."

Roaring Fire thought to himself, *White Lightning doesn't have to tell me about Joe and Mark's loyalty to Jacob.*

"Roaring Fire, Jacob is going to need your help."

He waited for Roaring Fire to make the pledge. They continued to stare into each other's eyes.

Roaring Fire hesitated, he was unsure. He then said, "Yes, White Lightning, I swear to you that I pledge my loyalty to Jacob."

When Jacob arrived back in the village, Josh and White Foot dropped them off then left for the Denver Camp. Phoenix fire approached Jacob as they walked to their teepee. Jacob could see Phoenix Fire was upset. Phoenix Fire told him, he and Joe needed to go to White Lightning's teepee immediately. Jacob asked him how serious was it. Phoenix Fire said he had been shot in the abdomen and they didn't think he had much longer to live.

Jacob was trying to hold back tears, while they walked over to the teepee. They walked in to see White Lightning laying on his bed. Roaring Fire was by his side talking to him. White Lightning excused Roaring Fire from the teepee.

Jacob knelt beside White Lightning then, he began to cry.

White Lightning said, "I'm thankful I'm able to see you, before I pass. When the three of you appeared in the village, at first, I didn't know what to do with you. I knew if I gave you homes, the people of the village would accept you. They are a caring people. I never imagined the three of you would have given so much as you have given to the people of the village."

White Lightning said to Jacob, "When my wife and son died it broke my heart. I knew I'd never have a wife again. I believed I'd never have children either. It's been an honor to have met you and I'm proud to call you my son. Jacob, when I adopted you, you became the heir of not only everything I own, but you also have rights to my title."

Jacob said, as he sobbed, "White Lightning, I can't take anything from you."

"Jacob, you don't understand, you're going to inherit everything, I have. You're also, going to be chief of the village the moment I pass into the realm."

"No, White Lightning, I'm not a leader."

"Jacob, you are a leader."

"You never taught me to be one."

"I didn't have to teach you, you're a natural-born leader. All I had to do was give you the tools you needed. Jacob, good leadership comes from life experiences, the good ones and the painful ones. The people and the warriors in this village look up to you, because you fight along-side them to help preserve their way of life. A good leader doesn't rule by fear. He's earned the respect of the warriors that he goes into battle with side by side."

White Lightning told Jacob, "You brought a lot of happiness to the people of the village. You also bring a lot of happiness to Joe. Joe's one hell of a man and you're lucky to have him."

Joe could see White Lightning was about to pass.

White Lightning's last words were, "And Jacob, you brought happiness to my life."

Please visit our web site at
www.thedemonoftablemesa.com
if you want detailed directions on
where you can view the landmark
"the Sleeping Demon" in person.
If you have any questions about Jacob's story
you can contact him at jacobjericho102@gmail.com